T0039326

Also by Terry Leeder

The Iron People

A Fighting Lady

The Long Sault

The Great River

The Soldier's Son

Pioneer Among the Mountains

White Forehead of the Cypress Hills

Daughter of the Old Pioneer

Brand 999

Canadians in a Far Country

A Trip Across Canada

Melissa's Daughters

PRESTON

TERRY LEEDER

iUniverse LLC
Bloomington

Preston

Copyright © 2014 Terry Leeder.

All rights reserved. No part of this book may be used or reproduced by any means, graphic, electronic, or mechanical, including photocopying, recording, taping or by any information storage retrieval system without the written permission of the publisher except in the case of brief quotations embodied in critical articles and reviews.

This is a work of fiction. All of the characters, names, incidents, organizations, and dialogue in this novel are either the products of the author's imagination or are used fictitiously.

iUniverse books may be ordered through booksellers or by contacting:

iUniverse LLC
1663 Liberty Drive
Bloomington, IN 47403
www.iuniverse.com
1-800-Authors (1-800-288-4677)

Because of the dynamic nature of the Internet, any web addresses or links contained in this book may have changed since publication and may no longer be valid. The views expressed in this work are solely those of the author and do not necessarily reflect the views of the publisher, and the publisher hereby disclaims any responsibility for them.

Any people depicted in stock imagery provided by Thinkstock are models, and such images are being used for illustrative purposes only. Certain stock imagery © Thinkstock.

ISBN: 978-1-4917-2784-3 (sc)
ISBN: 978-1-4917-2785-0 (e)

Library of Congress Control Number: 2014904185

Printed in the United States of America.

iUniverse rev. date: 03/21/2014

Note: The quotations in the novel "Preston" are taken from Dante Alighieri, The Inferno, as translated by Charles Eliot Norton (1827-1908), published in Boston and New York in 1891-2 and revised in 1902.

To Angela

They think

They think I can't hear. They're out there whispering. I feel like getting up and going out there and confronting them and telling them to their faces, I can hear you, I know what you're talking about.

"The man in the other car wasn't doing anything. He just started shouting."

I can't hear Beverley.

"What's wrong with him, Mom. What's happened?"

There is nothing wrong with me. Nothing at all. I am in perfectly good health. I am in wonderful health for my age.

I can't hear. They must have gone to the balcony. I should get up and go out there. Dare them to say whatever they've saying to my face. Whispering. He hasn't been here for ten years and he shows up and starts badmouthing me. A loudmouth. Name. It's been years. Richard. Richard, my own son. He hasn't been here for years. It's no wonder. He hasn't been around for years. Imagine, forgetting my own son's name. I keep forgetting things. It drives me crazy. I always had a good memory.

What are they saying out there? They woke me up.

I should get up. I don't feel like it. I could get up and go out there and confront them both. I don't feel like it.

Light across the ceiling. Faces. The shadows make faces. The way the, what is it, plaster, the plaster, the way the bumps and shadows make faces. It's hot in here. She always puts too many blankets on. She means well. She always puts too many blankets on. Beverley. At least I remember her name. Not that I would ever forget it, how could I ever forget. Imagine forgetting . . . . He hasn't been here for years.

"What happened to your plants?" Him again. I wish Beverley would talk up.

". . . tried to fix them. . . . carried away. He cut himself, the poor dear."

"That's not like him, Mom. What's happened?" Good. They're talking up. That's better.

"We had no idea where you were, my dear."

"I left you my address. You should have written. I had a right to know what was happening to my own father. You look terrible."

"And isn't that what every mother wants to hear."

That's my Beverley. She never took garbage, not from anybody. Not even from me, that's for certain. Good for her.

"What happened to the ceiling?" They're in the kitchen. What are they doing out there? I should get up and go out there and find out what's going on and dare them to say that to my face. Whatever they're saying. They stick me in bed so they can talk about me.

2

What are they saying? Is the door open? I can push it open, if I can reach, I always put my cane beside the bed, within reach, unless someone moved, there it is. I can reach out and push the door open, be quiet, have to be quiet.

"He could have burned the apartment down and fried you both."

"It did create some excitement."

"You should have told me."

"We thought you had enough to think about, Richard. It must have been terrible. All that starvation. I don't know how you coped with it, I really don't. And those children. Those pictures you sent us."

"You're changing the subject, Mom."

"We are proud of you, Richard. Nobody else could have done that."

"I was only doing what you did."

"It's not the same thing."

They've stopped talking. Maybe they've moved. Maybe I made a noise in here. Scared them off. No sound. They must have moved. Richard. Richard. I have to write that down. Imagine, forgetting your own son's, there's someone in the hall, coming along the hall. At the door.

"I can hear him breathing." What's he doing, spying on me. I should shout. I should tell him I can hear everything he's saying out there, badmouthing his own father. "He's asleep, I can hear him breathing. I thought I closed the door." A squeak. "Damn." That door's always squeaked, he's trying to close it quietly, the latch.

He's shut it.

Damn.

It's hot in here. I hate the door closed. I feel like I'm choking. I can just barely make out the ceiling, I feel like I'm choking in here. Beverley knows I hate the door closed. She should have told him. Nobody cares what I think. I might as well be a big lump of rock by the side of the road. A non-person. A prisoner in here. Where is that damn cane?

Here we are. Give it a push, not too hard. Gentle.

It wasn't shut all the way. They tried to be quiet, and they didn't shut it all the way. The latch didn't hold. I need to fix that latch. I keep forgetting.

"We have to get him to a doctor, Mom. You're worn out."

"Keep your voice down."

"You need some help. It's destroying your health."

"Your father was there when I needed him, Richard. I am not going to desert him now."

"I didn't suggest that. You can hire someone. I can help you find someone."

"We tried that." They keep moving. Beverley's voice is low, too low, I have to ask her to speak up. Not Richard. I remembered. Richard. Imagine . . . .

"What happened? Why did she leave?" I can't hear what Beverley said. "What did he do?" I can't tell what Beverley said. This damn cane. Don't want to drop it. Don't want to make a noise in here. "Four of them? You had four of them?"

"Not all at the same time of course."

"He drove them all out? One after the other?"

"They didn't understand him, Richard. He thought they were stealing his books."

"Yeah. . . . . All over . . . ."

What did he say, dammit? I wish he'd talk up. I always had to tell him to talk up.

"He didn't hurt you, did he?"

"He's your father, Richard. Your father doesn't do those things."

"The people you hired didn't think that, obviously." I can't hear what she said. "He needs to see a doctor."

"We have had enough doctors, thank you very much."

"You're not facing the facts, Mom. Your husband is not well. There is something terribly wrong with him. He needs help. You need help."

I do worry about Beverley, she works too hard. I can't hear what she said. I wish I could hear what she said. I'm trapped in here.

"I've got two weeks, Mom. In two weeks I start school. We haven't got an apartment yet, no Mom, we are not staying here, don't even think about it. Listen to me, Mom, we have to settle this now. In two weeks time I won't be able to do anything. If he has to go somewhere we have to deal with it now."

"I am not sending my husband anywhere."

That's my Beverley. If I ever lost her I don't know what I'd do.

As long as that person is out there I will not go out there. I don't care if he is my son, I will not go out there and talk to a man who talks about his father like he is. No respect. I'll get up and do something in here. I'll wait until he's gone. He's causing nothing but trouble.

Beverley, God bless her. All organized. Sometimes I don't appreciate her. I never appreciated her enough. I try to tell her and I hope she understands, if I lost her I don't know what I'd do. I want the door open. I can't stand it in here with the door closed. I won't go out there. They must be out on the balcony. Drinking wine. Without me. You'd think they'd invite me out there. As if I didn't exist. He comes over here and talks about his own father and then cuts me out, as if I didn't exist. As if he could just show up after how many years of never being here and cut me out.

She's got all my things organized. The scissors here. Ruler, to help me cut. It would be better with a sharp knife, I could run the knife along the edge of the ruler and cut out the things and paste them in. Paste here. Bless her. Mucilage. A new newspaper. I get out of touch. Wars wars. Murder and mayhem. Isn't there anything worth reading? It's not worth reading any more. Not much is worth reading any more. I've got out of the habit, I used to read all the time. All these books. I love the looks of them, the feel, newspaper too, soft, sort of spongy, not like paper. Easy to rip. I don't cut, straight the way I used to, can't make the old fingers, work the way they used to, hard to get my fingers in the holes whatever they are called, to operate this damn thing. They don't make these things, the way they used to. They used to have scissors that would fit your hands, that weren't so stiff, or awkward. All this plastic they use. Break as soon as look at you. I don't know why I'm doing this. Cutting out things. Things that sort of interest me. A policeman, getting some award. Mayor what's his name, what is his name? Never heard of him. Looks pretty stupid. Who was that woman, used to run circles around everyone? An old gal. Tough old gal.

"Hi dad. What're you doing?" God! "Sorry Dad, didn't mean to scare you." A strong hand on my shoulder. I'll give him that. He's a strong man. "So what're you doin'?" He grabs a chair from the corner and hauls it over here beside me, a big man, a little frayed around the edges right now, his voice is loud, Beverley must hear everything he's saying in here.

"Where's your mother?"

"Lying down. You wear her out." He's a big strong man, I always thought he'd make a wonderful football player, but he was never interested. Neither was I, of course, so I guess he followed me there. Not big sports people, either of us. "Do you know him? That police officer." He's pointing at a picture I don't recognize.

"No."

"This is a huge scrapbook. How long have you been doing this?" He turns the pages, as if it's any of his business what I'm doing. "You've always loved words, haven't you. Words words words. Figures, doesn't it, how you made your money. My smart dad." I reach across him for the newspaper. "Can I help?"

I don't answer. I really don't know what I'd say anyway.

"I forgot to tell you. I'm teaching Moby Dick." Who? "You used to read me Ahab's speeches. Do you remember? Like Shakespeare, you said. I always thought it was a boring book, to tell you the truth, but then my dad made it interesting. And now I'm teaching it. Incredible, right. You never know."

He's got some kind of blood veins like spider webs in the corner of his right eye, it makes him look sort of crazy, like he's staring at something crazy wild that nobody else can see. "You don't remember, do you?" he says.

"Moby Dick," I pronounce, just to satisfy him. He really isn't a bad type, it's nice to have him here, after all. It's good for Beverley. It makes her happy.

"I wanted to ask you," he never shuts up. "You used to have a book with pictures of whaling ships and so forth. A black book with gold printing and a picture of a whaling ship on the front, no two, I think, and the sea, with big sloshy waves humping up and the outlines of the waves in whitecaps and there's a small rowboat rocking up and down on the waves and a ship in the background dipping up and down and these magnificent sails spread up like tree branches one step above the other like wings. I loved that picture." I am cutting out something about road repair, I can't keep the blades of these damn scissors going the way they are supposed to go. "Do you remember? I thought that maybe, if I could have that book, if you've still got it. To help create interest. With my students. I'll probably have a lot of kids that are more interested in libido than literature, if you know what I mean. Something to distract them." What do I say to that? "Can I look for it?"

"Of course. We have to stick together."

He squeezes my shoulder. It feels kind of nice but I wish he'd go away, it's nice to have my son back, but I want to be left alone right now. Even a good thing. You need time to get used to it.

"Mom looks terrible, dad. What's happening to you."

"Nothing is happening to me, mister. I am in perfect health. Perfect. You do not have to worry about me. Worry about your damn kids with their damn libido."

"You do listen, don't you." He gets up. "Do you ever talk to, what was his name, he used to write books for you? He was one of your best friends."

"I don't have any friends." Why am I so upset? All of a sudden I'm upset.

"You have lots of friends, dad. You always had lots of friends."

"I don't have any friends."

"Everett McTavish," he says. Everett McTavish is dead. All my friends are dead.

He leans over me and whispers. "I didn't want to tell you, dad, but you sort of smell, okay. You should go to the bathroom." I changed your diapers, dammit, I remember how you smelled, you stank, mister. He goes to the door. "We're off to the mall when Mom gets up. You should do it before then."

He really is verging on corpulent.

"You're going too." He closes the door. I'm going too. As if I had a choice. As if I had a choice about anything now. I'm trapped in here.

It's good for Beverley to get out like this. She does look tired, but she's livened up now that her son is here. I'm not very good at shopping. I stay out of the way. I wouldn't know what my wife wants. She dresses me. I have terrible color sense. The crowds here liven me up, I must say. We stay inside too often. I keep telling Beverley, we have to get out more often. We shouldn't have gotten rid of the car. She says she doesn't like driving. She won't let me drive. Come to that she won't let me do anything. Nothing. I feel like those kids on that rope going around the aisles dressed in yellow and two big women, one at each end of the line, dressed in yellow too, and the one in front pulling on the rope and the kids, hanging on and going where they're pulled. Bored. They look bored. Poor kids.

I can't get distracted. I saw that sign, a sort of, brass plate, with that doctor's name on it. I recognize this place. We've been here before. The big store, and the office up above, and the elevator. Distracting me. We always shop. To distract me. Go to the doctors. Go shopping. And now, both of them, up to it, both of them. And I know what that doctor will say, I've heard it all before. They don't want me to know what they're up to, they let me lag behind, as if it doesn't matter, as if everything is just hunky dory. Where did that come from, I wonder. Richard looks back. He waits and then his mother goes on and he starts after her. Distract me. Then, we'll drop by the doctor, since we're here anyway, dear. I know what they're up to. Make me think the whole purpose of this trip is to get my wife out. As if I didn't want to get out.

There's lots of people here. They see me with my cane and they sort of shift away. Maybe they can sort of guess what I'm thinking. A good sharp rap. They used to do that in the army. What did they call it? The officers carried, a small sort of stick, under their arm, covered with leather. Something. British army. We hated the officers, with that stuck up British accent. Strange. We hated them, and the song we sang said bless them, and kept repeating that, over and over, bless them, bless them. I can still hear that song, in every pub I ever went to. Funny, how songs.

They've turned the corner, some sort of cosmetics counter or perfume counter up there, Beverley loves that, she needs to get out, I'm glad, they'll be there for ages, Beverley loves cosmetics and Richard will be looking at all the women and those raunchy pictures at all those cosmetics counters, turn the corner the other way, double back, keep the crowd between me and the counter, over on the next aisle, keep the counters between me and them, I'll head a different direction, not the way we came, so they won't know where to find me, excuse me, I'm sorry, I didn't mean to knock against you, hope you're not, nice little kid, what's that man got the stick for mummy, I carved it myself, sonny.

Concentrate.

There's an opening up ahead and a long aisle and crowds on both sides and sort of apple carts in the middle with stuff, little plastic tablets and kids with, what do they call it, scribbles on their skin, black blue red arms all streaked and the lipsticks, black lipsticks, purple stuff around their eyes like they're, vampires, that's the word, vampires, ten years old they have to be, older maybe, I can never tell ages, and the noise, the music, drums and pounding throbbing, crazy kids on a stage, I have no idea where I am. I'll sit down, look around. Calm down.

I have no idea who these people are. These people with crazy makeup and scribbles on their skin and kids with heads completely shaved and laughing like inmates in some crazy nuthouse and this is supposed to be normal. A woman with a little child, sitting in a sort of little cart, she pushes it in front of her, a stroller, that's the word, she's so young and she doesn't look happy, and there's people of all different kinds, women with hoods completely covering their faces, and one over there with nothing but eyes showing, completely covered, head to foot, and she's a young woman inside, I can see it in her eyes, those are not old eyes, I know old eyes, "Can I help you sir?"

A woman about, young, twenty one perhaps, beautiful golden skin, some sort of uniform. "You look sort of lost, sir."

"Could you tell me where a taxi is?" It's the first thing I can think of. There are stores all along this aisle on both sides, and this thing is like a street that never ends, it goes on as far as I can see with these old eyes. She helps me up. I'm weaker than I thought, stress perhaps, stress gets me, I don't like stress, she's nice though, chatters away, asks if I've come with someone and I tell her I've come from a home and I need to get back, if I could find a taxi I'll tell him, the driver, where to go and he'll get me back and I'll be there in time for afternoon tea. I must be convincing, she goes along with the story. She's a nice little girl, actually. "Where were you born?" I ask.

"Right here sir. Watch the door. There's always taxis out here, you can find one in five minutes, I can wait if you like."

"You have been wonderfully helpful," I say. I feel like asking her to stay but I don't think I should, the sooner I get away the better. The only thing I want right now, is to get away. There's a big parking lot and cars pulling up, by the entrance here, and people swarming around.

The taxi cab driver's name is, I can read it on his card, A H S A N, he looks Indian, I don't think that's an Indian name though, D' S O U S A.

"It means 'Compassion,'" He's watching the road and sort of tilting his head backwards so I can hear him, but not turning around, so he can keep his eyes on the road, which is crowded, people are driving crazy, cutting in and out, he uses the horn. "Noontime, sir," he explains.

"D'" I can't pronounce the name.

"No, the first name sir. Ahsan. It means compassion. So I'm told. Something to live up to, as it were."

"I see."

"And what is your name, sir. If I may ask."

"Preston."

"A vigorous name. It sounds powerful. Like a person who definitely knows what he is and where he is going."

"Sometimes." I like this man. I have to get out of the apartment more, I have to get out and see what's going on in the world with the cars and the trucks driving crazy and the buildings tall and the people on the sidewalks looking glum and angry and confused. Hundreds and hundreds of people, going both ways and no ways. His picture and his qualifications are posted on a card inside a plastic sort of slip cover right above the glass sort of sliding panel that he's opened up so we can talk. They still use the old flag to tell you what it costs. Some things haven't changed. This is an old car, though, the dash is scratched and the back of the seat is ripped in two or three places, one long tear, like a knife has been run along it and something written in black ink, some rude remark undoubtedly.

I can think more clearly out here, when I have to take control. It's enclosed in here, away from all that confusion outside.

"And where do you want to go? Downtown," he asks.

"Anywhere. Where would you suggest?"

"That depends, of course, what you want to do."

"Out of the house."

"House bound." I nod my agreement. He doesn't say anything more. We're stopped. There's a truck turning the corner, going the same way we are. A huge thing with a long trailer and it looks like the driver may not make it, the back of the trailer is getting pretty close to the sidewalk, it keeps going. The truck stops. Backs. Swings farther out so the cars heading the other way, have to crowd over or back up, as much as they can.

"Where do you live sir?"

"On the mountain."

"Beautiful view." The truck is moving slowly again, it's making it, the back of the trailer lifts and the front swings into the traffic lane and the truck takes both lanes going way out and we'll just have to wait. "Trucks like that should not be allowed on the road at this time of day," he says.

He tells me the cost. I don't have any money, she didn't give me any money. "Sixteen fifty, sir."

"That's too much."

"I agree sir, but that's what things cost these days."

"We haven't gone anywhere. We've hardly gone anywhere." He turns and looks back.

"Perhaps you've misplaced your wallet, sir." I take it out and hand it through the window. He hands it back. "Perhaps you can get the money out yourself, sir." I pull out three bills and hand them through. He hands me back two. "I'll make your change," he says, turns away and looks down at a console or something and hands me back change. I try to shove it back and he holds up his hand and refuses.

As I get out, he is talking to someone and they talk back, he just sits there and talks and they talk back, like his cab is a person. And he thinks I'm crazy. I may be crazy but I don't talk to my car.

That smart mouthed young squirt took my money and laughed, as if I didn't have a right to buy a bottle of wine. I know the type, I've dealt with that type all my life. I've dealt with all sorts of types. Types like him will never get farther than some dingy warehouse. They'll spend their whole lives sneering. I know the type.

It's a nice bottle, though. Red wine. Beverley loves red wine. I'd open it, only I can't. It needs something to open it, I should have gotten one with a twist top. I'll save it. Beverley will like it. She always likes red wine. We used to sit down every Friday, when I got home, if it wasn't too late, and have a glass, or maybe two. We don't do that any more. Things have happened. Maybe I've done things. There's people all around me here, another of these malls. I don't know where I am. I have no idea where I've been taken. I saw the liquor store and thought I'd get Beverley some wine. It's like my life now, I don't know what will happen. It's confusing. I'm getting nervous, I feel totally alone here. I don't always understand what people say, I don't like the way the people look here, it's a rougher crowd, I don't like the way that group of kids over there are looking at me and laughing, and there's some really rough looking characters here, unshaved, faces dark, and the way their eyes stare. I can't let it bother me. The cabin boy the cabin boy, The dirty little nipper, He stuffed his ass with broken glass And circumcised the skipper. The first time I heard that I must have been, what, twelve years old. I remember how embarrassed I was when it had to be explained to me. Why do I remember something like that when I can't remember something that happened to me five minutes ago?

"Excuse me sir. You were singing, sir." He's leaning over me, speaking respectfully, a policeman. My daughter was a policeman, when women weren't usually policemen. We were so proud of her. We used to talk to policemen all the time.

He's left the door open. To keep an eye on me in here. In case I jump up and yank out the window and jump out. Beverley is asleep in her room. I won't get any sleep, none, I can't sleep, I'm staring at the ceiling, trying to make out the faces in the plaster. Sometimes I see one kind of face, sometimes I see something else, sometimes I only see spackles of plaster. Spackles is a good word, I always liked the sound. I'm just getting old, all old people have memory problems, it comes with the territory, old age is not for sissies. Old age is not for sissies. He'll wake Beverley, talking loud like that. Talking talking talking. Lying here, listening to him talking. Making trouble.

"No, he was found by the police." Who is he talking to? I wish he would keep his voice down. Beverley is sleeping. "Apparently he thought we were spiriting him off to see you. What gave him that idea I don't know. We'll have to take him now. Yes, if you would, what day?" I feel like the CIA or the RCMP, listening in. "That should be all right, I'll check with my mother. Apparently they have a wandering something or other they make out, any cop that sees him knows to bring him back here. They've brought him back at least seven times, I'm told." What the hell is he talking about? "Only because my sister was a policeman, Renata, she was run down by somebody she tried to stop for a traffic ticket . . . . Thirty years ago . . . . No, he doesn't seem to be bothered by it now, it

19

was thirty years ago. Eighty two." I am not eighty two. "I'm sure he doesn't. My mother can't take it any more, it's destroying her health. He needs proper care and so does she, she's over eighty, for godsake. Eighty five. What I want, I want my father to be looked after properly, if it means he has to go to a home of some sort, so be it, as long as he gets proper care. I won't be satisfied until he does." I am not going to any damn home. Not now. Not ever. They'll have to drag me out of here. "No, sometimes he makes perfect sense and then he goes off like this morning . . . . We were coming in a parking lot, it was full and we had to wait. The driver behind us was getting agitated, actually no, the driver looked harassed, it was the old man beside her getting agitated. They drove up beside us and the old man started shouting and my father went ballistic . . . . No . . . . I've never heard him do that, ever, he was always controlled, he always let people know what he thought, no problem with that, he was completely controlled. Always . . . . He almost burned the place down. She didn't tell you that either, did she? He was trying to make breakfast, it was kind of sweet actually, he thought my mother needed breakfast in bed and he almost burned the place down and them too. And don't ask me what he said to the women my mother hired to look after him. She won't tell me that either. I know there's a lot more, all I have to do is look at my mother's face." It's hard being old, he has no idea what it's like being old, nobody has any idea what it's like, of course his mother looks old, what does he expect? "Twenty. A nurse. The Northwest Territories somewhere. All by herself. That's why they got together, my dad admired her guts. She's always been gutsy. Too gutsy sometimes."

He's stopped talking. The doctor must have gotten a word in.

"Can't you see him today?"

He's managed to get another word in.

"Not until then?" Does he have to talk so loud? "Well this is why he hasn't been looked at sooner, because of what you're doing right now, putting me off. I will not be put off . . . . And what did he say? So you've seen him already . . . . Don't tell me about patient's rights. The patient has the right to get proper treatment, I understand that, and so does my mother. What about caregivers' rights? When do caregivers get rights?" He's managed to wake me up completely, I'm too mad to sleep, I'll never get to sleep now. "I'll have to look into that, if we have to do it, we have to do it."

At the top of his voice. He doesn't need a telephone, all he has to do is stand on the balcony and aim his voice.

"Did you hear all that?" He's standing at the bedroom door and flipping shut that phone thing. "I've made a doctor's appointment. I think we need to get you some pills or something."

"Do I get a say in any of this?"

"I'll come over on Thursday. Four days from now. I'll call and remind you."

"I am not stupid, mister. I do not need some royal reminder. I am not dead yet."

"See you on Thursday." He puts that thing in his pocket, turns away from the door, goes down the hall, I can hear him, he has heavy boots, he's a big man. The door closes, not very gently.

Why did he come back? We were perfectly fine without him. He's done nothing but make trouble, ever since he's been back.

So now we're alone, just me and Beverley, on the balcony looking down on the parkette, sitting at the edge of the escarpment, and the city below spread out like a map for a king and his queen inspecting their domain. Domaine, from French meaning home, from Old French meaning estate, from Latin, domus, meaning home. It comes back sometimes, all the things I enjoyed, like old friends dropping by to say hello, to sit and have a drink, and savor each other's company. "Wine?" I ask.

"Not right now dear. I'm still digesting."

"Wonderful dinner."

"Thank you."

"Did he wake you?"

"I slept right through. I was tired."

"You looked tired."

Far to the west, down below the hill, along one of the streets that stretch away among the factories and warehouses there is black smoke, rising. Not a lot. It's a perfect day, in the middle of the afternoon, we used to be able to see a train moving along on a track that ran in the middle of a city street straight toward the foot of the mountain and all the box cars and flat cars and oil cars following behind until just before the mountain when the train would turn and head east, I always get east and west mixed, I've never been able to get it straight. That smoke is east, not west. It's a little thicker now, a little more than someone burning rubbish out behind some building, but still it rises lazily, I'm trying to think of a word that suggests that it makes no threat, innocently I suppose, it fits in with the warm domesticated sun spreading out across the city. "What's that smoke?" Beverley asks.

"I've been watching it. It looks a little odd, don't you think?"

It's getting darker and spreading out as we watch, like a warning bell in the night, who said that, when did they say that? It isn't night of course. There's a ship in the harbor heading toward the entrance underneath the skyway, though of course it's leaving, it isn't entering. It looks like a big ship.

"That smoke is spreading," says Beverley. She is right. In five minutes or so we can begin to see actual flames in the smoke

23

and it's boiling up and rising and scattering out when it reaches a certain height above the city and is beginning to draw a smudgy line downwind, and the flames are more obvious and Beverley is beginning to feel insecure, though of course it is so far away it can't possibly touch us in any way. "I hate fire," she says. I can hear a siren, and we can follow it by the sound all the way along that distant industrial street, and then a second, amplified by the mountain, ascending like a warning, who said that anyway, it's beginning to bother me, something I used to know. There are people at the lookout at the parkette down below us, at the edge of the escarpment, pointing. Another siren.

"Let's go inside," Beverley says. I reassure her, we're safe here, that smoke must be five miles away, maybe more, it's way in the west—no, the east end of town, the fire trucks are on their way, you can hear them. "I hate fire," she says.

The smoke is beginning to turn slightly more grey and in another five minutes there is definitely a white section though it's still pretty extensive, and in ten minutes more, it's all white. "They're putting on water," I tell her. "They're putting it out."

"I wish you'd come in." I get up and we go inside, because that's the way she wants it, and I really want to make Beverley feel better, everything is all right we have a wonderful apartment, here, we've been here, I don't know how long and we'll have many more good years yet, if she'd just relax. I don't feel so relaxed now. I wish we could have stayed out. I love our balcony.

"Richard is coming over tomorrow," she says.

"He said Thursday."

"He told me tomorrow. I think I'll make us something special. A celebration. Sort of." I offer to help, but she insists, no, she enjoys cooking, she wants it to be a surprise, she says, it's all right if she surprises me once in a while, isn't it.

"You always surprise me," I say. She suggests I listen to my music. I haven't for a while, the machine is broken. She talks me into going to the bedroom, where the CD player is, and sits me down in my easy chair, over in the corner of the room beside the window, with my earphones on.

"Beethoven?" she suggests. I nod. She gets out a score from the shelf where I keep them and opens it out, Sonata 32, Opus 111, she fiddles with the knob on the whatever they call it, at first the volume is too loud, then she turns it too soft, and finally she gets it adjusted. "As you can see," she says, "It does work. Or as you can hear, I guess. You used to say that, didn't you, how our ways of talking don't always fit what's happening."

I said that? She starts the music over from the start, wiggles her fingers, and goes out softly.

The first part I've never quite liked. Too intense. Maestoso. I used to be able to visual this music, or hear it, when I saw it laid out like this. A whole shelf of scores. Symphonies. Beethoven sonatas. It's better, just to close my eyes and listen. Beethoven never— what is it—never disappoints. The music is so clear, etched in the darkness some place far beyond where we walk and live our petty lives. I still love music. I can't say what I like exactly, but I always do. It calms me. Music hath charms . . . corny saying. Beethoven. Incredible. He takes a simple, almost ridiculous, scrap of music and weaves it into something beyond—mystical. Corny. It sounds corny to say it, it's wonderful to hear it. He knew he was dying. Those last notes almost touch you with a sort of blessing, a tremendous peace, as if everything no matter how awful, is, in the end, somehow all right. Touches the heart. Spreading peace. He knew he was dying. He knew he was dying. Like me. I know I am dying. Slowly. Bit by bit. Everything is being taken away, bit by bit, one thing after another. I'd rather it was just over with, once for all, shoot me and get it over with.

This is awful, dying by inches.

Old age sucks.

Death sucks.

Life sucks.

I can't put my finger on it, I'm losing one thing after another, everything is getting farther and farther away, everything and everybody. The ones I hate and the ones I love, are leaving and I'm trapped here, all alone.

I don't understand, if he knew he was dying, how could he be so peaceful, almost joyous?

I feel her touching me first. "You've been asleep," she says, she takes off the earphones, I open my eyes and stare at her. "Hello dear. Sleepyhead." She has such a lovely smile. No matter how old she gets, she has a smile that would conflagrate the universe. I used to say that, joking of course. Strange, how that comes back. She has a smile that is better, more brilliant, more beautiful than any beauty queen that ever lived. My beauty queen.

"You won't be able to sleep if you don't come to bed."

I try to get up. Sometimes I have problems, getting out of this damn chair. One of these days they'll have to yank me out with a damn crane. She puts her hands underneath my shoulders and tries to lift me. "Don't," I say. "You'll hurt yourself."

"Well then," she steps back, "how are we going to get you up, pray?"

"I'll fall forward and push myself up. Like a horse or something like that." I manage to pull myself out of the damn chair, grunting and groaning, and stand up, but I'm wobbly on my legs and tip forward. She leans against me. "We could both fall," I say as we stand here like two damn trees in a forest holding each other up.

"If we do that," she wonders, "who would pick us up then?" We chuckle and manage to straighten ourselves and she leads me to the bed.

"How was Beethoven?" she asks.

The bed can only sleep one. I wake her when I snore, we sleep in separate rooms. She doesn't say anything when I flop out and lie here looking up at her, sort of imploring. I want her to join me but I don't think she's in the mood, I've caused her enough trouble for one day.

I lie awake for a long time before I know I'm awake. It's the middle of the night. I hate it when I wake up like this. Night is a hideous time. I don't want to wake Beverley. It's good she didn't, maybe I'll just swing around and sit on the edge of the bed for a while. I'm tired but I know I won't sleep. I don't want to crash around trying to get the CD on. I can't see. I don't want to turn the light on. If I get up very slowly and sort of use my cane to feel around. The hall is full of hazards. The table beside the door with, there's a light down by the floor, I can see in a kind of way, the shadows are confusing. There's a light outside, on the street, at the corner of the building, glaring. It's almost daylight in here. Well, not quite. I can make out the recliner chair, and her cabinet with the glass and cups and her Royal Doultons. They're worth a lot, she can always sell the Royal Doultons if I'm gone and she needs some fast cash. Lights in the city like, little stars on a chessboard. Quiet. It's clear. The lights at the harbor entrance, flashing, red, a long way off. The harbor black, except a slow line of lights, reflecting on the water, a boat, moving out. Cars on the skyway, pinpricks crossing in an arch above the blackness. Blinking where the lights pass the girders. A red glare from the steel plant.

I don't know anybody. People pass me and call me by name and I don't know who they are. There's all those books over there. I can just see them. Shelves of them and I don't know any of them. I open them and my name is stamped on the cover and I don't remember doing that or why I did that or what the book was about, or what it means. They feel familiar and I don't know them, I'm a stranger and I know I should know them and I don't know why I should know them and I don't. I feel dead. People talk like I don't exist, like I'm some sort of object. It's like I'm a part of that blackness out there, an emptiness where the lights pass across slowly and then it's blackness again.

I need the light on. There's a switch or something, I know there's a switch here somewhere, there.

Three whole cases of books. Packed. Books behind. I should know these books. This green one. A circle, a whole set of circles and pictures, white printing on the cover. I know the people who did this. I know their names. Everett McTavish. Nothing. This Everett McTavish and these two other people, Allison I can't even pronounce the last name, Norman, Norman, that, rings a bell. What was that, I was trying to remember what that, ringing a bell.

He'll be coming tomorrow. Beverley was making something, a surprise, I remember that, and he'll be coming, I know the name, I wrote it down, somewhere. Goddammit I know the name, it's right there, it's lurking right there, back in my stupid goddamn head somewhere. I am not going crazy. I am not going crazy. Useless, useless, all these books and they don't mean a thing. What the hell is the use?

I have to calm down and take this slowly. I can never get anything done if I panic. There is no need to panic, I'm here, this is my apartment, this is my chair, I'll sit down and keep myself calm.

I've made a mess over there, haven't I. All those books, flung on the floor. I have to write things down. I know I've written things down. Where did I put it, all those notes to myself? That McTavish character, whoever he is. Was he tall, short, did he have a moustache? What were his outstanding features? Who is coming tomorrow?

"Come to bed dear." Beverley. I woke up Beverley. "You need to get some sleep. This doesn't help anything. It will only shorten your life."

"Some of those books are missing."

"Richard took a couple. You said he could have them." Richard. Of course. Richard. "Don't you remember?"

"Of course I remember! Why wouldn't I remember!"

"That book with the pictures of ships or something. He needed it for school. You said he could have it."

"I said I remembered!"

"You don't need to shout. It's late. It must be two o'clock. The neighbors will be knocking on the ceiling."

"They can come right up here and knock on the ceiling right here. I'll spit in their faces."

"That wouldn't be very nice." She always, always says something like that. She's always been able to calm me down. "Come to bed."

"I can't get to sleep."

She goes by me and picks up some books and goes to the dining room table, in the half dark, and sits at a chair. She looks white in the partial light from the lamp by the bookcase and the light from the lights outside, and the sheen of the city and the clear night. The Moon has risen while we were talking, or maybe before, I thought there was more light than the lamp.

"Who is Everett McTavish? I've been driving myself crazy trying to remember who Everett McTavish is."

31

"Is that why you got up?" She sounds so tired, so tired in every bone of her body, tired of everything, tired of life, tired as if every bit of spunk she ever had has been drained away, so tired it will take years and years to recover all the energy she's lost, if she ever can and maybe she doesn't want to. I haven't been fair. I haven't been fair. I woke her up crashing around out here. "Everett McTavish was the author of the first book you ever published, when you started in publishing, centuries ago," she says, as if she's said this again and again for years and years, which she probably has. I am so sorry I woke her. She is so tired.

"Everett McTavish." It still doesn't sound familiar, even as I say it. "Where is he?"

"He died at least twenty years ago."

It is

It is another lovely day. It's hard to feel depressed when you get up
and the sun is out and the air is cool when you step on the balcony.
Beverley is still asleep. I may not get out of my pajamas all day. Or
shave. I look pretty good as it is. I feel like shouting, just to hear
my voice. I have to pick up the books. Someone threw them off the
shelves last night. Some of the paperbacks have got damaged, pages
opened and bent, one has come apart completely. A big fight, that
one, to convince the powers that be that we had to find a glue strong
enough to hold them together. A book is no good if it falls apart.
I wish I could remember those people, what they looked like, but
I'm not worried about it today. How can I when the air is so fresh
that I can stand out here in my pajamas with the breeze blowing up
my, whatever, and feel warm, comfortable anyway, and look out at
the harbor and the cars going across the skyway, little specks with
sun flashing off their windshields. I don't understand this, how my
mind can be clear one minute and then I get confused. I need to
be realistic, I can't take on things I can't do, what does it matter,
there are things around this apartment that need to be fixed and I'd
only screw them up. I used to do stuff. What's the difference? Let
someone else do it, I've earned it. I have to write that down. Where

is my damn notepad? I had a notepad. Not in my pajama pocket. Damn. Oh God. Oh God that hurt. That damn door. I hit my toe on the goddamn door thing. Sill. Sill. I think it's bleeding. A bloody big toe. Oh God, can't I have five minutes? I have to watch everything I do, all the bloody goddamn stupid bloody time, I can't look for a goddamn bloody stupid notepad without banging my bloody goddamn stupid bloody toe. If I'd had my bloody sandals on. Why didn't I have my bloody sandals on? Oh God, I'm bleeding all over the place.

Relax Preston. It doesn't matter. Your toe will get better. You'll find, what was it? This always happens. I get excited, or upset, and I can't think straight. I used to be cool. Cool under fire. I was actually cool under fire. I was lucky the war ended. Cool under fire and my head blown off.

I've bled on the carpet. That stupid toe is beginning to sting. Did I rip off the nail? Don't think so. Bleeding all around it. Probably lose it. How could I be so stupid?

I don't remember sitting down. I must have, when I came in and stubbed my toe. Relax. Sit back. Recline. If I can figure out how to. There we are. Pull the lever. And pinch my damn finger. I'm an accident waiting to happen.

"What happened to your toe?"

"Good morning dear." She bends over and looks at my war wound.

"Honestly," she says and goes off, probably to get some bandage and iodine or something stinging. Thank god she was a nurse. She kept me in the fight.

The Sun's come out. It was behind that big cloud, right at the horizon. Pretty soon it'll probably get too hot out there. I have to put up the umbrella. If I can figure it out. She kneels down and tells me to hold still and, wow. That hurts. "I don't know how you manage to do this," she says.

"The stupid sliding door."

"Probably," she says, bending over and stinging me some more with her medications. Keeps me sharp. I need to keep sharp. I was going inside for something. It was lovely out there and I was going inside for something. She stands up and doesn't say anything, usually she'll say something.

"You didn't get enough sleep," I say. She goes off, back towards the bathroom, maybe I was going to the bathroom. Good idea!

When I come back out, she's picking up the books. "I'll do that," I say.

"That's all right. I'm almost done." Poor Beverley. She's never done.

So my toe is bandaged and we've finished our breakfast sitting out on the balcony and the sun goes behind the clouds and comes out and there's a breeze coming up the mountain and sliding across the parkette and then lifting up the side of the apartment like another escarpment and cooling us here. There are buses coming up the hill and stopping at the top at the traffic light and then roaring off and others gearing down and cars, impatient, drivers going off to another stressful day at jobs they hate and bosses they despise or looking for work at the start of another frustrating day because they've been screwed after twenty-five years of hard work and someone new comes in and fires them all. I know where that is. Don't I know where that is.

"What are you thinking about?" Beverley asks. I shrug. "You seemed uptight."

"I'm okay." She offers me some more orange juice, do I want another piece of toast and I decide, yes, I would love another piece of toast. I would love to see our pictures. I have thousands of pictures. Life isn't bad. I'd like to see our pictures, all the things we did, and the good times we had, me and Beverley. My toe is neatly wrapped, sticking like a finger puppet out at the end of my sandal. "Watch the door sill," I shout at Beverley, who is off in the kitchen making me more toast. I should give her a break, she deserves breakfast in bed, something relaxing, some kind of luxury.

"I'll make lunch," I shout. "I don't want you to make lunch. You are forbidden to make lunch."

"That's nice," she says, and steps carefully across the doorsill where the sliding glass door comes across and sets my toast on the table beside my lawn chair, what do you call it, the thing that stretches out so you can lie in the sun and get baked and I can half lie here fingering my toast and contemplating my toe.

"I think I'll get the projector so we can look at some pictures," I announce.

"It's too bright right now, isn't it? Wouldn't it be better to wait until Richard comes? He'll probably want to see them." So he can show me how to work my own damn projector.

"I'm doing it now." I get up.

"Relax dear. Eat your toast. You need to relax. We've got all day." I go inside. Once I start a project, I have to get on with it.

In five minutes I have to shout out at Beverley, "Have you seen the projector?"

I have to watch everything I'm doing, every minute, I never get a rest. There are so many things to screw up, I can't do anything automatic, as soon as I do anything automatic, as soon as I stop paying attention, every second, something goes wrong. The projector screen is ripped at the top. It jams when I try to pull up the, what do you call it, the long rod that holds up the screen. Someone has taped the screen back to the crosspiece that holds it up, that I hook to the sort of elbow or crook or whatever that comes out at the end of the long sticking up rod that keeps jamming when I pull it up. Probably I taped that thing. Looks like something I'd do. I was never good with technology. Not lately, anyway. As soon as I turn and look at something else, to make sure I'm getting the screen up so it's at right angles to the projector so the picture won't get distorted when I turn the machine on, I lose hold of the screen I'm pulling up and it rips down and bends over and creates another crack on the white sparkly surface that the picture shows up on. It's not important, there's already lots of marks on the damn thing. We can see the pictures anyway.

I should sort out the pictures. There are too many to show, I have to make a selection. The screen slips again, and I curse to myself, goddamn frigging thing, I'm glad Beverley can't hear what I'm thinking, so much of what happens happens inside my head now. She's beside me, pulling the screen up. "I'll get it, dammit. I'm not dead yet."

"I'm afraid the neighbors will hear. You never used language like that. I'm embarrassed."

"Screw the neighbors."

"I hope not."

"Bev, go out and relax, have another cup of coffee. I'll take care of this." She's in her fussy mode. "Please. I promise."

"Do you want another coffee?"

"No thanks, honey. I've got enough stuff to screw up as it is."

"Do watch your language dear." But she does go back out, after I promise that I'll sort out the pictures and wait until she's had another coffee before I tackle the projector.

Richard could never look at any pictures of his sister without getting upset. It's a long time ago. There's nothing any of us could have done about it, none of us could help it if the man who ran over her got off on a technicality, though I have to say it infuriates me. My son gets really angry and that sets me off. It's better if he doesn't see something that sets him off, it spoils it for all of us, especially Beverley, who doesn't like to see us like that. You can never trust the law, I had authors who could have told him that. Don't ask me their names.

There are pictures of Renata when she was young, a baby, by herself. When it happened, Beverley was distraught, who could blame her, and after that she clung to Richard, and spoiled him, I'm afraid. Afraid she'd lose her son too. These pictures help, there's so much I forget, they help. All the things that happened when he was young. Except I have to make sure I cut out any pictures of Renata with her little brother. Sometimes I have no idea what's going on and I have to ask Beverley, who is that, what is that all about. I cling to Beverley far too much, like she's my mother. She isn't, of course. I don't want to tell her, she'd think she's married a baby. I've tried to be strong for her. She's sitting out there right now, with her coffee in a fancy little teacup, with the saucer on her lap and her right index finger on the handle of the cup, I can almost hear the tinkle the little cup makes when she sets it in the saucer. She's just staring. She can't sleep. She's beyond sleep. She's living purgatory. How do these damn pictures fit this goddamn carousel? They rip. I've cut one down the middle, jamming it in. Three already on the floor. I can't be sure if they are right side up or upside down or sideways. This whole thing has never worked. It's broken. The stupid thing is broken. Dammit.

"Please dear, don't say that," she's standing in the doorway again.

"Aw Bev, have your coffee."

"The language, really."

"Was I talking?"

"I can close my eyes and tell everything that's going on in here." She steps into the room and slides the balcony door closed.

It's getting hot in here. I sweat the more I work on this goddamn carousel, shoving pictures in. I don't know what I've got in there, and by the time I fill the stupid thing I am sweating like hell and I'm completely frustrated with this whole thing. Whose idea was this anyway? She tells me it doesn't matter, we can look at them tonight, when Richard comes, there's probably things he'll want to see and it would be interesting, wouldn't it, to see what someone else decides we should see, we've already seen these pictures again and again, we know what's there.

"I am perfectly capable of doing this myself. I don't need help from my son Richard or any other self important . . . ."

"Now dear, watch your tongue," she knows what I was going to say and it's just as well she stopped me. I need to take this calmly. The worst is yet to come. The projector.

Which so infuriates me that I finally have had it and I fling the damn carousel and hit a Dresden figurine that Beverley displays on a little low table over against the wall where it's protected from traffic and by the worst of bad luck, the carousel smashes it. She picks it up. The little lace ballet skirt has been broken off on the one side and one of the arms, the one that the sweet little figurine was holding above her head has been snapped off and there's nothing left but a pointed stump.

"Renata gave me that when she was eighteen," she says and takes it and goes to her bedroom.

Oh my god Renata, I am so sorry. I am so sorry. The phone rings. I yank it up. "Who is this!"

"Excuse me sir, I am sorry to bother you on a beautiful day like this but I wonder if you would take a few minutes . . . ."

I scream every obscenity I can think of and click the receiver up and down several times so the bastard can hear the clicking in his idiotic ear and slam up the phone so hard that for a second I think I've broken it, but I pick it up and am relieved it isn't. The receiver buzzes its objection and I apologize for being so stupid and using such language to a phone that hasn't done anything to me.

She has so much to put up with, it amazes me she comes back for more. She really must love me. She's laid out some really nice clean clothes for me, and I've managed to shave myself without cutting myself once, except maybe a little nick just by the side of my sideburns on the right and I've stuck on a bit of torn-off toilet paper to absorb the blood, and she scrubs off some shaving cream I've apparently left behind my ear. She straightens up my jacket and tugs up my pants. "What are you up to, madam," I say. She smiles.

"Now this is the handsome man I married. So many long years ago. The first time I saw this handsome man, I was twenty one, just going off to the Northwest Territories as they called it then, not the Inuit name they have for it now, Nunavut, I think they call it. We used to call them Eskimos then, it's much better," she's around at the back pulling down my shirt and the jacket over top, "calling things by the names the people actually use, magnificent people, just like my handsome managing editor who knew so many people," back in front, "and helped so many authors publish things they could never have managed without his help, do you remember how we met, in an airport, I dropped my luggage, I had so many things, and you helped me get them all loaded on the carousel and you carried a bunch of things out for me, why," she brushes my shoes with her foot, "do you think I was bringing so many things, when we went to Europe, and Asia for heavens sake, we carried one bag each, and we carried it on, such a handsome man I have." She smiles and leans up and kisses me full on the lips. "Enjoy your walk. Don't go too far, promise. Just around the building. Maybe over to the park, where I can see you. I'll keep an eye on you, so some little schemer doesn't carry you off."

"My collar's tight." She loosens my tie.

"Now go off. I have some things I have to do. The exercise will be good for you."

"You need help."

"You need the exercise. You had a hard night. You need to get out, see the world. Talk to people." She turns me and opens the door and practically pushes me out in the hall.

Well she's right, I do need the exercise, and it was a rough night. I let things get to me. I mustn't. I can handle things. I just need, to stay calm, stay calm.

"Hello Preston. How is Beverley?" She's older than I am. She's wisen and bent over and can hardly manage the elevator. I let her get on before me and take off my hat. I have no idea who this person is, I've never seen her before in my life. How does she know my name? It's embarrassing.

"Isn't it a lovely day," I say.

"Oh isn't it. It's not so hot as it's been the last few days, it was terrible, I thought I could have died. The air conditioning isn't working. Is your air conditioning working? The superintendent here is absolutely useless. He comes in and I swear, he takes ten seconds and tells me someone else will be up here this very day, this very afternoon and that was three weeks ago. I love your cane."

"Carved it myself."

"You don't say." I let her get off ahead of me and leave her in the lobby, waiting for a taxi, whoever she is. It's a little breezier than I'd expected. I'll have to shove my hat down. I lost one like that. Right across the road, underneath a bus. I could turn right, and go along by the stoplight, and then up the road. Too busy. Bus fumes. Better to the left, I think. Along the road by the escarpment, into the suburb where the houses . . . . How much do they cost, I wonder. That's what we should have done. Bought a house. Beverley needs to get out more often. I keep telling her that. She doesn't look well.

Now that is a big car. It must be fifteen feet long. Another one right behind it, turning in the lot by the park. Parkette. A strange one, the second one, more like a truck, big and boxy and long like the first, and the windows all black. How can they see out? Must be someone big and important. A man with a peaked cap, and a blue uniform with buttons. Opens the door. I didn't think young men wore tuxedos any more. Live and learn. All white. She's all white, her dress keeps coming out, she's got enough dress for three people, all puffy, and it keeps coming, trailing, a train, of course, and more of them, young ones in the second car/truck outfit, all so young, and all the men spiffy. And more cars and older folks, and a little girl with a white skirt puffed out like that statuette and running to the lookout, all excited.

This is worth looking at. There's a number of benches. I can look at the view, and watch the proceedings here as well. A man setting up equipment, a camera on a tripod and a funny metal umbrella pointing sideways.

We're attracting a crowd. Me and all these people. A couple of young men over at the apartment door talking to a taxi driver, having some kind of argument or discussion, no jackets, white shirts. A taller one, and the shorter one, in charge, pointing.

"Hello." I have to say hello, she is the cutest little girl I think I've seen for a long time, no, the cutest little girl I have ever seen. "Now that is a pretty dress." All white and frilly and smiles and the most lush and incredible dark brown almost black hair that a child has ever grown with ringlets all down her back. She hands me a bunch of flowers all tied up with a handle and runs off, back to the lookout. How do they get the energy?

So here I sit, watching this show, with the bride in her long enormous dress and her thin, almost starved figure, brides were filled out, in my time, they had some meat on their bones, they looked healthy. She's pretty, though, brides are always pretty. The girls around her arranging her dress and laying the train on the grass in a curved line, beside the flower bed, and the men in their tuxedos standing around in a big group laughing, with the guy who I guess is the bridegroom. The two young men, I can tell they're young, they're close enough now, coming across the street to see what's going on and me sitting here with my cane and my hat and my jacket all dressed up and up there, probably, Beverley, looking down to make sure one of these pretty young things doesn't carry me off, or probably just enjoying the wedding. Me, with my cane and a bouquet of flowers.

"Give me those!" A burly young ignorant man, in a tuxedo, thick curly hair, thick neck, broad across the shoulders, with a thick forceful nose and thick lips, a sort of caricature of every bully that was ever born. He grabs at the flowers and I hang on and we tug and

I think he's surprised that a stupid old man who means nothing to anybody has such a damn firm grip.

"Stop it!" A sharp female voice and the man steps back. "I'm sorry," she says. One of the wedding party, in a dress like the others, blue with a sort of cape and blue shoes thin little shoes with thinner straps scuffed with grass stains. "I think my daughter gave you those," she says. She's more mature than the others, somewhat more broad at the hips, with lush long black hair beautifully twisted into a sort of weave pattern at the back of her neck. I hand her the flowers. "He doesn't mean it," she says.

"Your daughter is very beautiful."

"Thank you," she says, there's a sort of catch in her voice that is partly humiliation and partly appreciation.

"I'm enjoying the wedding."

"I wish I was."

"You're too beautiful to let it bother you. You have a beautiful daughter and it's a beautiful day and the wedding is beautiful and you fit in perfectly. If you weren't tied down already I'd marry you myself."

"Don't tempt me," she says and goes off and she and the burly fellow stand aside from the rest and have some sort of angry discussion and in the meantime the little girl stands away from everyone by the stone fence with the iron railings at the edge of the escarpment, looking down at the city.

"It's quite beautiful, isn't it sir." The shorter of the two young men, sitting down right beside me and looking over at the wedding party. In charge. Slim. Purposeful. Dedicated. With a slightly thin long nose and a slim face tapering in at the chin and slightly thin lips, it's his hands, oddly enough, that most remind me, long fingers and palms slightly calloused and a very faint white mark at the base of the fourth finger on his right hand where Richard had an operation when his hand got infected and swelled angrily and the doctor had to suture the hand and drain out the infection, it kept coming and coming. The other young man is taller, a little more meaty and not distinguished in any way, he doesn't talk. It's the young man sitting beside me who goes on, like Richard would, like his mother would. I must seem especially stupid because I can hardly make out what he's saying, the resemblance to my son is so wrenching, it's the hands, Richard is taller and bulkier, it's the hands, I'm choked up.

". . . for example, that couple you were just talking to, I don't think they get along, it's pretty obvious, of course, what do you think, the way they're lining up for the picture," all the wedding party is over by the stone wall with a panorama of the city behind them and the young women in their matching dresses and the men who accompany them standing behind them and the bride and groom in front with parents on each side, "how they've lined up the bridesmaids and you'll notice that the couple you talked to are not matched, the man with the woman, the short one standing behind her, is different, and the man who came over and tried to grab the flowers from you is standing on the far side behind an entirely different woman and you can see how he's acting, the way he's looking at the man behind the woman he is apparently with, and you can tell by the way he's holding himself and getting tense along the arms and across the shoulders that he doesn't like his woman to be matched with somebody else. I'm sure you've noticed it, older people can judge these things."

The young fellow stops. I can't comment, I didn't hear half of what he said. "What is your name?" I ask.

"Tom O'Neill, sir. Thomas, as in Doubting Thomas. I think the name my parents gave me without realizing it, was some kind of warning. I tend to doubt. It's a warning. I need to fight it, this feeling. Faith is never a gift, we have to work at it, we have to fight for it. Haven't you found that?"

"I suppose." Not really.

"Jim doesn't agree. We argue about it. The apostle James never doubted, he was always solid, at least that's what it says."

"Jim Havlichek," the other fellow announces, leaning forward so I can see him on the other side of Thomas.

"We've been sent here," says Thomas. "The people you were talking to aren't married. You can tell. They don't have sufficient conviction to commit themselves, you can tell, just by the way they carry themselves. Look at the way he's looking at the man who's standing behind the woman. What I feel sorry for is their daughter. It's a sickness we see in our entire society and it has to stop. I'd be willing to bet that half the couples there are living with someone and not married and never intend to get married, and if they are, not necessarily with the people they are living with today." The photographer is arranging the parents and the bride and groom for a separate photograph and the little girl is holding her mother by one hand, and her flowers in the other. The burly chap is off joking with a couple of his buddies and looking over here. He says something and they laugh. "I'm sure you agree," says Tom.

I don't answer.

"You have a beautiful city," he says. "We came here just over a week ago and we've been going door to door, just down the street here. We were hoping to talk to some people in your building and we were hoping you could help us, perhaps introduce us to some people."

Another long limousine pulls into the parking lot, followed by a number of additional cars, the place is getting crowded. Tom tells me that he and his friend have been sent here from some place out west I don't catch the name and their task is to go around house to house, door to door, to talk to people about everything that's important. They are both quite young, Tom is twenty three and Jim his friend is two years younger. Tom is in charge, very intense, full of conviction, still certain that the world can be changed and that things will change as long as he approaches his appointed task with enough fire and conviction. The only thing that Jim will tell me about himself is that his name is spelled without the c before the k and that his family has disowned him. They're both short of cash, Tom interrupts, they've been given a limited budget and what with the rising cost of air fare and hotel accommodation and bus fare and every other little expenditure, such as food, they have just been scraping by. They eat the most basic things, the cheapest meals they can find and they'd go to some place like the Salvation Army if they believed that those people were doing what was right, but they cannot compromise their beliefs. There would be no point coming all this way if they did that, they are here to be tested, to show that they have the fire of their convictions, that they will risk everything to spread their message. I give him my wallet and tell him to take the credit card, they can draw what they need and mail it back. We cross the road and I can't remember the apartment number and he looks at an identity I have in there, something that Beverley made up with my name and address and phone number and pushes the correct button. There is no answer. He pushes it again and I look up and there is Beverley, sitting with two other women in the lobby. She smiles and wiggles her fingers and I point her out to my new friends. They hesitate, but Beverley is already at the door unlocking it and holding it open.

"I took your suggestion," she says to me, "I could see you down here, you were having such fun. I watched you crossing the road but I guess you didn't see me. Maybe you can introduce your friends." Which I do.

Tom hands her my wallet. "There's a credit card with your name on it," he says.

"Oh Preston, what have you been up to," she asks. "He is such a fox," she tells Tom and Jim, and introduces the two ladies she's been sitting with watching us from the lobby. Soon after that, the two men go out the door, just as a police car pulls up. As we get in the elevator, the policeman is standing with a notepad talking to them.

"How the hell did you get my credit card?" she asks me as the elevator door closes.

She is angry with me. We're standing in the living room and the balcony door is open, she rushed out when she saw me down there talking to those men, she left everything open. "I was talking to your son. It's lucky I went out when I did."

"Didn't he look like Rick!"

"Not in the least."

"When he was young," I explain. I can tell when I'm in trouble, her whole tone of voice changes.

She goes to the kitchen with her credit card, takes out the scissors, and starts cutting it up. "I should have done this when I cut up all our other credit cards. I thought I could at least have this one. I don't know how you found it, but apparently you did. I can't believe it. You handed him your wallet. A complete stranger. Who looked nothing like Richard, by the way. I don't know what made you think otherwise. He isn't the same size or the same build or even the same color of hair," she keeps cutting as she talks, she's exactly like Renata, or vice versa, sometimes I see my daughter in my wife and it hurts, I can imagine what Renata would have been like, "never mind the eyes, which you never notice anyway. I am eighty five, Preston. I can't take this any more. It's been one thing after another." I sure do feel like a whipped boy. "You were always childish." This will pass off, she's been angry like this before, but it always passes off. At the time it seems like it won't, like everything is over. Then it passes. She takes a deep breath. "What made you think he looked like Richard?"

"The mark on his hand."

"What mark?"

"Where they operated." She has reduced the credit card to tiny plastic shards and takes the waste basket from underneath the sink and spills them inside. They make the sound of plastic rain.

"I'd forgotten that," she says.

"Right here," I point to the base of my fourth finger on my right hand. "A little white scar, like a tiny line."

"Strange you'd remember that."

"They took so much out of it. We were off on a canoe trip. We came back and his hand was all red and you were outraged, you said we were never going camping again. I felt horrible."

"I don't remember. But what I don't understand is how you could do all these crazy things and remember something like that. It's like you are two people in one skin. Several people in one skin. It's confusing."

"I may be crazy, but I'm not stupid."

"And yet at other times you can't remember a thing."

"It's not funny. You wouldn't think it was funny if it was happening to you."

That gets through to her and we spend the next hour or so working with a word game, teaching me to remember. Associations. In the end I get frustrated, I can't remember things I want to remember, I remember crazy things, things that she insists never happened but I know did happen.

Richard

Richard is here. He came over all smiles pretending innocence and the first thing Beverley did was look at his hand and give me a big smile. Richard wondered what the hell it was all about and I felt good, it was something between Beverley and me he couldn't interfere with. He seems so different. After a while they went off to my wife's bedroom and stayed there a long time and that really angered me, what were they up to, but I brought out an extra chair to the balcony and set up a little wine table with a table cloth. Well, a clean dishtowel. I found the wine I bought for Beverley, after looking around for some time and located it underneath the sink way at the back, where I probably stashed it. It was good I did, of course, find it that is, I was getting frustrated. It didn't happen, though. I was happy and worried that the sun would go down before they got out of their conflab, but they came out at last and I bowed, with another dishcloth on my arm like a French waiter and conducted them to the balcony. I'd found a candle stub and stuck it on a plate. So we're all set up, whatever they have cooked up, I'll wait and find out, Beverley has brought out some munchies she made for just this purpose and we sit down in a little circle on our balcony, which is much smaller now than it is when it's just me and Beverley, and it isn't just the size of my son, it's all these other things that are crammed out here.

"I am so glad you're back," says Beverley, smiling at Richard, "I kept worrying we'd see you on the CBC News, kidnapped or some horrible thing, and I kept wondering, how will we pay to get you back, we're not very rich and your father is retired."

"I forgot," he says and jumps up.

"Relax dear. Your father hasn't opened the wine."

"In a minute. I have to show you something. I forgot until right this minute, when you said that." He pushes out by the table and I have to lift the bottle up with the corkscrew, which I've been trying to operate since we all sat down. Back inside the apartment, looking for the leather file thing he was carrying when he came in, he hollers for Beverley, did she see that leather thing he brought and she calls back you're just like your father, on the table by the door in the hall. I set the bottle on the table once more and poise the corkscrew over the cork. Beverley touches my hand.

"Wait until he's back. It's better if we open it when he's here."

"It might take too long."

"For me." She smiles. I put the corkscrew down. Richard comes back out and sets a newspaper on the table, crowding out the candle on the plate, threatening to knock it over. Beverley takes it and sets it beside her on the deck.

"Read page 26," he says, sitting up proud but sort of nonchalant. He was always interested in something, enthusiastic. Pushy but enthusiastic.

So Beverley reads page 26 and I pick up the corkscrew again, put the tip of the screw on the cork, and start twisting. The cork resists and starts crumbling as I turn the screw. Half way down the entire upper half, or I should say quarter, of the cork comes loose and splits off and I pull it out and the other quarter as well. There are cork crumbles on the table and the grey balcony floor and the whole bottom half of the cork is still in there. The thinner half. And it's hard, the cork.

"Language," Beverley says, reading the paper.

"I can get it," Richard says. I wave him away. "You're shoving the damn thing inside, Dad."

"Language," warns Beverley, looking up from her reading. The entire bottom half of the cork is punctured and instead of coming out, it drops into the bottle and floats on top of the wine. "You must see this," Beverley says, and holds out the paper.

"Stupid goddamn cork," I say, louder than I intended.

"Everybody can hear you," Richard points out.

"Read," says Beverley. I glare at her. "Read. You'll be proud."

So I take the local paper and read about my son, who left a well-paying teaching job in Canada, I am informed, and cashed in all his investments and bought medical equipment and concentrated food and flew to Africa to one of the most dangerous places on the continent and spent two years living on local food, when it was there, and taught a hundred kids in the morning and another hundred in the afternoon and at night ran an impromptu medical clinic as long as supplies lasted and then, when supplies ran out, contacted people on the outside and organized them to keep him supplied and did this for two years, while the rest of us clucked our tongues and turned the channel when we saw starving children and fatal diseases and yammered about what was wrong with the world, why couldn't we all be nice to each other? Richard is leaning forward as I read.

"Well," says Beverley.

"Does everyone have their glasses?" I ask, and pour the wine, fishing out the cork bits and tilting the bottle several times as the cork inside the bottle stops the flow and I have to turn it up and then tilt it down again to get more wine out. When we're ready, I hold up my glass.

"To Richard. Our wonderful son whom we are so proud of. Here with a loaf of bread beneath the bough, A flask of wine, a book of verse—And Thou. Welcome home."

"The Rubaiyat of Omar Khayyam," he says and lifts his glass and the tears start from his eyes and down his cheeks as he raises and drinks and watches me all the time. "You used to recite the Rubaiyat all the time. My friends were jealous as hell. It's a jug, isn't it?" I smile. We stay out here until the sun goes down and decide to come in because we're worried the mosquitoes may start bothering us and there's a report that the West Nile Virus has returned and we shouldn't fool with that, Richard says, it's amazing how much medical knowledge he's picked up because he had to.

Beverley is facing out towards the bay and Richard and I are across from each other and I've been leaning against the railing feeling good about my son and our relationship, we've had our set tos, but it hasn't been as bad as all that. "Oh my," my wife says.

We turn in the direction she's looking as a sort of red blossom fades from the sky over beyond the skyway. The beads of light are sparkling across the skyway and a boat is just coming in the entrance and we can see a light at the prow of the ship and a white and yellow fountain shoots up and spreads out and shimmers in the lake. A faint streak spears up and an enormous flower erupts way above the water and a bright red blur spreads across below it. We watch for almost an hour. I can't remember any fireworks that have been anything like this, such a perfect setting, such a perfect time.

When it's over, we've been bitten a couple of times, not too badly and we pick up the empty bottle and the other debris and come inside. Richard goes to the shelves in the living room, the books are all back where they belong and searches until he locates a slim little paperback with a purple cover with a sort of white U and inside the U the sketch of a young smiling almond-eyed lady with a white veil and a red shift with an embroidered sash around her middle, bending forward and looking up shyly, The Rubaiyat of Omar Khayyam. "A flask of wine, a book of verse—And Thou," he reads. I smile.

"I guess you were wrong," Beverley says. "Your father does know these things. You don't always give him credit."

"More than you think," he says. "I have the best goddamn father in the world."

Beverley has the sort of dinner I'd expect for her son's welcome home and by this time the sun is down and we've lighted a candle and finished another bottle of wine that Richard has brought and started on the third, and he brings out a pamphlet from that leather file thing of his. "I'd like us to look at something," he says and turns on the lights.

We've had such a good time. I don't like the feel of this. "I got one for each of us," he says, and hands me a brochure with a big institutional building on the cover and old people playing cards and old people sitting at chairs before a fireplace and old people playing shuffleboard and old people in a dining room with women in white outfits circulating between the tables and a cat walking down a hall and a station wagon or something of the sort, a kind of miniature bus with windows and a big door opened at the side and a person in a wheelchair on a platform smiling as someone holds her hand and half of the logo of the Home painted on the side with the other half hidden by the wide open door, Hearthaven Retirement Home and Nursing Facility. With a view of the water, it says, and a caring staff and an in-house doctor and a bus to drive residents to the local malls and gambling casinos and enjoyable excursions and sometimes, for residents that are able to manage it, tours arranged to Atlantic City. "What is this?" I ask.

"I think it looks very nice," says Beverley.

"We are not going to a retirement home," I say.

"I am awfully tired, Preston."

"You love this place!" I object.

She shrugs and looks at the brochure once again. I stare at her, at Richard, back at her. Neither will look me in the eye. "You think I need one," I say. "You think I need to be locked up."

"I just brought it along to see what you think," he says. I rip up the thing and throw it on the floor.

"I'm prepared to have an open mind," says Beverley.

"I am not going to some kind of goddamn hospital for the senile, I am perfectly fine right here. Your mother loves this place." Richard stares right back at me. "That's a hospital. I am not going to a goddamn hospital. There is nothing wrong with me."

"You need to face reality, Dad. It's not fair to your wife. It's not fair to me."

"What the hell business is it of yours?"

"I hate to see you like this."

"Like this! What the hell do you mean 'Like this'?"

"Calmly dear," says Beverley, "we can talk this over without shouting. There is no need to shout."

"This was a perfectly fine evening and now it's ruined," and I get up and go to my bedroom and slam the door. And stand here in the dark. I will not go to some goddamn old folks lockup.

In a while, Richard knocks on the door. "I'm going, Dad. I'll be over tomorrow. Take care of yourself. Love you." I'm lying on the bed and I don't answer and I assume he must have gone though I don't hear the outside door closing.

"Preston." Beverley. "Are you all right? I'm making some tea. Do you want to have some tea? I think I'll go to bed. I'll have some tea and then I think I'll go to bed. Do you want some tea?"

"No thanks." She doesn't answer. She mustn't have heard me. "No thanks dear," I say more loudly. She doesn't answer and I get up and open the door but there's no one in the hall and I go to the kitchen, where she's sitting with a tea cup and saucer in front of her, just staring at it.

"You weren't very nice to Richard," she says. I come to the table and sit down. She's got a cup with little roses red and yellow painted around the edge, very delicate, and the same kind of roses around the rim of the saucer. The porcelain is very white and the cup is so thin you can vaguely see the level of the tea inside, when there is any tea inside. Right now there isn't. I put my hand over hers.

"I don't want to go," I say.

"Nobody said anything about you." She sounds angry.

"You need some help. We can afford someone. We should get someone in to help you out."

She doesn't look up, all the time I've been talking she's been staring at her tea cup. "Why don't you go listen to your Beethoven," she says. I go. I don't think that was a very nice thing to say.

I don't know what time it is. I'm still dressed. I took my shoes off but my socks are on and I'm sweating. I've got a shirt on and a tie and a long pair of pants. I can't get my collar loose and I finally tear at it and something rips and then I can breathe. I'm sweating like a pig. I don't want to go out there and wake up Beverley. I feel like I'm being swallowed up. I feel like there's some black hole eating me up from the inside out, swallowing me whole, from the inside out. I feel hollow.

I am less than nothing. They want to get rid of me. They've been scheming, both of them. She knew what it was all about. Beverley knew what it was all about, Richard came and they ran to her bedroom and they stayed in there for hours and hours and then they came out and acted like nothing had happened, all sweet and juicy, like nothing had happened. Scheming to lock me up. That's what they want. For all they care I might as well be dead.

My shirt is soaking. My underpants are soaking. I smell. I've been lying here shitting my pants. I'm nothing but smell, nothing but shit. That's all I am.

The ceiling is black. There's no light coming in. There's a grayness. I can't see. The ceiling is black.

I do not recommend old age. It leaves you with nothing, not even your dignity. It takes away everything.

I can't go out there. I might as well be trapped in here. Locked up. It must be a hundred and twenty in here. She's stuck a chair against the door. I heard her last night, shoving a chair against the door. If I tried to get out I couldn't. There's a chair against the door.

This is worse than a nightmare. This is worse than a nightmare, a nightmare gets over. Do not get old. Whatever you do, do not get old. I feel like screaming. Screaming.

So now I'm getting a headache. This always happens. I can feel it building up and my veins, my veins explode. I get a headache. Little triangular pills. In the bathroom. I can't get out.

God it's hot in here. It's hot and I'm getting a headache. I'm in the fifth circle of hell. Some goddamn circle. Stuck inside a sewer pipe with fire all around like a goddamn barbeque, like that movie I saw once where a man was plastered with mud and then baked and then put on a spit and turned around and around above a white hot fire, still alive, sizzling, with his mouth stuffed with baked mud and his screams caked inside his mouth, his screams gagged inside his mouth, stuffed inside a sewer pipe, head first, nothing but my feet sticking out.

Dante. Seven circles of hell. More than seven. How many?

He went through every goddamn circle of hell, right down to the devil in the frozen lake and never got a headache. Dante never got a headache. To hell and back and he never got a headache.

I guess she didn't put a chair there after all.

I wanted to get Beverley some breakfast, when the sun finally came up above the lake and I woke up with light on the ceiling. I don't know how I burned the toast but I did, smoke spreading across the ceiling. Beverley came out looking like a zombie and said, "Get out of the kitchen," and wouldn't speak to me for the rest of the morning. I decided to listen to Beethoven but the damn CD wouldn't work and I didn't dare ask her to help me. So I sat in my bedroom. It wasn't as hot, for some reason, and about an hour later, I came back out because it was cold in there. "Air conditioner," she said. "How's your foot?" While she was fixing it she said that Richard was coming in an hour and we had to get ready. "You'll need a better shirt," she added. All of this verging on rude, which I was beginning to find irritating. "How the hell did you rip your good shirt?" she asked. Her language shocked me.

So now I'm sitting in my recliner chair beside the sliding door to the balcony keeping the hell out of her way in a second best shirt and my jacket on the chair beside the table beside the door to the outside and Beverley in her bedroom getting ready. I don't dare move. I have to go to the bathroom. A pigeon lands on the balcony and I find my cane and rap on the glass door to shoo it away. It waddles along the balcony and stops. I rap on the window again. It doesn't move this time and I really give the door a good knock and the door rattles and I think my god I broke it. But I didn't. That's all I need, I'm already in the doghouse. "What's that noise?" says Beverley. She's putting her earring in, or trying to.

"Pigeon."

"You need to go to the bathroom. You'd better do it now. I'll help you if you want."

"I don't need your goddamn help to go to the bathroom," I get up, or try to and have to find my cane to help me, this stupid chair is too deep, one of these days I'll be stuck in here forever, in my own private circle of hell, a goddamn chair.

"I offered," she says.

Old age sucks. By the time I've finished my business Richard is sitting in my chair waiting to take us on this excursion he's got planned. "You look good," he says. Beverley fixes my collar and tie and hitches up my pants. I don't feel like reciting poetry today, I don't think I could, every poetic damn thing has fled, I'm tired, I didn't sleep well last night, I've got clean clothes thanks to Beverley and I'm not sweating, if anything it's too cold in here. Richard turns down the air conditioning when we leave. "It's getting cooler," he says. "Fall is coming. It's good to have you, Dad. We'll enjoy ourselves today."

It actually is interesting to drive down to the city along a road that stabs through a gully and suddenly we're at the edge of the mountain and turn right and go down an elaborate twisty road and come out among the scruffy old wooden houses in the east end and finally along a street that goes right through the steel plant and we can see, on each side of us as Richard drives slowly by, the inside of the steel plant with fire blobs jumping out and a long steamy aisle with dark happenings and men vague inside there, walking around.

"That is a horrible way to make a living," I say. And then we go through more scruffy neighborhoods and by vacant neglected lots with junk and weeds and finally along the road by the beach where the skyway soars above us and the cottages look even more run down than the houses we passed ten minutes ago. Just before we arrive at the lift bridge across the channel that leads from the lake to the harbor, bells start clanging and black and white striped barriers come down. While we wait, the entire body of the bridge in front of us starts to move up, a great blocky thing criss crossed with girders and an open net for the roadway when the bridge gets high enough that you can see it and hear it later when the bridge comes down and you drive across and your tires make smirring sounds.

I open the door and get out of the car because I'm getting cramped, even though Richard has got hold of a big white luxurious thing with a sliding door in the roof and windows that move up and down with a button and a car door he can lock by holding some black little oval with a ring at one end and four silver squares along one side and pressing one of the silver squares and the car locks itself with a clack. He doesn't have a key. He just gets in the car and pushes a button below the steering wheel and the car starts. What's to prevent anyone from doing that? I asked. "This," he said, and held up the same black oval.

We walk to the end of the road, by the barrier, and around that to the edge of the pavement, and watch an old lakeboat towed through the channel. The pilothouse at the front has a sort of visor hat and the railings and the decks are speckled with rust. A poor old boat going to the steel plant to die. To be cut up in pieces and melted down. Like the steel plant itself, now that the new owners have taken over, says Richard. I watch the old fellow, painted bravely black and white. It used to be young and useful and the pride of its fleet. Now it's being cut up, like the rest of us. No more use than scrap. But it moves by majestically. A big boat. Even now, a big magnificent boat. Paint her up and put a new crew on and she'll be as good as new. Not wanted. It always sounded strange, how the navy types used to call their ships "her." The pilots did the same thing, with bombers.

"That was interesting," I say to nobody in particular when we are back in the car and the bridge has slid back down and the barrier lifted up and we stream off with the rest of the cars that were waiting with us.

"Greasy," says Beverley.

Richard has been gone for two years, but he remembers, and we stop by a boarded-up store that used to be an art gallery, and grocery or hardware store before that, and many long years before, a railroad station on the train line that went across the sand barrier that blocks off the harbor and makes a roadway for the Skyway, which has been arching above us and gradually come down to ground level again. Up the street a bit is the old Mohawk Chapel, set back among trees, a small thing as far as churches go with a nice spire and a well proportioned front entrance and steps with a railing going up to the double doors and down the street an ancient tree knobbly at its foot, stuck out in the road and lifting three sections of the cement sidewalk up around its roots. The trees are huge and green and arch across the street and they won't last long, now that the city has decreed that the street will be repaved. So says Richard.

"I don't know how I'll manage the next few months," he says. "I've spent all my money in Africa."

"This is a pretty luxurious car," I point out.

"Rented. Just for you. Just for today."

"We can lend you something. We really don't need it," Beverley says. I can see what's been going on here. "It just sits there."

"No Mom," Richard replies and the subject is dropped, but it's clear it won't disappear. We eat at a place across the road from the lake and Beverley insists on paying and then we walk along the waterfront and I stop by a memorial to the corvettes of the war and their crews. These names sound familiar. I must have known some of these people. Nobody challenges me. They are both being very agreeable today, which makes me suspicious. I am somewhere on the other side of a glass partition watching everything passing by and nobody notices I'm even here, and talks as if I'm not. Where they are, everything changes, but nothing happens, everything remains the same, where I am. I'm tied up to a muddy bank with scrap and weeds in the long grass, waiting for the torches to cut me up and feed me to the steel plant. Head first with my feet stuck out. My toe is sore. A breeze is coming in off the lake and like Richard says, it's getting colder, some sailboats out there are flinging spray and leaning dangerously as they swing about, in some kind of race it looks like. There are people walking along the cement breakwater, kids and dogs and parents and young lovers and asshole young men acting stupid. A parade. I'm feeling good. I need to get out. This is good.

"The fireworks were over there," says Richard, pointing to the long spit of sand reaching out at the end of the lake and the Skyway curving up and down and the bridge, which is up again with the long double cement piers coming out in the lake and out beyond far across the water on the other side of the lake the escarpment vague and blue and fading out of sight, somewhere disappearing over the curve of the Earth. I went there one time, I think, on a lakeboat, I've got a vague recollection, going through the locks with a bunch of yachts that we were afraid we'd smear against the lock walls and I actually can feel the way the boat bounced off the entrance to the lock when the pilot, a young guy still learning, lost control a little, and the boat hardly felt it. And that was an old boat, fifty years old then, recycled as they say. Cut up long ago.

"Penny for your thoughts," says Richard.

"You don't want to know." I get miserable sometimes. I don't know why I said that. It was an innocent question.

We travel up the mountain on a four lane highway cut into the side, I remember, I think, I have this picture of standing in some park or something or other down at the foot of this hill looking up at a machine drilling in the rock, you could hear it for miles, a relentless hammering, making room for the roadway we are traveling now, and out there somewhere down at the edge of the suburbs in the greener area must have been where I was standing, it's the sound I remember, and the sight of this tiny machine, it must have been pretty substantial of course, with a pole raised up and whatever drill it was using at the end of this vertical pole, making drill cores for dynamite, which then blasted the space for the road and the line of scarred rock we can see to our left as we drive up, a long ragged straight run of rock forty feet high, I would imagine, with horizontal layers where ancient seas laid down sediment that solidified and lifted and there they are and inside the rock there, fossils, teenie animals petrified. Old guys. Whose time had come. There are trees at the top of the scarp and trees to our right fringing the road and dropping off and way over there, another section of escarpment that swings around like a horseshoe, and between the two, in the valley below us, houses and hospitals and buildings of various kind, a university, Richard says, the place where he's taking courses this year, and giving lectures it turns out. Everything is green at the horizon and lots of green between here and there and it's soft and lush and restful, and I should have known, because when we pull in the parking lot of the Hearthaven Retirement and Nursing Home, the purpose of this entire excursion becomes clear.

I don't want to get out, but Beverley talks me into it, I can't say no to Beverley, she never says no to me, my legs are wobbly, from sitting in the car so long and my toe hurts more and I won't take the wheelchair that Richard wants to offer me, they could strap me in, I want an escape route. I smile though, I don't want to embarrass Beverley and we wait in the lobby while Richard finds a parking place because all the parking slots in the narrow little lot in front of the building are taken, except one and he's afraid that someone will scrape the car, with all these old people, driving and their weak eyes and poor coordination, as if Beverley and I were spring chickens. I'm grumpy and I won't answer when people smile and say hello, not even when Beverley says something, but Beverley is used to that, she gets moody too. There is a line of sofas and chairs with their backs to the front wall of glass that faces the parking lot and we look at a long reception desk and, to our right, a fireplace, why

73

do all these places have fireplaces, there's never any fire, except in the brochures, at least not a real hundred-percent fire, just something you switch on and off as if fire was a machine like everything else. There's a group of old people, mostly women, at some tables on the other side of the lobby, this is a big two or three story space, there's a set of windows half way up and people walking along a hallway and some in wheelchairs looking down, wheelchairs are the transportation of choice here, and these old women at the tables on the far side of this lobby, at the other side of the entrance doors, doing something with beads and crayons and beyond them a square, actually a rectangular opening in the wall and beyond that inside some kind of tuck shop, a person moving around handing out cans of pop and the like. Everything is so bright and happy in here. But what's beyond those elevators, and what's along the corridor that goes off on both sides where people emerge and pass with wheelchairs and bent over old people, everyone here is so damn old, boats tied up ready for the blowtorches.

Richard comes back. "I had to walk forever. This is a decent lobby. Bright and cheerful. Don't you think?" So is a funeral home. A little darker, maybe. Same kind of furniture. And flowers. They've got flowers, and a big fish tank with bright colored swimming creatures in there trapped like everybody else in this place.

"My father has a sore foot," Richard says when a brisk tightly dressed woman with short hair comes up and shakes his hand and Beverley's hand and makes a special effort to be nice to me, "So this is Preston." How does she know my name? I've never seen her before in my life and never want to see her again. And I have to fight to avoid the wheelchair, which they've got all lined up at the counter for me, no, thanks, I'll hobble by myself thank you very much, I don't need a tugboat yet, I'm not ready for the furnace yet. The elevator has a button to open and close on the first floor and an elaborate keyboard on the second, which I notice at once when we get off. No button, just a keyboard. Down the hall to our left is a group of people milling about, stooped, sitting in chairs, walking aimlessly, like cattle milling about as a prairie fire closes in. A black cat meows as we tootle down the hall, the perky female ahead of us stopping and waiting while Beverley tries to help me along and I push her hand away, she's in on this, she knew about this. It doesn't matter how rude I am, they are all bright and perky here, the tall hefty guy and the short guy in hospital greens and the nurse at the counter around the corner and the staff of the dining hall, suitable for twenty five people, we divide our home into things we call houses here, and this is Waterside House with no water anywhere, except for the painting on the sign that announces the name. The cat follows us. The rooms are on both sides of a long wide hallway ending in a large window far down the corridor, and trees visible outside that, and a woman buzzing up towards us in her motorized contraption, the sports car of wheelchairs, and a bright smile on her too, it's some kind of disease, even though she can't move except at the push of a button, or the lever she operates, she could compete in a rally, she spins that chair on a dime. The beds are all hospital beds with machines that lift them up and down, the head, the foot, the middle if you want that, and tables that lift and lower to the height that the staff decides to set the bed, whatever whim they happen to have that day. Each room has a tiny closet, and a bathroom, and a clutter of sad mementoes. On the way out we pass a side room with a television set and a bunch of lounging chairs, but not so fast that I don't see the woman sitting two feet away from the TV screen staring at it like she's been nailed there.

As we're leaving, a woman at the front desk in the lobby says to me brightly, "Preston! We just got an opening! You can be here next week, I've got your name at the top of my list. We can't wait to welcome you to Hearthaven!" and her smile follows us all the way out the door as the rest of her vanishes.

I don't want to upset Beverley, because this was her idea, hers and Richard's, she's different when her son is around, not so nice, but I owe her and I don't want to make her sad so I don't say anything until we are well out of hearing, in the car and driving away. "I think it was lovely," she says, as if I hadn't said a thing, and Richard agrees, but it is up to me, my son declares.

I'm damned if I'm saying anything. From the silence in the back seat I know that Beverley wants me to say something. I'll be damned if I'll say something. I want to know who put my name on that damn list.

I'm waiting for Richard to leave, but he isn't leaving and it's getting dark. I lay down when we got back, but I couldn't sleep, I was too damn mad, but he wouldn't leave, he didn't leave, I'm going to have to confront them both. I don't want to.

The dinner wasn't so good, some ham and boiled potatoes, it's getting monotonous, Beverley isn't the good cook she used to be, I used to help her get ready but she won't let me any more and I just have to sit in my chair and shut up, seething with anger here.

We watch some television and I fall asleep again and when I wake up my goddamn son still hasn't left. "Why don't you go for a walk with your father," Beverley suggests. "I think you need some exercise, Preston. You won't be able to sleep unless you get some exercise." So I'm ordered around again. She's probably right, I sleep better when I get exercise. I don't have any choice. My name's on the list.

"It's cold," says Richard, coming in from the balcony.

"You'll need a scarf and a warm hat and a coat," says Beverley.

"I sweated like a pig last night," I say.

"Well it's cold out now," talking like I'm a child.

"I need to go." I should have said I need to go weewee, I am not a man, I do not go for a piss any more, I go weewee, like a child, like a baby, ordered around.

"I'll wait outside," says Richard and puts on a sweater and goes out the door while I go down the hall to do my business, to go weewee. When I come out, Beverley is standing by the door.

"He put my name on that list, didn't he?" I've got her alone. She can't hide behind her son. I've got her alone and I want some answers.

"No dear. It was my idea."

"Don't tell me that shit, I know it was Richard," I raise my voice, I am tired of being pushed aside like I'm a child, like I don't know anything, like I'm too stupid to know what is going on here. "He didn't even have the decency to apologize. He put my name on that damn list and didn't even have the decency to apologize."

"No dear. It was my idea."

"He didn't even apologize." I've really raised my voice now and Richard comes inside. "You didn't even apologize."

"There was nothing to apologize for," he says and I push by him and go out the door and slam it behind me and cane down the hall, bang thud bang bang thud I can hear him following behind me and Beverley saying something but I don't hear and I don't care to hear bang thud bang thud, yank open the fire door and stump down the stairs, six flights of stairs I can hear him behind me, thump thump down the stairs, six flights of stairs "Slow down," he says, "You'll hurt yourself," I've always been stronger I'm stronger than both of them, even at my age, I could outrun them both, I could beat them both, down down, thump thump, it sounds like he's slipped, "Dad," he's farther behind he starts to move faster thumpedity thumpedity thumpedity, I reach the bottom of the stairs and yank open the fire door and head to the rear exit to the parking lot and open the door to the parking lot and he's right behind me and I hold the door and he comes out and I swirl and rush back inside and slam the door shut and he's locked out, it's a fire exit and there's no latch on the outside, he hammers on the door but I'm thumpeting down the hall, thump bang bang thumping and hammering on the door behind me and an indistinct sound that I know is my son hollering but the door is thick and I'm far down the hall I'm faster than he is and when I reach the front entrance there she is the hunched-over lady I saw yesterday, who says "Hello Preston" as I rush by but I don't know her I don't have time to pass the time of day thank you, the parking lot for the apartment comes out by the main street and if I turn that way I'll meet Richard as he comes around the building but there are houses on the other side of the parking lot and at the back, so it's blocked off there by privacy fences so I turn left and walk to the end of the block, reach the corner and turn up the long residential street with trees and lights spotted all along from time to time and dark patches between for blocks all the way down there, I'm thumping along, cane ahead, feet following cane supporting, feet ahead cane behind cane ahead feet following cane supporting, I am fast and I know what I am doing and I will go up this street until I reach the end, I can see it way down there, this is a long street with cross streets a car blares its horn and someone shouts but I'm across the street stumping along if anything I'm faster than ever faster than ever an old man speeding along there are houses on both sides and verandas and fences with yards and flower beds right out to the sidewalk little one story houses that people have been looking after and tall yellow flowers on long stalks leaning out brushing against me as I pound by he didn't apologize he didn't apologize he didn't apologize putting my name on that goddamn stinking list I will not go there there is nothing the damn wrong I may forget sometimes yes but I am perfectly fine another street across I almost trip on the curb shuffle my feet but recover and keep going I used to run marathons I ran marathons when he was still shitting his pants it's cold I fart I haven't been out for days it loosens my bowels I fart that's a good sign I need to have my bowels loosened I am not going back there they can all go to hell I'll spit in their faces and tell them to their faces another street, light on the sidewalk in and out of the light, darkness on the house fronts it's cold, my head is getting cold, my ears are getting cold my toe is hurting I'm limping I've been limping for a long time now and only now just noticed my toe my foot is hurting I might have broken the bandage and the toe may be bleeding I keep stumping I'm going faster than ever I will never go back there's a man and a dog walking toward me the dog barks the man holds it back it barks as I pass it barks after I pass stump stump in and out of the light, "Hello dear," I jump, I must have jumped twenty feet straight up, Beverley, panting, she's hoarse, "You really can go," she says, whatever in the heck is she doing here, it's cold here, she shouldn't be here, it's far too cold but for some reason I'm actually going faster again and she's keeping up, panting hard but she's keeping up and she tries to talk and she can't and I slow down so she doesn't have to go so fast and finally I just stop. We're both panting. My side hurts. I'm gulping air. I can feel my heart pounding. I'm out of shape. I wouldn't be like this if I wasn't so out of shape. I have to get out every night and get exercise. I've been listening to Beethoven too much. Beethoven is fine. But my body needs attention too.

I'm bending over.

My legs hurt.

My foot hurts.

My side hurts so much I'm slightly bent sideways.

"Can we sit on the curb?" Beverley gasps.

We do.

She looks blanched, even in this light, everything looks white at night in a streetlight, but Beverley looks hideous. She leans against me. "You sure can run fast. Cane and all."

"You shouldn't be here." I put my arm around her.

"You neither."

"We don't get enough exercise."

We say this between pants. My head feels strange, dizzy across the eyes, for a moment I fade out, at least the light sort of fades out though I know where I am and who is with me and why we are here.

"Maybe I should go too," she says.

"We just need more exercise."

"Well we got some tonight." She always has an answer. Whatever I say, she always has an answer. One of the reasons I loved her. That I still love her. One of many reasons.

"I wonder where Richard is."

"He'll be okay," I say. "He's younger. It's a world for young people."

"I had a feeling there was something wrong. I don't know why. I lay down and I thought, is he having trouble with Preston?"

"Sorry to cause so much trouble."

"You're no trouble really. No more trouble than you've ever been." She lays her head on my shoulder again and takes it away. "It's hard I know. It's not nice getting old. We each react in our own way."

"I won't go there."

"You made that pretty clear."

"I won't."

"You always were a pretty determined man."

"That's why you married me."

"One reason." We haven't been like this for a long long time. "You have to have some kind of help, Preston. I'm sorry. I wouldn't say it if I didn't love you. You'll have to accept that. It tears my heart, what's happened."

"What has happened?"

We are standing up and starting back and Richard runs towards us along the sidewalk and throws his arms around me and squeezes me so tight I think he'll break my ribs and stands on my hurt toe. "Oh my god," he says. "Oh my god." He lets me go and I stagger back a bit and get my balance and he grabs my shoulders to prevent me from falling and says, "Oh god."

"Your father was worried about you," Beverley says.

"I thought I'd lost you," he says. I smile. "Mom said you were out in the park yesterday talking to some people and I thought you'd jumped over the wall and were down on the road there squashed flat. I couldn't see a thing down there. I thought you were dead and it was all my fault."

"The report of my death . . . ."

He hugs me again. He's never been like this. I've never seen my son like this. He was always so standoffish.

"We'd better get in out of this cold," says Beverley.

"How did you find him?" Richard asks and they come on both sides of me and we start limping me home, though I worry about Beverley, she's older than I am and was never as strong and she should be the one we're helping not me, I'm still pretty strong for my age though kind of winded right now.

"I could see someone way down the street," says Beverley, "and I wondered if maybe it was your father and then he walked in a streetlight and I could see the cane and I recognized the coat though he was too far down to be sure, but it looked like him. He jumped a hundred feet when I said hello."

"I ran down the street," Richard says, "I literally ran. I must have gone ten blocks and almost got run over at least three times and then I thought, oh my god, he's gone over the escarpment and I ran back and went straight to the park and leaned over the wall and looked in all the bushes at the bottom of the drop and I couldn't see anything but I thought it was so dark down there he could be dangling in a tree with branches stuck all through his body or maybe he bounced and landed on the road and a bus ran over him and dragged his body a hundred feet and I'd find my father mangled beyond recognition."

"You have a good imagination," I admit. I have to smile, the picture of Preston mangled beyond recognition is amusing in a weird sort of way.

"Doesn't he though," Beverley says. "I almost saw your body there myself, the way he described it."

"Neither of you are very damn funny," says Richard. "Could we stop for a minute. I need to get my breath. I'm actually kind of weak." We've reached the end of a block and he sits on the curb and after a minute we join him. We get up, finally, when Beverley says,

"My bum is cold."

When we get back to the apartment, we all lie down. Me in my black bedroom. Beverley in hers. And Richard on the antique sofa that Beverley lays out for him with pillows and blankets and an extra soft quilt underneath. My wife worries it will be too warm, but Richard is asleep by the time she's got him all tucked in, so the old folks go to bed after the young one.

"Don't do that again," Beverley says when she puts me in bed, and kisses me on the forehead. "Your wife is too old."

I promise. Never again.

I lie awake thinking, and I don't realize I've fallen asleep until I wake up I don't know how many hours later from a hideous nightmare and I rush to the living room and there's someone on the sofa and I've got my cane which I picked up when I jumped out of bed to protect myself and I start whacking at the person on the sofa it's dark and I miss the person jumps up and runs to the kitchen where the light is on and it's Richard and Beverley screams, "Preston!!!" because for some reason I've started flailing about smashing the glass cabinet she has with her Royal Doultons and I drop the cane and stare at Richard who is staring at me horrified and I start bawling I can't stop and they take me back to bed and I say, "I thought it was somebody, I thought it was somebody who had broken in, I thought it was a stranger, I was trying to protect you!" and Richard is calm, "You know this can't continue, Dad. We have to do something before something terrible happens. You don't have control any more."

They knock on the door and I can hear the bustle as they come in and Beverley gets up and goes out and a big burly man like the man in the park says, "Hello sir, how are you feeling?" and I say something that he probably doesn't hear but wouldn't have paid any attention to even if he had and another man comes in, a corpulent woman actually, and they click up some sort of device beside the bed, and the woman says, "We are going to move you to a gurney sir, this won't hurt, we'll have you on in two seconds and then we'll take you downstairs, are you feeling all right?" and I say something to her too and she ignores that also and then they pull off the covers and lift me and place a sheet under me and wrap it all around over my arms and legs and up around my head so that I'm bundled like a mummy and then they lift me underneath my legs and my back and set me on a kind of table, very hard, and wrap long wide straps around my legs and my body where my arms are and tighten them, not too tight, and wheel me down the hall, they have trouble negotiating the corner by the door and decide they'll have to do it differently, and unstrap me and lift me off and take me back to the bed and while the woman does something the man stands by the bed and remarks how the weather has turned cold it looks like fall is coming on though we've still got some summer left and we'll probably get another spell of warmth and the woman is back and they lift me off and carry me down the hall and out the door where the gurney as they call it is now and strap me in again and wheel me along the hall of the sixth floor and I notice that the hall lights are set in round wells, which I've never noticed before and while

87

we wait for the elevator the woman asks the man is he's getting any holidays this year and he says probably around Thanksgiving, the family is coming, his mum and his dad and a couple of cousins and their kids and the elevator door opens and they wheel me in and I can feel the elevator lurch as it starts down and it's daylight out when they take me off the elevator and some people in the lobby look down as I slide by and I can see the canopy above the driveway where the cars come in, it turns and I slide forward, "Easy now," says the man and I'm lifted slightly and my feet tilt down a bit and I can feel something bumping underneath me and I slide in and the man says, "There we are" and for the first time I see Richard and Beverley who get in at the back of the ambulance on each side of me, "Do you have to have the straps on?" says Beverley but no one answers and I can hear doors slam and it gets darker inside and Beverley strokes my face and Richard has tears and doors above my head slam and the woman calls back, "Everybody okay back there?" and Beverley says, "Yes, fine, thank you," and I can feel the vehicle start off and I start to yank at the sheet and the straps and feel the needle going in and Beverley says, "I am burying him alive."

This place

This place is right across from a school. There's a whole line of cars across the road in front of the school. Adults dressed up, kids dressed up, tiny ones waving goodbye or clinging, a mother walking her girl up to the door and swooshing her inside, adults, mostly women, talking in groups on the sidewalk, green leaves blowing across the view between my window up here and down there. Happy sunlight.

"We almost sent our kid there," he says. "My wife doesn't like private schools." What am I supposed to say to that? He sounds angry. "Do you sit here every morning?" he asks. "Drinking coffee, relaxing after breakfast." I am not impressed with this man. "Pretty good, I'd say." He's short, younger than me, in a sweater. I don't think lawyers should show up in sweaters. It's not professional.

"I give my son fifty dollars," let's get on with it, you're here to do my will, no damn conversation, "and the rest to charity."

He takes a sort of electronic slate from a small black bag he's set on the floor beside him, lights it up, and makes some kind of gesture above it.

"All of it?" he asks.

"All of what?"

"All of your estate, except the fifty dollars."

"All of it."

He makes more gestures and punches at his slate.

"You're sure?" he says.

"All of it, you fool!!!"

He shrugs. "Your wife's name is Beverley?" He knows that. I've already told him that. He's irritating me. "She's not included?" he asks.

"Of course she's included!" What kind of an idiot is this?

"Her share as well?"

"What do you mean?" Doesn't he understand the English language?

"Her share as well? To charity?"

"No!" I've got the wrong lawyer. The man is an idiot.

"She's included then."

"Of course she's included, you idiot! She's my damn wife!"

"Maybe it's best if I come back with a copy of your will."

"Why?" What the hell is this? Come back? What the hell is he talking about?

He can see I'm angry. He doesn't say anything for a moment. To get me to calm down, I suppose. Well I am calm. I am perfectly calm. I know what I'm doing.

"In case there's something else we need to have a look at," he says and doesn't look at me and puts the slate thing away, in a compact little holder he's brought along, black with a handle, slim. "Unless you have a copy of it here."

"I don't have a damn thing here!" What does he mean, unless I have a copy of it here! Didn't he bring a copy? What's he up to?

"I'll bring a copy," he says really quietly and stands up. He didn't bring a copy! What kind of a fool have I hired? "And there is no need to be angry with me, Preston, I haven't done anything. I didn't put you here."

"Whose side are you on?"

"Yours, of course."

"Like hell."

"Was there anything else?" What does he mean was there anything else? What the hell is the man's problem? "Nothing else? Maybe I misunderstood."

What is so difficult about changing a will? The man is incompetent. He doesn't deserve getting angry over.

"There is nothing else you want me to deal with at this time?"

"No!!!"

He picks up the chair he brought over here when he first came in. "I wouldn't be able to do anything about it anyway. Not until we deal with the incompetency business." What does that mean?

"You'll have to excuse me, Preston, I have another appointment. I'm late already."

"Where do you think you're going?"

He carries the chair to the end of the bed and turns and faces me, holding the chair between him and me. "I'll be back with a copy of the will. We can't do anything until we look at the will." He is walking out on me. I am stunned. I don't believe it. "Until we deal with the incompetency business I won't be able to do anything, Preston. From what I see, I'm not sure I can."

"What is that supposed to mean?"

"I have another appointment." He goes to the door and places the chair beside it as he leaves.

"Come back here!" He ignores me and keeps going. Nobody pays any attention, they all walk out. "Come back here!!!" I shout as loud as I can, but nothing happens. "Come back!!!!" Nobody comes. I'm left here, sitting here, outraged. Who the hell does he think he is, who the damn hell does he think . . . !!

He's a fool. He's not worth it. He's a fool. I have to calm down. I get excited and then I can't decide anything. I have to calm down. I was always cool. I always kept my temper. That's why I was good, that's why I knew what I was doing.

Deep breath. Calm down, Preston. Calm down. The man is an ass. The man is an incompetent ass. You made a mistake. You hired a fool.

Calm down. You'll get another one.

Incompetency. What did he mean, incompetency?

Calm down. I didn't used to be like this. I was always calm. I know I was always calm.

Deep breath. Really deep breath. Think about something else. Concentrate on something else. Come back to it later.

Calm. Be calm. Calm.

There's more cars and people standing around out there. A bus trying to get through the traffic. I feel sorry for those kids. They have no idea what it is they're getting into. They think that life is so damn exciting. They think there's nothing but good things coming. What do they know? Poor kids. I feel sorry for them.

Calm.

This is the only thing I like about this place. This view. I don't know why exactly. They are so free, those kids. They are so protected. They have no idea what's coming. Who will stab them in the back. They don't have cops standing guard and men in shabby suits writing out reports and making decisions. I like this view. Who knows, maybe it reminds me, when I was a kid. So long ago. So damn long ago. I enjoyed myself. We had a really wonderful little country school. I used to play outside every day, ball games and swings and jumping the fence and hiding from the teacher, did I really do that? Probably not, I was a pretty obedient little kid. Why do I remember that? We didn't have much, not like these kids, these kids have everything. We enjoyed it. I wonder, where all those people are, the children I used to play with, they'd all be grown up now, most of them dead, probably. Well, some of them. A lot of them probably. I'm getting up there.

When I was like that. Like those kids. It makes me so damn sad.

I like this place. A hell of a lot better than that other place. They don't have policemen at this place. Not like that other place. No shabby suits. The people in charge here are better. They are nice, I have to say that, in fairness, they are nice. They let me roam around, not like that other place, there's a TV in the main room, I have the run of the place, after everyone else is in bed. They go to bed so early here. The only thing good about that other place, I wasn't there long. Policemen and shabby suits but I wasn't there long. I've already been here much longer. Much longer. God help me, it's beginning to feel like home. And it's not home. Beverley is my home. I could go out for walks. They won't let me out here. Not unless there's someone with me.

There are crazy people here. No matter where I go, there's crazy people. Including lawyers. Especially lawyers.

From here I can see the basketball court but there is no one there right now and the swings are empty and the shadows of the trees are half way across the playground, there's some paper blown up against the fence that has a sort of criss cross sort of grid thing, there's a name for this, I can't think what it is and a black small rat like animal with a long tail is crossing the concrete, nosing around, stopping and chewing at something, kids are always dropping food, the animals love it, sometimes one will chase away another, it's quiet, the Sun is slightly yellow on the yard, a car goes by on the, squirrel, it's called a squirrel, I can look down on the roofs of the trucks and cars as they drive by, a car down the road, I can see it if I lean forward, stops and someone gets out and opens a gate of some sort and drives in, a bus comes along and stops and a woman gets out and comes in this building, my old mug, with a thing, a dot and lines spraying out and writing on it all around a circle, this feels good, my own mug, and coffee, and the machine in the corner that I play my CDs on, it doesn't work, I'll have to get it working, there is a tree right outside this window practically and sometimes the leaves make shadows dancing on the wall and across the door, which is closed, I ask them to close the door and they do, this is a big room, I like it private, I don't like people looking in, when the door is closed no one can look in, can't look through the wall, not yet, no window in the wall yet, haven't thought of that yet, not like that other place, I've got a table and a chair and a computer machine thing, not turned on yet, and the picture of an old man sitting on a dock in a wooden chair, dozing, and two kids at the end of the dock fishing and a canoe to one side, tied up and water stretching out to a line of trees far across and a bank of trees on one side with some white birch trunks peeking through. It's restful. I would have liked grandchildren. Looking at that picture makes me feel like dozing in this chair. But my favorite, hanging on the other wall beside the door, jagged mountain peaks and a man standing on the peak closest and the Sun just emerging and the sky painted with brilliant reds and oranges and blues, Zarathustra, imagine that, remembering that name and not being able, I don't understand, it's all so random. No one here has a name. The woman who comes in. Older. Wrinkle faced. Harsh voiced. Kind enough, like a mother. Thinks I'm a child. Some smaller pictures along the wall on the other side of the door, small things that I can't make out from here and really don't mean much, pictures of people standing rigid and smiling, in groups, and the shadows of the leaves dancing across them, and all along this one wall where I'm sitting, big windows letting in the Sun and heavy curtains to pull across if the Sun gets too bright, which I'll have to pull across later on when it starts glaring in, but not now, I like it right now, I just got up and have my coffee and I like it right now. The curtains are dark blue when they pull them across and they really block out the Sun and almost make it too dark in here. There's a dark glass half globe above the door that almost looks like an eye when you go right up to it and stare at it like it's almost staring back. The walls are a light sort of brownish I've forgotten the name, almost white with a suggestion of brown. An easy chair for me to sit in, and lean back, and watch the show outside. If I want TV I can go in the other room, later on, when the crazy people who circulate around here are resting and there's nobody in there and I can have it to myself. A dark green and orange blanket on the bed, woven with holes all through it, and yet it's warm and I don't know why, how can a blanket with holes all through it be warm, especially that one, made like a grid with huge holes you can see if you hold the thing up. I like it though. Still haven't figured out how it works. It seems like I should know, for some reason. I don't know why, but I like it. It's homemade, I can kind of see the person who made it, knitting like they're making a scarf, sitting in a chair, for some reason I think of a hard back chair with carving on the back, at the top, scrolls.

The first car. A van. Maroon red. Two kids get out the side and one turns back and then the van drives off, I can only see the roof and the kids going in the door and one minute later, out another door in the yard and the boy, can't tell what age, with a ball bouncing and throwing at the loop, and missing and the girl standing watching and a car pulling up now and five kids getting out, tumbling out and running towards the door and out in the yard and one kid grabs the ball and throws it to another and the kid who came first stands for a while and then goes and sits down and watches and the girl goes off with the other girls who've come in the car and two more cars arriving. I used to, when I was that age, in a one room school, throw a ball right over the school, it was a game we all used to play, throw the ball then run around and try to catch it, as it came down the other side. The trick was, just get it up the roof so it'd roll over and then it would start running down the roof on the other side and you'd have a chance to get around just in time to catch it. I think we used to have points. Sometimes we'd have teams and one team would stand on one side and one team on the other. If we slipped up and threw it through a window the teacher would confiscate the ball. I can't remember any of the kids I used to play with. Most of them are dead by now, I'm sure. Most of my friends are gone. The only thing that's left, are memories, and those are going. I don't understand, how I can remember all of that so vividly and can't remember what happened yesterday. It's like, when I look down at that school yard, I can feel what it was like, so many years ago, when I was that age and could run around and didn't have a worry in the world. And some day . . . .

No. I won't think that. I have my coffee and I'm enjoying this and that is all that matters. Let what happens some other time, happen some other time. That isn't now. Right now I'm relaxed,

I have pleasant thoughts and I'm enjoying this and I feel that, for some reason, I'm more like those kids down there than anyone in here, just sitting here enjoying the Sun, not worrying about anything, enjoying their games for the sake of enjoying their games. And sort of wishing I could play them myself. No, I won't think that. I'm too old for that. Let them enjoy them, I'll enjoy them enjoying them. More cars coming, delivering kids, and an adult, out there in the yard now, supervising. A teacher, I assume. The road is narrow. With a car parked on this side, and cars pulled over on the other side, letting off kids, there's only room for one more car to squeeze by through the middle. And it's a problem, cars going one way, have to wait until cars going the other, get through the gap. One guy, looking like he's impatient. Driving a van. I can see his arm stuck out the window, drumming his fingers on the roof. Looking down on things like this, I feel like a god, looking down on the world. What are those foolish humans up to now? Like Zeus. Like, what were the other gods? I used to know.

Notebook. Yesterday the—8th. So today is the—9th. Tuesday. Tuesday the 9th. Who was here? Beverley. The doctor. No name doctor. I can never catch their names. Doctor not recognized, I've written. Watching kids. Watching kids again. Watching kids, gap of two days, then watching kids again. Back and back, watching kids, watching kids, every day. Hockey game, Sunday afternoon game it says. Leafs lost. Exciting game. It says. Funny. I can't remember that at all. Must have happened. It's written right here. Lawyer. No name. Must get a new lawyer. Should have written his name. Competence. That's not his name. Change my will. Maybe. Depends on how they act. Right now they're on trial.

So. Tuesday the 9th. Watching kids. The start of another day. The shadows are getting shorter out there. I was always organized. I am not so organized any more. I feel better if I'm organized, so I know what's going on, so I know I'm in control. I have to write down everything now. Instructions, how to turn on the computer. Instructions, how to turn on the CD. Still doesn't work. Can't make out what I've written.

Hard Nose wears a green outfit, pants and top, the pants are baggy and the top has long sleeves and is not pressed, it's been thrown in a washer and it's clean all right, but nothing fashionable. She has white hair, curling in below her ears cut like a cap with a few hairs straggling out, over her forehead, she's got glasses with thick arms tapering towards her ears, her nose is coarse and her chin curls underneath her mouth and joins a thick neck that hangs like a pelican below her jaw, her skin is coarse and wrinkled, she looks sixty at least, seventy maybe, older than the rest of the people here. She's square built and muscular. "Do you know what day this is?"

she asks and pulls the sheets on my bed straight. "You need to do this yourself."

I can't remember what my notebook says. "A good day," I guess.

"Tuesday. The day you came here."

"Do I get a cake?"

She goes around the room moving things and picks some clothes off the floor. "I should." She clips a plastic thing on my finger. "Leave that there. Have you gone to the bathroom yet?"

That's a pretty personal question, so I don't answer.

"Probably not," she says. "Open your mouth." She puts some white and blue things in and tells me to drink my coffee. She watches while I do that.

There's more kids in the playground and more cars pulling up in front.

She unclips my finger, writes down something, takes my coffee mug and puts it on the window sill.

"Let's get things going here," she says and lifts me up and gets me to the washroom. "We'll get you dressed after. Breakfast in fifteen minutes."

She closes the door. She's a little bit military. I don't know why she's still here, at her age. How long did she say I have been here? She has soft eyes behind those glasses. Her mouth is small, it's not harsh, sort of neutral, not hard like her voice. When I'm done here

I'll wash up and brush my teeth and the rest of it and go out and choose something to wear and she'll probably criticize my choices. I could resent her, but I think she's had a hard life. Must get a new lawyer. Have to write that down.

I get a little dizzy sometimes. I hate being dirty. This toilet flusher doesn't always catch at first, they need to get the thing fixed, but it does work. I'm glad to have a toothbrush and something to shave with and mouthwash to gargle. I'm dizzy but I grab the edge of the sink and reach for my toothbrush and my legs go limp and I crash against the ledge above the sink and there is a big smash and I'm down.

"Good heavens, Preston," she says. I can feel her hand reaching around my head and pulling back. "I don't want to move him," she says. "Get me a first aid kit." I can hear some kind of scuffling, someone else. "Can you hear me?" she asks.

I nod.

"Don't try to move. How did you fall?"

I shake my head.

"You don't know?"

I nod. I can feel hands moving around my body.

"He's conscious," she says. "Preston. Can you hear me?" Her voice is louder. "Can you get up? You've had a bad fall. I think you're all right, except for a cut on your head. You're a lucky man. You smashed the glass shelf. You need something to steady yourself." I can feel someone lifting me, my legs are rubbery, I scramble my feet around but I'm not doing much good. "Just lean on me," the voice says. White hair helmet, glasses with heavy dark brown arms, harsh voice.

I feel dizzy, my left eye is blurry, I stumble hands are underneath my armpits and gripping my arms hard the room is seasick.

"There we go. We had a weak spell. You're okay, I'll have a doctor look at you, but I think you are okay." A head, eyes squinting at me, everything vanishes, cloth wiping my face. "Your eyes are sort of glazed. How are you feeling?" The room reappears, my eyes aren't so blurry.

I nod.

"Good." Her voice is still loud, like she's talking to a child.

"Considering I just fell and cracked my head," I say.

"Good. You're conscious. You know what happened. That's good, Preston. You'll survive."

I close my eyes, I feel really tired, I can feel a bandage being stuck to my forehead. "You may need stitches. There was blood all over your face, I was afraid you'd done yourself some serious damage." Still the loud voice. "You scared us, Preston. I can't leave you alone for five minutes."

"Don't worry about it." I don't open my eyes, I don't know if I've said it so loud, my throat is parched, I need a drink, I can't talk loud, the sound came out harsh and hoarse.

"Not for five minutes," she says, not too friendly. I suppose I'm a bother. "I was afraid you had cut your eye, especially your left eye. Not so much damage done. Except for the bathroom." I open my eyes. She smiles and pats my face. "I wouldn't know what to do without you," she adds.

"My legs just gave out."

"It happens, Preston."

It doesn't happen. I'm not like this. I used to jog. I'm fit. I'm a hell of a lot fitter than you are, you're old and you're not in shape, you do well just to get done what you do around here.

"Let's get him back in bed," she says in a lower voice and I am lifted, I can see someone else on the other side of me, I can't tell if it's a man or a woman. "It'll probably happen again." she tells me, gets me settled and asks if I want breakfast.

"I'm not hungry."

"We're okay now," she says to the person who has helped.

Thank you, I try to say to the other person but the words get lost in my throat when I try to talk.

"I'll get you some toast," she tells me.

"I'm not hungry," I repeat but she's already gone and I didn't say it so loud, I just want to rest, I've had a shock, I don't fall, this was a stupid accident.

"Preston! What happened?" I open my eyes. Beverley. My Beverley.

Sitting here with Beverley, watching the schoolyard, wind in the trees out there, some leaves red, yellow, green. "I mustn't have played with the other children a lot," she says, holding her coffee mug with both hands. "I remember I used to stand beside a fence looking at a fish pond, at a house next door to the school. You wouldn't think I would do that, if I used to play with the other children a lot." I can picture her, a short little kid in a skirt with a coat over top that came down just below the skirt and fur around the bottom and fur around a hat that comes down below her ears, it's windy out there, the kids are running around but they need a coat today. She must have been a shy little girl, with a mind of her own. There are a couple of kids standing, over beside a fence, watching the others play ball of some sort. "Do they skip any more?" Beverley asks. This is good, sitting here with Beverley. She doesn't come to visit as much as I want her to. This is really good. Sitting here with coffee, watching the schoolyard with my wife. The kids down there running around, you can hear their shouts, muffled. A truck pulls up and parks by the fence, partially blocking our view. We can see above the top but it blocks out part of the game and the kids standing by the fence. A man in a blue suit gets down from the truck and walks around to the back and a flap folds out and slowly moves down. He steps on it and it starts back up. The kids are shouting and raising their arms, some of them, and others are bending and making wild gestures with their arms. The flap stops rising and the man bends down and straightens up and disappears inside the truck. The angle is wrong, I can't see inside the truck, but I can see the edge of a round drum tilted and straightening up and most of a drum now sitting on the flap. The kids are running again, the ball appears in a tangle of limbs and a kid kicks it and it vanishes behind the top of the truck and the flap moves down. Above the truck and the schoolyard, closer to us, a black animal runs along the limb of a tree, in among the red and green leaves. "You used to tell me the way you played when you were young," she says. "Something about throwing the ball above a roof and running around to the other side and catching it. Our lives were so different. The city gal and the country guy."

"I can't remember names."

"Neither can I," she says.

"That thing."

"Thing?" she asks.

"There. That black thing."

"Black thing?" She is puzzled. I point to the animal, which is moving among the leaves, making it harder to point out. It stops, twitches its, its . . . tail.

"There." I point straight at it but she doesn't seem to see it.

"The telephone pole?" she says.

"There. There!" I'm pointing straight at it, doesn't she have eyes? "There!"

"In the tree?" The thing starts moving again. "The squirrel?"

"Yes!" It's frustrating, trying to get people to understand. We watch it moving. Squirrel. Black twitchy thing, tail. Something in its mouth. It reaches the main part of the tree and goes around the other side so we can't see it any more. The man is rolling a barrel on its edge, tilting it sideways, rolling it along by the side of the truck. A bus stops until he reaches the front of the truck and rolls it out of the way. He lets it straighten up and waves at the bus as it burbles by. "Imagine forgetting squirrel," I say.

"We all forget," she says. "Most things aren't worth remembering."

"I forget everything."

"I'm satisfied."

"I can't remember people I went to school with."

"Neither can I. That's a long time ago."

"I feel like I should . . . . It's like, like my life has . . . ." She is incredibly patient, my Beverley, she waits until I say what I want to say, until I find the words. I didn't used to be like this. I would never shut up. I never, let her get a word in. I remember bits, like that, but I can't remember, faces, faces maybe, not names. "Who is . . . ." I lean forward, and lower my voice, like we are whispering secrets. "That woman. Hard nose. I call her hard nose. I can't remember her name. I know . . . It just . . . ."

"Emily."

"It's not important."

"You should write it down."

"Yes! Yes! That's an excellent idea. Where is my paper?" She finds it for me and I'm sitting here, hoping she'll find it while I remember, and I write it down and she puts the paper, a book, back on my bed.

"You've been writing a diary," she says.

I take it back and flip the pages open. Dates and numbers. "Beverley looks good today," it says, "patched me up, made me feel better," and again, "Beverley was here, looked at the schoolyard. Children noisy. Woman came in to change the sheets." I strike out "woman" and write "Emily."

The children are going inside the school, and the truck has gone. "I wonder what the barrel was?" Beverley muses.

"How long have I been here?"

"A month. You've been gone one month and one week." I reach behind me and take the book back again and open it up. One two, sixteen twenty-three entries altogether. Beverley here, Beverley here, Beverley here, Beverley here, Beverley, Beverley. Richard twice. I don't remember that.

"How is Richard?"

"I was wondering," she says. "Looking at the children reminded me." The yard is empty, the animal is back running along the branch, in among the red and yellow leaves. "I've never seen his school. He's terribly busy."

"I enjoy this," I admit.

She brushes my forehead. "I'm glad that bandage is off. I couldn't have looked after it. I'm tired, Preston. Terribly tired." Her hand is small and wrinkled, her face is slack or something, it's seamed, her eyes are sad. Terribly sad.

"When you are old and grey and sitting by the fire."

"Who is that?" she asks.

"Somebody. It just popped in my head."

"You always had quotations. You haven't forgotten everything." She leans over and kisses me.

"And wonder rather sadly . . . . I can't remember the rest." All the things I have ever done are like sheep jumping through a hole in a barbed wire fence, the only thing left are bits of wool.

"Forty." She says nothing. Hard Nose says nothing.

"Thirty eight." Nothing.

"Thirty eight?" She says nothing. She sits here staring at me, giving me no hints.

"Forty minus . . . . thirty six." This is harder than it seems. A ridiculous exercise and harder than it seems.

"Thirty one, no two. Twenty, thirty one, no thirty two minus four."

"Twenty eight . . . . Seven. Eight. Even number, twenty four."

This isn't getting anywhere. She isn't saying anything, no hints at all. Sometimes I can tell, from her expression, if I'm right or wrong. Think it through.

Minus forty. Down to twenty eight minus, twenty four.

I'm all confused here.

"I'll give it another shot, okay? From the first?"

She nods.

A ridiculous question. Stupid test. I was no good at math. What does it prove?

"Okay. I'll give it another shot."

She nods again.

Count down from forty, by four, all the way to zero.

Deep breath. Here we go.

Forty minus four. "Thirty six." Minus four. "Thirty two." Minus four. "Twenty, twenty six. Twenty . . . ."

Forty minus four.

"I'll write it down."

"No, Preston. You're not allowed to do that."

"No?"

"Let's try something else," she says. "I'd like you to count backwards, from twenty. By two."

New question! Down from twenty! By two!

"You're trying to frustrate me." I'm only half joking. I'm getting angry. Frustrated. "Right?"

She shakes her head solemnly.

Okay, my dear, I'll give it the old college try.

Twenty, minus two "Eighteen," minus two, "Sixteen," minus two, "Fourteen," minus two, "Ten," minus . . .

Twenty minus two, "Eighteen, sixteen, fourteen, twelve. Of course, twelve!"

Eight, six, three.

"I can't write it down?"

She shakes her head. I was no good at math. It's tiring, I'm already exhausted. I'm tired today.

"Ask me tomorrow."

I didn't sleep very well last night. It's the street light, right outside my window. It didn't used to be so bright.

"That's okay, Preston," she says, "I was terrible at math too. Let's do the next one."

It's embarrassing. She knows my name and I can't remember hers for the life of me. I see her all the time and I can't remember her name to save my soul, not that I believe I have a soul, but if I did, I couldn't save it worth a damn. I've written it down somewhere. I write everything down. I have a note how to get here. Down the hall, turn to the left when you pass the fourth door, then pass by the locked rooms where the violent men sit with nothing but a chair and a mattress to sleep on at night, the men who used their canes for other things, I've been told. I remember that. I remember being told that.

"Can we start the next question?" she says. I'm not sure she is suited to this job, she doesn't have the patience.

"Another test. I may not remember everything but I remember that. Ridiculous questions." The window is cold, the cold comes through, Beverley is gripping her coffee mug to warm up her hands.

The tree branches are black, snow piled along in lines, chunks falling off in the bright sunlight hitting the branches below and spraying, like a white explosion, plopping on the ground if they last all the way down. The kids bundled, everyone in parkas and fat little suits in bright colors, the smaller ones anyway, the bigger ones in boots with pants tucked in the boots and hats, the timid ones with a sort of knitted thing that comes all the way down to their necks with holes cut out for eyes and nose and mouth, and a kid with glasses sticking out the hole where his eyes go, nothing but glasses, the tougher ones with their knitted things rolled up so their faces are bare and a little red and raw, kicking a ball around in the snow and kids throwing snowballs. One tree branch with the line of snow still sitting on top, not fallen off yet, but saw edged, where something has been running along the branch. Sun, painting everything, too bright. I need sunglasses.

"How is Richard?"

"He promises he'll be over," Beverley says. "He's terribly busy. They have lives of their own, the young people. It's only old folks like us who have time to sit here doing nothing."

"You're entertaining me," I point out.

"You're not bad yourself."

Two boys are rolling in the snow, fighting. A bunch surround them. Beverley yanks the drapes across the window, it's actually a good idea, it's much too bright in here, it's too white out there, it hurts my eyes. "He's found a place," she says. "I think I'll stay where I am, for now. Besides, I think he's found a friend."

"Who?"

"He hasn't said. I know it's a female. She's a female. You never know nowadays. They live such different lives."

"Who has found a friend?"

"Your son. They're moving in together. It wouldn't have worked, in the middle of all that confusion, he's better on his own without his mother, his mother would have . . . just been in the way." She drinks some coffee. "I need our money, Preston, I can't take on a mortgage at this stage in my life." She looks up from her coffee and smiles. "Our life. Besides that, it isn't really my money, it's ours. He didn't understand that. He says it's only money. I guess it's only money when it isn't your money." She looks good today, she's been much better lately, not so tired, she's getting her sleep, and eating properly, though the snow bothers her, she says, and the taxis are terribly slow, and some of the drivers downright rude. "I miss sitting out on our balcony," she muses. "Of course it isn't the weather to do that right now."

"We can see . . . . schoolyard from in here." She drinks some more coffee, placidly, waiting for me to finish, she is a marvel of patience. "Too noisy . . . . Out there." She nods. "Always wanted . . . . balcony." She looks in my eyes very intently. "Always."

"Anyway it's too cold," she says, talking a little too fast, I have to ask her to slow down sometimes. It's easier to listen though, I know what I want to say, it's hard sometimes to get it out, I'm better some days than others, some times than others, it's best when I'm calm and not upset, it comes on, this panic I call it, for no reason, sometimes when I think I'm feeling good, when things seem good.

"My head," she doesn't move, I have more of her attention right now that I have had, for a long time. "Like champagne sometimes," I say, "it feels like . . . . little bubbles inside. Really an odd . . . ." She nods and waits for me to go on, but I've said what I wanted to say.

"You said you feel numb sometimes, that your head feels frozen." She strokes my face. "I used to tell you if I only had half of you," she brushes a bit of hair from my eyes, "it was better than all of anybody else."

"There's something wrong. I feel . . . ." I like this place, it's comfortable, I feel trapped inside my body, inside my head, the people are good here, I . . . .

"Have you used your CD lately? You wanted me to help you get it going." I pull the drapes open. The Sun isn't so bright out and the schoolyard is empty. The yard is scuffled with footprints it's almost clear in the middle where the kids have been running. Someone tried to pile large chunks of snow over in the corner, one on top of the other, three, they've been pushed over. She wipes around my eyes, I do that sometimes, I get upset. "You don't remember our balcony, do you?" she says.

They are walking cocoons. Colorful. Trying to pack snowballs, but they can't. Wind is swirling threads of snow, spinning, sculpting. There are very few of them out today, mostly the brave ones. Someone, a teacher, is standing at the door, and they go back inside and there's nobody out in the yard now except the wind and the swirls of white and the piles up against the fence. The branches of the tree are empty, ridges of snow along the sides of the road and rutted tracks in the road itself, three cars mounded with snow, carved into white shapes, sitting at the side of the road in the piles of snow, wind lunging against the window, the cold coming through, frozen frost on the inside I can scrape with my fingernail, someone outside the school again, a big person hunched and disguised, leaning to protect himself, I assume it's a man, against the wind, smoke blurred away by the wind, coming from his head. He throws something in the snow and goes back inside. A car, slewing along the road. Wind creaking the window, hurling snow. I can sit on the thing with wheels, turn it backwards and sit, the seat is damn cold, I've got a blanket over me, coffee warming my hands. I'm glad to be in here. A taxi, the glass tablet on its roof, stopped in the road on this side, the driver's door opens, the driver huddles around with his hands on his ears, bends at the back door, opens it.

This day. The night over. Cold here. Heat coming up, welcome. My hands cold. My eyes feel squinty. Sheets piled up on the bed. Mattress bare. I'm wearing pajamas I haven't had before, they smell, a sharp not very pleasant odor.

I haven't seen Beverley for months. "Oh." The woman is dressed in a hat and snow and snow on her coat too and boots that trample, she tramps her boots on the floor, looks around, takes black shoes from a bag, takes her boots off, puts the shoes on, standing on one foot while she pulls the shoe on the other foot, reaching down, balancing. "It's terrible out there!" She comes over, by the bed, kisses me. "I have to get coffee! I'll be right back. You look handsome. I want to know what you've been up to since yesterday. All the gory details." She leaves.

I didn't recognize her at first, with all those clothes and the snow. I can hear her chattering out there. The cold makes people chatter, they've been chattering all morning.

Chattering all morning. How do you spell chattering? Where's my breakfast? How long do I have to wait for breakfast? I've been up here sitting for hours, waiting for breakfast. I didn't recognize her, with all those coats and the snow. "Beverley," I say when she comes back.

"Some people are so lucky to be inside on a day like today!" she says and sets a coffee mug on the windowsill. "Aren't you cold here? Why don't I take you somewhere warm? It's freezing here. Why don't they have the heat on?" She helps me up and turns me around so I can grab the handles of this thing I stand up at with the wheels and we go to the door and along the hallway, she walks beside me and I move along holding the handles, I want my cane, the cane is better, I like the wheels though, there's a basket to put things in and some kind of foolishness on a loop on the handle of the thing, some kind of multicolored snake made of plastic fuzz, they want me to put it on my neck, it's better where it is, I can squeeze the handles, there's a brake, I have this joke, that I don't have my driver's license, someone put some kind of tablet with numbers on the front, between the wheels. "You had a good breakfast today. You ate everything. That's what I've been told," she says.

"I haven't had breakfast. I'm . . ."

"I'll get you some toast. I could use some myself," she turns me in a door and there are people sitting around and the people in green sloppy coveralls shout some word, a TV on and someone talking about the weather, loud and chirpy, like it was all a big joke.

"Aloha," says someone in a green outfit and takes the thing on the handle and puts it around my neck. "You have to wear your lei," she says and puts one on Beverley's neck too.

"Damn foolishness," I say. Someone has turned some music on, it's loud and confusing, I can't think, Beverley says something but I can't make it out for the music, twanging and croaking and irritating metal string things. All the green outfits are talking, loudly, and the other people aren't saying much and one woman is sitting hunched over with her lips stuck out, why am I living with crazy people, why am I here, everybody's talking and I can't understand anything, they don't know how to communicate, I can't answer what I can't hear, everybody's asking questions, laughing, handing me drinks, they taste thick and too sugary and there's a stick hollow thing I'm supposed to suck it up with and the thing it's in is picky and fat and I can't hold it and give it to Beverley, she's the only one here who is sane, wonderful Beverley, if I ever lost Beverley I don't know what I'd do.

"Waiting for a better place," she says to someone, the loud woman in the green outfit thing, she has a sort of helmet of hair and her face is wrinkled and she has a neck that melds into her chin so you don't know where her chin ends and her neck starts, her neck kind of droops.

"He hasn't called me that for at least a month," she says to Beverley. I can't make out what Beverley says.

"That's where we want him to go," Beverley has to lean forward and shout, it's so loud in here. It's not cold but I'd rather go back and freeze and talk to Beverley, she's the only one I can talk to, she's the only one who listens, she's the only one who knows I exist.

The mist clings to the tree up among the branches, it fills in the spaces between the branches, it fogs the school, everything is wet, the road, the people walking on the sidewalk with things attached to their coats up over their heads, the kids in the yard some with yellow rubber things like blankets and yellow boots. The window is cold when I touch it, coffee is not. Patches of dirty white mounds along the fence, along the side of the road, a bus splashes water as it goes by they get wetter and dirtier. Everyone walking with their head down, avoiding puddles. Sometimes lines of rain, sometimes just mist. Dirty patches of white.

A piano, I've forgotten what this is, I know this, piano. Relaxing, something from another world, going to another world. I think there's things missing, those things we put in the machine . . . . I know there were more music things there, people come in at night, I can see them even though the light's turned out, dark shadows moving quiet so they don't think I hear, so they don't think I see them, they steal things, I holler and they run out. What is the name of that thing that's playing? Beverley brought it. The man who did it, the man. Why can I remember some things and not other things, things I know, there's something wrong, I know this, there is something terribly wrong I can't remember.

Grey outside. It feels like the sky is pressing down. Everything is grey, pressing down, closing in. The mist fills the spaces in the tree.

"Hi Dad! Listening to your Beethoven." He is chubby, burly, pulls his boots off and comes over in sock feet and shakes my hand and sits down beside me. "It's good to see you sitting here listening to your Beethoven, it's kind of like home. I know this. It starts quiet and gets complex, he plays low and high, and then low and high together, and it ends so peacefully like something ascending, like he knew he'd be ascending. He wrote it in the last year of his life didn't he? Isn't that what you told me?"

There is nothing I can say to this person, whoever he is. What am I supposed to say? He gets up and goes to the washroom and starts hollering from there, "I brought you some more CDs. A bunch of Mozart. Mom says you love Mozart. She said you really got into it when I was off doing my thing in Africa. I'm just about to start in on Moby Dick, by the way," sound of water cascading, it gets louder, "I showed them those pictures from that book you gave me. We talked about saving endangered species. The kids brought in a video of fishing boats slaughtering whales with big guns at the front of the ship," he's back sitting beside me hollering in my ear, "and hauling them up inside factory ships, I kind of remembered they used to do that. It was a real shock to the kids. We talked about the morality of killing endangered species that are maybe smarter than we are and maybe it was okay for Inuit to hunt them, after all they are Inuit, they've done that for thousands of years and who are we to tell them what's right and what's wrong, they didn't have us around to tell them what was right and what was wrong for thousands of years, and that really confused them, how come it's wrong for us to kill whales but it's okay for Inuit to kill whales?" I can't make out what he's talking about he keeps jumping around, "How are you feeling?" he says.

I shrug.

"Dad? I'm Richard. Your son, Richard."

"Richard."

"You don't know who I am, do you?" He frowns. "What happened to your forehead?"

Where are

Where are they taking me now? They might as well put the shackles on me and bring in a paddy wagon. I don't need a damn wheelchair. Some place next to a cemetery, probably. I've seen places like that. I've never thought of them before, I've just seen them. But now I am. Some place where they bury you and dig up your bones afterwards and put your skull in a big pile with all the other skulls, grinning.

So here it is, some kind of a van with windows, and a pad that comes whining down at my feet and everybody stands around me making happy noises and someone behind pushes me up wham onto the pad and everybody talks like this isn't what it is.

I don't want to go. Nobody asks me, nobody listens, if they asked, they wouldn't listen anyway. I don't want to go, I liked this place, I had my window, I could watch what was going on, there was always something going on, I liked it, I could remember the way it was when I was young, it made me feel young, I might as well say goodbye to it all because I'm strapped in this damn thing and they are strapping this thing to the floor of this damn van or truck or whatever it is and they're all waving goodbye and turning around and going back inside and that's the last I'll see of any of them.

I hammer on the arm of this damn chair and scream no like a kid, like those kids I can hear at that schoolyard across the street and the woman who is strapping me down tells me to stop moving, it makes it harder and only holds things up, as if I gave a damn, as if that wasn't why I'm doing this. I swat her hat off and she stands up and makes a gesture like she'll swat me back and goes and sits in the chair of this truck thing and a woman I think I recognize steps up in the truck thing and comes and finishes the strapping and kisses me and gets out again and the door closes and the building moves away. "Pull that stunt again," the woman at the bus wheel says, "and you'll wish you hadn't. Do we understand each other?"

I am not answering.

She stops this bus thing and turns around and says, "Do we understand each other? Don't say a thing, just nod. Do we understand each other?"

She's burly and I don't want to take her on, so I nod and she turns back and starts off again.

"Where the hell are we going?" I demand.

She doesn't answer. No matter how often I say that, she doesn't answer and I finally give up. Wherever the hell it is they are taking me, I'll know when we get there. It reminds me of something, this ride, something I've read, something I've heard, maybe something that's happened before, I want out of here, I'm strapped in and strapped down this reminds me of something something trapped something horrible I start yanking on the belt and try to pull the straps from the floor but I can't reach that far down the strap on my waist is too tight they won't let me bend down to yank out the straps they must have locked it shut and finally I give up and sit and wait, for whatever is going to happen, whatever it is they intend to do with me, wherever it is they are taking me, to some dump somewhere, to bundle me like a mummy and dump me on a pile of lime, to fill this truck with gas. I have to go to the bathroom. How long is this damn thing going to take, get it over with, get it over with, I have to go to the bathroom! I am desperate, dammit. They won't even give me my dignity. I liked that place. It was home. They are taking me away from my home. Dumping me somewhere. On a pile of lime. She is driving so goddamn slow. Hurry up. I have to go. This is so damn undignified.

This thing rattles and bangs. We're going up a hill and I can see a long distance out over houses and smoke coming up from a blocky building far away near the water and there are trees beside the road and dropping off down the hill and we keep going up and one car after another is going down on the other side of the road there's six seven I don't know how many cars in front of us and they are all turning sharp to one side, there's rocks up above us straight down like they've been cut with a knife and there's cars coming towards us from the other direction and we are all turning one way and going up a gully and the rocks are on both sides of us straight up and down like a wall and we're driving in some sort of trench and the thing rattles and the driver moves a stick back and forth and we stop in the gully and the cars in front aren't moving. "I've seen me sit here three quarters of an hour sometimes," she says. I'm not answering. "This is a nice place you're going to," she says.

I doubt that.

"It's interesting, the way people act," she says. "There was one old guy," the cars in front of us move and we go for a little bit and then stop again. "They've got this light at the top of the hill, in the worse goddamn place possible" she says. "How are you coming back there? Still with me?" She turns and looks back. "Everything okay?" Her seat is in a hole and I'm sitting above her, there's a big slab of something up above her that I can look through sort of, it's on a thin round bar sticking out from the side near her window, there's an empty seat beside her that blocks my view, I can only see out between her seat and that one. There's some cars and a truck coming down on the other side of the road, but we're not moving. She's facing frontwards again. "I was telling you about this old guy, in this place like the place you're going to. You don't talk a lot, do you?"

"No."

"Nothing personal," she says. "Back there. Are you okay?"

"Where are we going?"

"I've got the name here somewheres," she says, and picks up a board with a clip thing she's got at the front, where the window comes down and makes a ledge thing. "Hearthaven. I hope you're okay back there, I wanted them to send someone, to look after you back there. Like I don't have enough to do already. Come on!" She pushes on the wheel and the horn blows, and pushes again, "come on, come on, what's the holdup!"

"Traffic," I say.

"Tell me about it!"

"What's Hearthaven?"

"You'll find out when we get there. Your wife says she'll see you there. She wanted me to tell you that. Come on, come on!" She pushes on the wheel and the horn goes again. "What did you do?"

"Gave people shit."

"I'll bet." The cars move and stop again. "Shit! Excuse my French. Like what? Like what did you do?" I need to go. I really need to go, we're moving again, forever, this damn trip is going on forever, the cars are spreading out we're going faster and she hasn't stopped talking, "this old guy gets horny and comes up behind some old lady in the hall and puts his hands on her breasts and she turns and says, "Fuck off!" and the old guy is outraged and takes it to the residents' committee thing they have there, and would you believe it, he complains about her language. Her language!" When are we getting there? "There's one middle age guy comes to visit his mother, a sweet old thing, and discovers she's lying in bed with the door open, inviting guys in. You've got to watch yourself, my friend, what's your name?" For godsake! She roots around in front of her and picks up the board thing again. "Preston." Damn damn damn. "My name is Sharon," she says. "I forgot to introduce myself. Not very polite, was it? So you're Preston and I'm Sharon. And it looks like you've had an accident."

All I want is a blanket to cover me, we turn off the road and there's some kind of canopy or roof or something we drive under and then Beverley is there, standing back while the driver operates the door open and the pad whirrs down and a man who must be six foot and a young Asian woman ease me off the damn thing and the man asks if I can walk, and I tell him no, could they get something to cover me and he ignores that and Beverley follows us in by a whole bunch of people in chairs around tables and a big counter like some kind of hotel and a woman behind there who asks is this Preston and the man says, "yeah, it looks like," and they take me to an elevator and up and along a hallway and a woman behind another desk says "Welcome back, Preston," and I crouch and try to turn so she doesn't see what I've done and the big guy takes me straight to the bathroom thank god and practically elevates me off the damn chair to the pottie and tells me to say when I'm done and goes out and closes the door and I'm alone, finally, I don't want to leave here, I just wish everything out there would go away.

But it doesn't. In ten seconds the big guy raps on the door and calls in, "Done yet?" and I say no, but I guess I don't say it loud enough because he opens the door and looks in and says, "Oh, you're not done yet," and closes the door again. "Tell me when you're done," he calls on the other side.

"Are you okay Preston?" Beverley says, she's out there, the only woman, the only person in the world who makes me feel human.

"Yes." I talk louder, I'll answer her, she's the only one I'll answer. What has happened to me? In hell they bolt down steel doors and seal you inside and turn up the heat.

I don't deserve this.

"Do you want me to help you?" the big guy calls.

"No," I shout. "I'll do it myself."

"I'll help him," Beverley says, softly and muffled.

"Are you sure?" he says, he can't ask a simple question without bellowing. She says something and then I can't hear anything except for noises of something rolling in and out and voices of other people, talking to Beverley, I can't make out what they're saying, something about me, if they hadn't been so damn long getting here they wouldn't have a problem now, I'm only human, I can only hold out so long, don't they know about old people, don't they know what it's like, our bladders aren't strong like they used to be, nothing is strong like it used to be, don't they have any heart? I finish up and clean up and stand up. There's a bar I can grab onto and I need that, I've been sitting too long, in the damn wheelchair and the damn bus and this damn pottie, the chair is in my way, I have a cane, I had a cane, they stole my damn cane, I don't need a wheelchair. As long as I can stand here and get rid of the dizziness.

I feel a little sick.

I am not going to ask for help.

"Preston?"

"I'm okay. I'm okay honey." I haven't been as good as I should have been, I haven't told her how I feel, how wonderful I know she is. As soon as I can stand up here and this dizziness passes. "I'm okay."

She's beside me, with her arm around my waist. "I should have come with you."

You're here now. I'd like to say that, it's hard getting the words out, choosing them. The right words. My brain works slow. She helps me and tries to coax me back in the chair but it's wet and I don't want to go there and we manage to get out of this damn room and someone brings a chair and I sit and they wheel the chair off, the chair with wheels, I never want to see the damn thing again. As soon as this dizziness goes away. "We'll get him something," a voice says nearby.

"Some soup maybe," Beverley says. "Do you want soup?" she asks me. I shake my head. "Tea?" I nod. Tea would be good. We used to have tea in the afternoon, didn't we, I can't remember, maybe you'll help me remember, now that you're here. As soon as I get some rest I'll be better, things come and go, I'm not so clear right now, I have good times and bad times. What did I used to do? I gave people shit. I ordered them around. Doing what?

They keep interrupting, all these people, isn't it enough that they've put me through all that crap but they have to keep coming in, interrupting, like this room is a freeway?

"I should have come with you," Beverley says. "I had no idea it would take so long."

"Traffic," I say.

"I don't understand that," she says, "We came straight through."

A TV is here and it's on, I keep getting distracted, if it isn't the damn TV it's some other interruption. There is a goose neck lamp on a table beside a chair beside a window. The TV is in a corner facing us, there's a big high bed with white sheets and a blanket of orange and brown and yellow patches with holes. Big glaring white lights on the ceiling, there's a yellow blob on the TV above grey mist and triangle shapes at the bottom and a trail of white smoke that slowly goes through the grey mist and I can see hills outlined by the smoke and there's a pounding chuffing sound, "Richard is coming tomorrow. He says he wants to see your new place."

"Too many people coming in here."

"Are you tired?" Beverley asks.

"I want all these damn people to stop coming in here," the big guy walks in again, what the hell's his problem, he asks Beverley if there is anything we need and talks to her about meals and the cats and the TV room down the hall and the pills I am supposed to take and what time breakfast is and when he comes in every day to get me up and Beverley nods and there is no point of my saying anything because nobody is paying any attention to me anyway they think I'm a dead animal splattered on the road the smoke in the mist on the TV is slowly dispersing and beside me out the window I can see some kind of tiny house on the end of a stake in a kind of geometry of grey shapes down below and some wooden chairs painted red and blue and orange and then the little Asian woman comes in with tea and smiles at Beverley and at me, she's half his height and half his width and she speaks so small nobody can hear her and Beverley has to ask her what she said and she smiles and talks louder and I guess Beverley can hear because she nods but I still can't make out a thing the little woman says. She brings a pillow from the bed and puts it behind my head and I lean back and close my eyes, I'm much more tired than I thought but Beverley is here and I want to enjoy my tea with her and talk with her and enjoy her company but I can't because everybody keeps coming in and I can't hear what they're saying because everybody is making so much noise and someone is talking loud on the TV and I can't pay attention to the TV and to the other people in this room talking and they all talk at the same time so I don't know who to pay attention to first but nobody thinks I'm important anyway I might as well go to sleep, "he gave the driver trouble," someone with a gruff voice says in the blackness with my eyes closed except I can sense the light from the window, I wish I could make it all black and I can see a sort of shadow passing across the whiteness and someone whispers and everyone thank god shuts up and

I'm in a bed wherever, I don't remember, wherever this is, my head feels odd, clearer though, my bladder is emptied, more or less, though now that I think about it, it isn't, Beverley is sitting in a chair by the window, this bed is sideways to the window and she's got her glasses on and her hair is nicely combed and she's bending over reading, she loves romance novels, I remember that, I'd be able to tell her the plot by glancing at the book for ten seconds, all I needed to know were the names of the main characters, the woman, the grumpy older man, a bit jaded, sometimes verging on violent, and she was shy and a lion tamer, it would always turn out, the plots were always the same. We didn't take on romance novels, we were more staid, we did educational things and staid thought pieces, I used to call them, very, what is the word I am looking for, something that suggests what, something serious, very, what is that word? Very earnest. I used to send all the poetry that budding authors sent in, send them to other places, if I thought the things were good enough, or if I thought I could irritate some competitor and waste her time, it was usually a her but not always. I wasn't always a nice person, I couldn't afford to be. How is it all this is coming back? It's like my mind is a camera and once in a while I get the right lens and everything gets clear and I can see back, like a mirror opposite a mirror, down a long corridor and the mirrors get gradually out of line until the view sort of bends out of sight, far far away. I used to sit in a barber chair when I was young, a teenager just starting out on manhood, looking in the mirrors, fascinated, as if there were fifty rooms next to the room I was sitting in, in both directions, and when the barber turned the chair around, there was another view, in the other direction, bending off in the distance, like there were worlds next to ours where people did the same thing, at the same time, and went on with their lives in different directions when I wasn't looking til I came back for my next appointment and there they were again, imitating everything I did.

How odd. Maybe the sight of Beverley. She looks so young. Except for her white hair. And the glasses. She didn't wear glasses, when I met her the first time. "Hi honey."

She looks up and smiles, a nice, warm, sort of sad smile, glad I'm awake and I can call her by her right name, because she really is a honey, my little Beverley.

"You had a good sleep," she says.

I did?

"I'm just sitting here, waiting for my handsome man to wake up, so we can go down for lunch."

"Good book?"

She folds the book shut and lifts her glasses to her hair. I always loved that, she looks so young and with it. "You haven't asked me that for years," she says.

"I thought it. Couldn't you hear me?" She gets up and she's crying and she leans over and kisses me.

"I am so sorry," she says.

"For what?"

"For everything. Putting you here. For not riding in the bus thing when they drove you here. For all this confusion. Everything, mostly." She's staring down at me, with a look more tender than I've seen her look at me for years. It's been really hard, on my dear wife, what's happened to me. I didn't want it this way, and neither did she. She looks more relaxed than I've seen her for years, it's like my Beverley is back and the old, tense, worn out woman is gone. The old tense worn out woman that I've created with all my nonsense.

"I don't know why things are so clear now. It makes no sense really."

"We'll just have to grin and bear it," she says.

"You look wonderful."

"Not half so wonderful as you look. It's marvelous, talking to you. I haven't had a real good talk with you for years."

"I've been going away." Her face changes, her eyes are filling up, I pat her face. "I'm not gone yet, my dear, you'll have to put up with me a little bit longer. Maybe I'll be a bit more sensible now. You did the right thing. This is where I should be. It was too hard on you, it wore you out."

"I wish I thought that."

"You did. All I have to do is look at you now."

"Do you want something to eat?"

"If you can help me up, I think I'd like to go to the bathroom first. I'm not as spry as I used to be, my grandmother used to say, do you remember," I pull the sheets off and swing my legs out and ease myself down from this bed, which is much too high, as if whoever has put me up here wants me to fall off and break my neck, "I don't think I've used that word for years, have I, it has a kind of atmosphere, don't you think, of the last century and a whole different way of life."

"Careful," she says.

"I'm okay. I'm feeling a lot better. Now that you're here."

Now that I'm down I have to steady myself against the bed, so it's lucky it's so high, I can lean against the mattress, it's exactly the right height. Beverley wheels over that damn upright wheelchair. "Get that thing out of here," I sweep it aside. She tries to steady me and I tell her I'm fine, I can manage just fine, I can take care of myself dammit, I'm not in the box yet.

"You should use the walker," she says, "you've been using it for months," but I growl and she steps back and I get to the bathroom and close the door and grab for something and find the counter, hold myself up, wait for a moment until the dizziness goes away. "Are you okay, Preston?" she calls in.

"Fine," I say and get myself to the toilet and finish my business and when I'm back out and we've got me freshened up and she's chosen some good matches, the pants and shirt and socks matching, I invite her to lunch. She says I should take the wheelchair or at least the walker but I offer her my arm and we tootle off down the hall although I have to say she grips my arm a little too strongly and I'm glad she's there, there's still a bit of unsteadiness in my legs, it's the trip over here sitting in that chair for so long and then waking up and having to get out here and down to, whatever the meal is, lunch, before they close the place. They run these lunchrooms like restaurants, it seems, if you don't get down at the posted hours, you're out of luck, which is what a somewhat corpulent but actually quite nice middle-aged I'd say woman tells us and stresses that they are actually closed but since my beautiful wife is here today they'll make an exception, but only this time even for her, their hours are noon to one and they close at one, sharp. There are tables for four people all around the dining room and nice clean table cloths, at least at the table where we are seated, by the window with a cat wandering on the balcony outside, a black cat, a young black cat that looks in at us, stops and meows only you can't hear it meowing, only the shape of its mouth as it does, and then it paces on, as regal as all cats have ever been from Ancient Egypt on. The food is sandwiches and soup, the sandwiches have no crusts and the soup is apparently made for dipping, I'll bet. I'm a little tempted but my wife is here and I'm on my good, no, my best behavior. The Sun comes in the window and lights up the table top and Beverley gets up and draws across the flimsy curtains that are pulled back to let the light in and I raise my water glass and she raises hers and we click and I say, "To my beautiful girl," and she toasts her handsome devil of a man, and I tell her I haven't had much chance for devilry lately.

On the way back to my room we are turning the corner where there's a crook in the hall, to go back to the room they've assigned me, when my legs suddenly disappear and I go down before either of us realizes what's happening and I hear Beverley yelp with pain.

They tell me she's okay, no bones are broken, she's had severe muscle strain and the doctors want to x-ray to make sure there is no ligament damage, but I don't trust any of them and the question is, what do I do about it, I'm using a wheelchair, after that accident yesterday, I feel terrible, if I hadn't been so damn stubborn my wife wouldn't be, she'd be fine, I muscle along the hall, lunging downwards and propelling this vehicle, the hall branches in two directions just beyond a fire door and swerves to the side opposite the desk where all the supervisors sit, the way I take is around the other side and I come to an angle where I go sharply in another direction that leads to the elevator, right by another section of the desk but the people there are usually looking out at the residents they call them as they wheel or totter themselves by the lunchroom where there are big windows that sort of make them stand out in profile against the light as they go by, but this way I can bend down and keep a low profile, below the level of the counter where they sit there looking out, I'm sliding by like a soldier crawling away from an ambush, using the contours of the ground to conceal himself, and so to the elevator. There's a punch board by the elevator with numbers that everyone who comes or goes has to push, using a certain sequence of numbers. I watched when they took Beverley out and am pretty sure I have the numbers right, I kept repeating them and as soon as I got back to my room, jotted them down, on the paper I've managed to fumble out here, and half stand up from the wheelchair to reach the punch board to punch in the numbers, remembering to put the lock on the wheelchair so it doesn't slide away while I do this. That's happened already and I bruised my ass when I sat back down and discovered there was nothing there but the floor, 7253 the elevator opens and in I go and press G, I saw them do that too, I'm still upset, sitting in here in this lighted moving room playing music remembering how my dear wife looked when they took her in a gurney they called it and she kept telling me, I'm okay, I'm okay, I don't know why they have me in this foolish thing and the little Asian girl kept cooing over her and telling her, that is all right, missus, we just want to make sure we have everything checked, we don't want to damage anything, "That isn't already," I added, I remember saying that, I felt so, here we are, this elevator takes forever to go down one floor and even longer for the damn door to open once it's arrived, the taxi should be there already waiting for me, that's one thing I have in this place, a phone, the room is small, horribly small, but I have a phone. Surely he knows the hospital she's in.

"Oh hello Mr. O'Shaughnessy," says the little Asian woman when the door opens, I dodge around her but she manages to take hold of the handles at the back of this thing and I can't propel it as fast as I need to, she's got the brakes on.

"Let go," I say, but the big guy is standing in the hall ahead of me and beyond him is the wide place where there's all the tables and the front door to the side where my taxi is waiting. He puts his hands on both armrests and I am completely stopped. "I have to see my wife," I tell him, I glare up at him. "My wife is hurt. Dammit, I want to see my wife."

"Your son is coming to take you there," the little woman says behind me, almost whispers it her voice is so small, not the big guy, he leans over and uses his weight to hold me where I am. I try to stand up and he puts his hand on my chest and holds me down. "I want to see my wife!"

"Your son will be here in ten minutes," she says. I don't believe that at all, it's a trick to get me back, but the big guy has turned me around and she steps aside and I'm moving back to the elevator, where a woman I've seen at that guard station is standing, half in and half out, "Where were you going, Preston?"

"A taxi is waiting for me." She nods, not at me, but at the big guy behind me who is holding me in the chair with one hand and has wheeled me to the elevator with the other, "It's taken care of," he tells the woman as he pushes me onboard and the door closes behind us and the elevator starts instantly, not like when I tried to use it, it took forever then, if it had been quicker when I tried to use it I would be out of here by now in my taxi, going to see my wife. "I want to see my lawyer," I announce.

"When we get back upstairs," he says, and the elevator door opens as soon as he says it and I'm speeding down the hall to the room they've assigned me. He actually straps me in bed and the little Asian woman comes a minute later and bends over me and says, "He will be here right away, Mr. O'Shaughnessy, he was already coming over, to get you, when you went away, take those off," she says, and I can feel the belts being undone. "Mr. O'Shaughnessy will be all right," she says it so soothingly and strokes my hair, "Your wife phoned us, she asked to speak to you but I said you were asleep, she told you not to worry, she knows you love her, she was upset that you thought you'd hurt her and she wanted you to know that you did not hurt her, she is not hurt at all, she is very lucky to have a man who loves her so very much," she washes my face with a warm washcloth and assures me that my son will be here soon, to take me to see my wife, everything is all right, my wife is all right, I do not need to worry.

"I have to see her."

"Your taxi isn't here," she says, soothingly, she is smart, she knows the big fellow makes me nervous. "I told the taxi driver you didn't need him, you had someone else to take you to see your wife, a family member, do you think you would want something soothing, tea perhaps., your wife tells me you enjoy tea, perhaps a little tea."

"That would be nice." I can be manipulated. I hate to admit that. Preston can be manipulated, all it takes is for someone to be a little nice and I am fine. I am not fine, of course, but it makes me feel that someone notices, that someone cares, that I have not left the human race, that I am not on the outside looking in on the human race, at least not yet. My little Asian girl has left to get the tea and I can hear her at the door, talking low, telling someone he is all right, he is under control, there is no need to worry, I'll call him, she says, maybe he will come and take his father to see his wife, he'll need to take responsibility in case his father does something.

The door to this room is never closed, anyone walking by can look in here, or come in here. How do I know I won't wake up tomorrow and find myself cleaned out? There are crazy people wandering the halls, one woman has already come in here and claimed that the goose neck lamp on my table beside my bed is hers and I had to shout and get the big guy and he steered her out, which I do appreciate. Everyone has a use.

If it was up to him I'd be strapped down for everything but meals. He's folded up my wheelchair and put it over by the corridor where he can watch me. They'll probably put some kind of alarm button around my neck, or a bell like we used to put on the cows so we'd know where they were. I can remember being down by the lake on a dark night and hearing them, wading in the water and the sound of the bell, the dumbest ugliest clanging you can ever imagine, but at night like that with the sound of the animal sploshing in the water and the bell clanging, it sounded mysterious and peaceful, especially with the sound of the water.

That little Asian woman is trickier than she seems.

She hasn't tied me in but she's tucked the sheets in tight at the bottom of the bed so my feet are tied down and I fight to get them out.

Which I can handle.

And taken away the little stool that I use to get down from this bed. I want this bed lower. I'll break a leg. I have to make a note. Lower the bed. I make notes to myself. I've got a bunch of them on the table. I meant to write the directions to the front door. I have to do that. There has to be a back way. There's always a back way. They think I don't notice and that gives me an advantage, I listen and learn things. I've still got that sheet with the code. They'll probably change it, now that I'm in on their secret. Old age is a tricky dude. To use the language the kids use.

Nobody in the hall. This wheelchair is stiff. You have to be a muscle builder to get it open, it comes open one way at the front, but the damn thing doesn't open at the back where the wheels are.

Careful, Preston. Don't want to fall. How does that happen? Suddenly my legs just, there we are!

Okay, us old guys know a trick or two.

"Mr. O'Shaughnessy." Damn, I didn't hear her coming. "You're up. I thought you'd be napping." I sit down in the chair even though it isn't opened up yet and she spreads out the arms so the seat goes flat and slides a cushion underneath my ass and a pillow behind my back. "You should have called me. I didn't know you wanted to get up." She tussles my hair. "You'll fall and hurt yourself." She adjusts the pillow. "I have your son on the phone." She raises a tiny black tablet to her ear and talks at it and then hands it to me. "It's your son."

What am I suppose to do with this?

She takes it back and turns it so the long side is up and points to a teenie opening at the bottom.

"Talk into this."

"Hi Dad," says a voice. Where's it coming from? I turn the damn thing around to find the thing I'm suppose to talk into and where the hell I'm supposed to listen. She takes it again.

"I don't think he's used to it," she tells it and listens for a while. "Yes." She talks some more and puts the thing away. "He'll be calling on your phone." And the phone by my bed, on the table beside my goose-necked lamp, rings. The little girl leaves me here and goes over and picks it up and says hello, he's right here and signals for me to come over there.

I am not going to do that.

After a bit she realizes that I am not going over there and walks back here, wheels me to the phone and hands me the receiver thing.

"Hi Dad. Can you hear me? Mom is all right. It's better if you don't go over there right now. Can you hear me?" I sort of mumble. "She's upset that you wanted to go over there, she thinks it's her fault that you're all upset."

"Slow down."

"It's better if you don't go over."

"I'll do what I damn want!"

"She's in isolation. She can't have any visitors."

I don't know what to make of this. I want to visit my wife. What's wrong with that?

"They'll tell us when we can, Dad. I'll come over there and take you. As soon as we can."

"How is your mother?"

"All right. As good as can be expected."

I can't make heads or tails out of this and hand the phone back to the little Asian girl, "How is your mother?" she asks and listens for a long time, cocking her head and taking a sheet from a note pad on the table and writing, she straightens out some other sheets that are lying there and reads them while she listens and picks up one of them, what's on that, what have I written on that, "He will be very happy to hear that," she says and hangs up and wheels me to the window where she unloads me in the chair that's sitting there, "I brought you tea. Your wife is getting x-rays, they're keeping her there another day. She'll be home tomorrow."

"When can I see her?"

"Your son will be over," she goes to the door and wheels in a tray with a pot of tea, some cookies and what looks like hard stale bread, "when your mother can have visitors. Probably when she's back at the apartment. Your son seemed upset that you tried to go over by yourself."

"He tends to go off the deep end."

"I understand you were a smart man," she pours tea, "I want you to tell me all about it, what you did with your life, some time," she puts the tea pot back on the tray, "when I'm not so busy," and she goes out like she's turned off a switch.

Some of my things are here. My dear Beverley brought my CDs. They came here before I did, in a cabinet with a glass door beside the table with my goose-necked lamp. The CD player is on a shelf inside the cabinet. No speakers. My earphones aren't here. I need my earphones to listen to my CDs. I'm sure the earphones were here when I came yesterday. I saw them on top of the cabinet when Beverley and I went out for lunch. The bottom shelves are full and the CDs are falling over on this shelf, Haydn, Mozart, Schubert. No Beethoven. Beethoven goes here. All my Beethoven. She's folded up my wheelchair again and I don't know where that walker is, the walker's gone too. I'm standing at the end of the bed, no cane, my walker is gone, the wheelchair is over at the end of the corridor and there's a space of floor between me and it. I don't want to fall. I've never had this problem before, if I go straight to the wall and prop myself on the wall and then work myself over to the wheelchair. I don't want to give people warning, I was looking after Beverley, making sure she got down to the ambulance on that gurney and no one was looking after things around here and the door was wide open like they always leave it open, there is no lock on the door, it's impossible to lock the door, steady on the wall, I don't want to give people warning someone's a thief out there, maybe I can catch them damn them, careful old boy, by taking them by surprise, work my way carefully along the wall, this is not so bad, I'm not half so bad as I think, that wasn't so bad, now to get the damn thing open, why do they clam it shut like this, I'm deliberately immobilized, why don't they just put on handcuffs, there, dammit, one quick yank and it's open, wrenched my shoulder a bit, not bad, get myself into it and here we go.

No one in the hall. The sound of TVs. The big guy.

"Off somewhere?" I'm looking up at him, he looks bigger from this wheelchair, if I was able to stand up he wouldn't be so damn tall.

"Someone stole my CDs. And my earphones."

"Why don't we go look for them?" He puts his hands on the chair arms and spins me around.

"I've already looked! Someone stole my CDs and my earphones. All my Beethoven!"

"Keep your voice down, Preston," he's right behind my ear, talking in my ear. "They're probably somewhere you haven't looked yet. We'll go have a look."

"I don't have to look. Someone stole my CDs!"

"Calm down. We'll find your CDs. I promise."

I wish I had my cane. I'm waving my hands but he's behind me and I try to swat backwards but it doesn't work. The chair jerks stop and he's set the brake. I try to get it off and swat behind me and he's standing back out of range. "They stole my CDs!"

"He was out in the hall shouting about his CDs," he's talking to someone but I can't get the brake off or turn the wheelchair and I try to turn around but it's too awkward and he's back there somewhere talking to someone else, it looks like a woman, I can't see, she's back in the corner of my eye, I can't turn any farther. "That's all right," a soothing female voice says, much stronger than the little Asian woman, soothing but firm and loud, coming from a diaphragm that is much bigger. "We'll find your CDs. Let's go back and have another look."

"I know they've been stolen! People walk in my room all the time! I've already lost a sweater."

"Lower your voice, Preston. Everything is all right. There's no need to make a lot of noise. It's not helping anything." I cannot swat at a woman and she does have a soothing voice, for a big woman.

"I've lost all my Beethoven CDs. I loved those CDs. It's damn cruel."

"Maybe they weren't brought in yet." She's bending down slightly, like you'd bend down to soothe a child, "You just got here Preston," it's the woman on the elevator, the one who sits at the police station at the end of the hall. She's wearing white and looks official and she stands up and nods to someone behind her, the big guy and we're speeding back to my room and swinging in the door and I can hear her marching behind. "Where do you keep your CDs?" she asks.

We look, on all the shelves, and in all the drawers and the closet and under the bed and all sorts of insulting places and she wheels me to the chair by the window, the big guy has gone, and she says when she's done, "I'll tell you what my thought is, Preston. I don't think they've been brought here yet. You just arrived, after all. Your wife told us she had more things to bring. I was happy to hear your wife is all right, by the way. It must be a great relief."

Then she's gone, and the Asian girl comes to get my tea things and when she is gone also, and things are quiet in the halls, I get out my pencil and some big sheets of paper and think and puzzle things out and scribble and cross out words and try different ones and finally, after a long time, I've got something I feel good about, it gives me a good feeling, it makes me feel alive to actually create something:

<u>To the Thief</u>

You like to skulk around

And never make a sound.

But if you really want some fun

I'm prepared. I have a gun.

Beverley has left me some scotch tape and a paper scissors and I wheel myself to the door and stick my sign up as high as I can reach. And wheel back inside, and close the door. It won't lock, but at least I can close it.

It isn't very long after that when the big guy comes in and practically lifts me from the chair and lays me out in bed and puts on the straps and maybe twenty people come in my room and search everything and everywhere, including the mattress, and they have to unstrap me and lift me off to do that and the big guy sits me in the wheelchair and stands behind me and holds a hand on each of my shoulders, his hands are huge they wrap around my shoulders with no problem at all and he squeezes hard and I think he's left bruises.

"If you ever do anything like that again," says the big woman sergeant major in the white dress, "you will be out of here, right back where you came from. Do you understand, Preston? I don't mean the place you came from to get here. I mean the place you went to when you were taken from your apartment. One more incident and you are gone. Do you hear me? I know you have seen the ward for violent men. I know you have. Nod your head. That is exactly where you'll go."

I don't argue with women.

The big guy lifts me back in bed and straps me down I ask him to turn up the TV, but he ignores that and they all go out, and then they go parading by my door, one and then the other, and look in here, to make sure I'm still here and I'm still here, strapped down, and where am I supposed to go, and my son calls, when is it, later, some time later, I don't know how long later, I don't have a good grip on time any more, some time, he sounds angry, "Dad, why the hell did you tell them you had a gun!"

"I don't have a gun."

"I know! You've never had a gun in all your life! Why did you tell them you had a gun!" He's getting hysterical, he needs to calm down, he'll give himself a heart attack.

"It rhymes."

He was never very creative.

I have

I have had phones before, it is not a mystery. I know the number, I used it all my life. She's home now, that's what they said. She was spending the night in the hospital and then she was going home. I don't remember everything but I know that. I also wrote it down. Over on the table by this bed. Someone has taken my notes. I had more notes. I can see there are not as many notes as I had when I first came here. Swing my legs out. I'll put them away. In this drawer here. I can't get upset about it now. I have to get through to Beverley. It's light outside. It's taken so long. It was pitch dark when I woke, and I've been waiting long enough. If I turn I can almost see that funny little house on a stick and some birds dropping down to it, it looks like, I can't see the house though, I can swing my legs over and sit on the edge of the bed on that side and look down, birds on a ledge thing on the house. I can't hear them, this window is too thick. Slide over and drop off on the far side by the chair by the window, I can't open it, it would be good to be able to open the window. I am trapped in here, I don't get out of here, I can't take walks, I used to get out, at the other place. There was someone who went out with me, for walks.

I'm getting distracted. I get distracted easily now. I don't think I was like that. I'm pretty sure I wasn't. I wish I could remember.

Sometimes it's clearer than other times. There's a glaring light at the top of the window up there, blazes in here, hurts my eyes, I'll have to pull the blinds, curtains, whatever. Sometimes I can't remember what these things are called. They work, so what does it matter. It's much lighter out there. I think I can almost hear the birds, fighting, always fighting over things.

Stand here. Listen. Quiet. It's quiet in the halls. It's usually too noisy, it's hard to concentrate when there's all that noise going on, women whining, fighting with the nurses, mostly complaining. No, I guess they don't fight that much. Come in and steal things. I'd like to know who did that, every time I look at that big gap in my CD shelf, I get mad all over again. I should prop up the CDs on both sides so the gap is more noticeable, so I won't forget.

I don't have a walker and the wheelchair is over by the door again, folded up, so I'll work my way back around, holding on the bed. I am tired. Everything takes so much concentration. I have to think all the time, what is this word, what is that word, I'm living inside my brain and it ain't workin' so good. It's harder and harder to say what I mean. I do good. Someone used to say that. I do good. Everything is so tiring, even getting around this room.

Whatever that bright flash was, it's not there now. I can probably slide the things open again, so I can see the birds out there. I think I can hear them now for sure. It means working my way back, so

I'll leave them closed. The view is rotten, come to that. The only thing I can see, when I lie in my bed, is the windows on the other side of the gap. I have to get up to look down to see anything down there, the house, the birds, the flowers in a circular thing, chairs, one tipped over, a couple of glass topped tables and one big ugly wooden thing, tough though, hard to smash or beat up. Little brown birds. I don't think I was much for bird names, I can't remember if that was really much of my thing, I'm pretty sure it wasn't though. As the saying is. I do remember some things. They pop in, like old friends.

I must phone Beverley. That's why I worked my way over here. I think I wrote the number down, on one of those sheets. There's no sheets here. Dammit, can't they leave me anything! Do they have to steal my damn notes too! I should run out there and scream and wake them all up. One of them will be the thief.

Relax Preston. You've got yourself all wound up. Here they are, in this drawer. I need to organize these things. I don't organize these things. Just a jumble of pieces of paper. I'll have to lay out every one, and read every one. And organize them. I had more. I know I had more.

Success! Beverley's number. Dear Beverley. I can't make this out. It would help if I turned on a light. One, eight six. You push the numbers. One. Eight Six. What's the rest. Seven. Is that a seven or a nine? My writing ain't so good. Seven. I think it's a seven. One

Eight Six Seven. Six sex six. Latin. One eight seven six three two one. What's these? Something, fold out the paper. Two eight. Push the numbers One Eight Six Seven Three Two One so many numbers Two Eight. Every time I push a button it beeps.

Come on. I've pushed in the numbers. Work dammit.

"Hello! Hello!" This damn phone is broken. Beep. Oh. How did that happen? Oh. I push the numbers and it beeps in my ear.

Try again. One Eight Seven Six Three Two One Two Eight.

"What? What was that? What was that?" Why won't she answer. She said something, please hang up and try your call again? "Hello!"

"Hello Preston! What are you up so early for?"

A small little Asian girl.

"What are you doing?"

"This damn phone is broken!"

"It's just past six o'clock in the morning, Preston. Nobody is up now. I suggest you phone later."

"I told you, this damn phone is broken!" I hadn't intended to be so mad. Stupidity makes me mad. It's not her fault.

"Let me see," she says and steps between me and the phone and I stand back. "What number are you phoning? You should sit down. You seem a little wobbly this morning. I'll get you a chair." That is actually a good idea. "I don't think anybody will be up at this time of the day, it is a little too early." She talks as she brings the chair around and places it in front of the table and I sit down, in fact I'm glad to sit down, I was getting tired, stupidity tires me. "I can help you puzzle it out, if you like," she says, "I can get you some tea, or maybe a bit of toast, and then in a little while Jim will be here to help you freshen up and get down to breakfast. We start at eight. Then we can figure out just what is wrong with your phone. When you come back. Does that seem like a good plan?"

"I wish you would." I react better when people treat me decently, she is treating me decently. I hope she's the one who looks after me. So far they haven't been very nice here, but now that she is here, maybe things will be better. "I'm glad you're in charge," I say, to be political, it's important to make people feel good, they do things better if you make them feel good about themselves, you get more with sugar than vinegar, my grandmother used to say. And it's true, she's smiling.

"You were a little upset yesterday," she says and suggests I sit by the window for a bit, I can watch the birds, they are actually quite interesting, she'll move the chair back if I like and I stand up and lean on the bed and let her do that, "it takes a little time to get adjusted," she says, setting the chair down on the other side of the bed with a little decisive clunk and turns and comes back to this side to assist me to get around there, I don't really need her to help me but I want her to think she is doing a good job and besides that, she is a nice little woman, her skin feels good when she touches my hand, "but I think you are getting adjusted," she says, "we are really very nice here, the staff is professional, there are a lot of people here and everyone has their own problems and issues and we try to do the very best that we can," spoken triumphantly as she sets me down in the chair by the window. "I'll have to go and help some people who really need my help. Not like you. I think you're all right now, don't you think. Jim would say you've got it all together." She smiles and pats my face and goes off and I am left here smiling, what a sweet little girl. I'll try to make that phone call later. That's what I got up for, I remember that.

There's a blind man over at the next table. A woman beside him who has had her leg amputated. An old man beside me so bent over it looks like he'll never straighten up again, he breathes above his food like he's praying to it. The woman on my other side grunts. When I first came in I commented on how bright the Sun was today and she grunted. I introduced myself. She grunted. My grandmother used to say, I think it was my grandmother, someone used to say that no matter how many problems we have, we can always find someone with worse. She sits there with a sour expression and her dress is a sack with a faded flower print.

The most interesting person is the woman sitting across from me, somewhat more fleshy than she should be, but sophisticated. She always wears makeup, she says, there is no need to let yourself go just because you happen to have added a few years. I've always liked someone with spunk. Like Beverley. I'll have to call her as soon as this is over.

"You don't remember me, do you?" this woman says. Should I? Where would I have met her? "I didn't think so," she says and continues eating and I'm sitting here, having my breakfast, wondering when have I met this person, where, how many years ago, why don't I remember her?

The food is not bad. Breakfast, the best meal of the day. Sausage, some bacon, scrambled eggs. The table is set up rather nicely, clean napkins, cutlery laid out, place mats and a flower in a little glass jar in the middle. A plastic flower. We're over by the balcony, next to the window. A black cat is sitting outside with its back toward us, staring at something down below. I was never crazy about cats, they always seemed sneaky. This cat is quite young. A woman sitting at another table calls to it.

The woman across from me is a pretty good conversationalist, she's up on what's going on, she talks about the Prime Minister of Canada and how well he is doing, and what's going on south of the border and how Obama is making out and the terrible situation in the Middle East and will they ever stop killing each other. Where have I met her? When? We trade impressions. I tell her what I think of the prime minister, she disagrees, he's too right wing to suit her taste, did I meet her when I was working, years and years ago, did I meet her socially, I hate this, I feel crippled. She's smiling, she knows what I'm thinking, she's not helping me and I'm damned if I'll ask.

The other two just sit. The old man eats, the woman beside me grunts. One of the staff comes over and encourages her to eat something and takes her fork and brings some eggs to her mouth, which she opens and moves around when the food goes in and slobbers. It's depressing. If I'm around these people long enough I'll get just like them.

When the helper goes off to assist someone else, the woman across from me jerks her head toward the other one. "She won't be here long." I feel like I should say something. "They shouldn't have brought her here." Where have I met this person? Why does she know me?

"Must have been a reason," I say, looking at the woman who made the comment and trying to keep my voice down so the woman beside me doesn't hear.

"I don't know what that would be." The woman across from me almost sneers when she says it. She is not a lady.

I should have said something stronger. I'm disappointed with myself. Where have I met this person before?

"What is your opinion?" she demands. She will not let it go and she has a loud voice. "Don't you think there is a better place for something like this?"

I don't answer. I don't know what to say.

"What I have found," she goes on, "is that people seem to think that the problems they have are the only problems in the entire world, as if there were no other problems anywhere else. And what irritates me is that they think they can impose their problems on everybody else. Like here. It would be nice to get a rest."

I don't say anything. I'm a wimp, I'm a damn wimp, I should say something, this isn't right.

"There is no doubt about that at all," the woman with the loud voice says, ending the conversation. She is not as sophisticated as I'd thought. Why don't I know her name, why don't I recognize her? What will I be like, if I can't remember someone who knows me, will I recognize anybody, will I know who I am? God, will I be like this woman they have to feed, or that man with his nose in his food?

I'm not so enthusiastic about my breakfast any more. The eggs are cold and taste like powder.

"What did you do with your life?" the loudmouth asks. "I always like to know who I'm dealing with. And don't tell me you don't remember. I know that game."

"I wrote books." I have no idea if I did or I didn't.

"What books?"

"School books." That seems to satisfy her. Who is she, dammit? What is her name? I'm not going to ask. I'd feel stupid. I'm supposed to know who she is.

I'm trying to push myself along the hall and the Asian woman is talking to someone, down there, I can't tell who it is, it's too far and my eyesight is getting worse, it's a muscular person, acts like she's, he's, I can't tell, it's too far, this person is carrying some kind of package, a long thin thing all wrapped up in brown paper. They haven't seen me yet, I don't feel like company, I've had enough company, I just want some privacy, I'm tired of damn guessing games, I won't know who this person is and I'll have to go through the same damn exhausting performance pretending I know who I'm talking to, if I turn around right now and go off, where, to the TV room, they'll

"Dad! Trying to sneak off are we."

Damn.

He comes along the hall and the Asian woman heads off in the other direction, having stirred up trouble. He bends over and squeezes my shoulder, "You've been causing quite a stir, old fella. The fastest gun in the west."

I don't think they appreciated that, the gun business.

"It's me. Richard. Your son. You don't have to stare at me that way, Dad. I'm your son, Richard."

"Of course."

He has a strange look on his face, it's my fault, whatever this is all about, whatever the hell happens it's all my fault, I whirl around him like a sports car peeling off and head for my room and he follows and he doesn't shut up, "Mom is feeling better. She doesn't have a broken leg. There's no damage to her ligament, thank god for that, it's just a severe sprain," he's still behind me, I turn in my room, maybe he won't follow me, "she'll be bedridden for two or three weeks so I'm delegated to fill in," he's followed me, this place is too small there's nowhere to go when I reach the window, I'm trapped.

I turn and face him. It is my son. He talks like my son.

"Why did you say you had a gun? When they called me they were all set to throw you out. I had to talk real fast and to tell you the truth, Dad, I didn't think I could do it. It was touch and go. You're damn lucky to be here." He stops. Finally. "Still."

"I'm feeling all right."

"That's good."

"Sit down. Have a visit." I might as well be sociable, I am not going to get rid of him.

"Why don't we get you in a chair."

He's turned me around and pushed my wheelchair chair between the bed and the window and has squeezed in between the bed and the wheelchair and has his hands underneath my arms to get me up in my leather chair which is set back against the wall in the space between the bed and the window, a ridiculous position. "Where will you sit?" I ask as he turns me and settles me in the leather chair, this chair is too big for the space between the bed and the window.

"We'll have to get you another chair for visitors," as if I hadn't said a thing, "there's no place for visitors here. My name is Richard by the way."

He's put a pillow at my head and turns my wheelchair around to face me and plops himself there like he's threatened to. So we're facing each other, me in this big leather chair he's put me in, and him in the wheelchair he took me out of. "We have to get you a new one of these," he says. Everything has to be commented on. He shifts his ass around, inspecting the wheelchair he's plopped himself into. "This thing belongs to the home. There's much better wheelchairs out there, Dad. Maybe something motorized. I think you'd like that," he turns and looks back at me and gives me a big smile, "you'd like that, buzzing down the hall, scattering all the natives."

I must admit that is kind of attractive.

"I have your Beethovens, by the way, they're in my apartment for safe keeping, in case you were wondering. We're getting you some new earphones, as soon as you tell us what you want." I nod. "What do you want?"

"You decide." For some reason that irritates him. "Richard." I do remember. Sometimes I remember.

"I want you to decide, Dad."

"Whatever you want."

"Well don't complain if I don't get what you want, all right. I brought you a mirror, by the way." He points at the package on the bed. "Where do you want it?" He can't wait to get this visit over with.

"I don't have room for it. This place is crammed."

"On the wall, opposite your CD cabinet, so you can see what a handsome dude you are."

I smile. "That would be good."

His foot is twitching and he can't seem to sit still in that wheelchair that he wants me to change for some kind of motorized death machine. He looks out the window. "You've got a good view here."

"Some kind of house with birds."

"What kind?"

"I have no idea." And we have no idea what to say next, either of us. We sit here, staring at each other. His foot keeps twitching. I don't know what happened, we just never got along, he could always talk to Beverley, but my son and I never hit it off. I tried. I suppose he did too.

"Mom's had x-rays. Nothing is broken. Just a severe strain. She'll be bedridden for at least a month and a half. Maybe longer."

"It was my fault." He doesn't contradict me.

"I'm working, you know," he says. "Teaching takes all my time. You and your wife don't seem to understand that. You think teaching is the easiest damn thing in the world."

"Is everything okay?" I try to reach across and pat his hand, which I hope will satisfy him but now he's off describing his school and his classes and all the things he is doing and the kids in his home class as he calls it, every one of his kids, the tall and the small and the cute and the ugly and the vicious and the sweet and every variation in between, I can see the birds at the house and the black cat, walking across the cement down there looking up, "Am I boring you?" he says.

"No."

"You're more interested in whatever the hell is down there than paying attention to your own damn son."

He stops and I look at him straight to prove I am paying attention and now he's not saying anything. He glares at me. We could never talk. We always invented things to talk about.

"Your mother is all right?"

"I told you."

"I'd like you to do me a favor. Could you take my CDs. They keep stealing them."

"Okay." I'll need half a day to recover from this visit, he wears me out. "Just remember, okay, I've got your damn CDs, Dad, so don't go accusing somebody of stealing them and creating a big scene and making them throw you out because nobody's stealing your CDs, Dad, you're just imagining things, it's just like that thing with your cane all over again and that stupid poem about guns."

"Someone is stealing them."

"I'll have to take two or three trips, okay. I'll have lots of time. Mom won't be up and around for at least two and a half months, the doctor thinks longer. Thanks to you."

Whatever I say is wrong. Whatever is wrong is my fault. He takes a deep breath, to cope with his impossible father. We've always butted heads. I wish we hadn't butted heads.

"I'll put up your mirror," he says, making a big concession it seems. "And I'll take your CDs, all right, as many as I can carry. Remember I've got them, okay, don't go accusing people of stealing them. It's not nice."

He gets up and unwraps the package and puts up the mirror, I've had enough company, if it isn't my son it's some woman I'm supposed to know that I've never seen in all my life. I just want to close the door of this room and lock them all out and let the whole world do whatever they want. They do anyway. I can't lock that door. I've tried. There aren't any locks. The doors in this place have no locks. Anybody can come in here and take whatever they want. I want to be like that song. Let . . . . Let . . . . Goddamn brain. That song. I can't remember. Something about sitting back, letting things happen, something, I used to sing that song all the time, I sang it to Beverley. I don't deserve this. My brain used to work. I could remember. I could do things. What did I do to deserve this?

I'll put some tape across the glass doors, I need something stronger, whoever is taking my CDs can break through this tape in no time, it's see-through and it breaks easily, damn it breaks easily. But it sticks. I can run it all across the front of the glass door, but I'm already running out, it breaks but it sticks when I start a new bit. Where are my scissors? Someone has stolen my scissors. I can't keep anything here. I know they come in at night and steal my scissors. All my things. I can see them, dark shapes, I can hear them breathing. I have to shield what I'm doing with my body, that person is looking at me, watching to see what I'm doing and then when I'm asleep that person, that person will come in here and take my things. They've already taken my Beethoven. I can see the gap where they took them. And there's more gaps. A whole shelf. I can hear people in the hall. The door is open. He didn't shut the door when he left. That was deliberate. He's in with them. He tells them what I'm up to in here and they come when I'm asleep. I can't even get any damn rest, as soon as I get some rest they come in. I should put a chair across the entrance, so they make a big noise. I need more tape. I've almost used up all this tape and I've got tape all up and down the door but it's broken and I can't get enough to go all the way across and I have to break off bits to seal the edges but, that's not so strong if there isn't tape all the way across, I can almost pull it loose myself, damn I did. I can seal it shut again. Except some of these pieces have snapped around and pasted themselves on the other side of the glass so I can't tape it shut. I need more tape. Stronger tape. Lots of it. That person is watching me. All this time he's been watching me. Up on that wall right behind me. He doesn't move. I don't want to say anything, I don't want to look behind too much, I'll sort of pretend I'm glancing casually, he wasn't there before,

I'll put a towel across the thing he's looking in, I don't understand why a window's there, it wasn't there before, I don't remember any window there before, when I get back from the bathroom I'll put a towel across it, I hate to leave my CDs while he's up there staring, god knows what will happen, I'll close the door and put my wheelchair across the entrance, I have to go to the bathroom, I don't have control any more, everything is fine and then suddenly it's urgent, I'll have to remember to bring a towel when I'm done, I can use this thing from the bed in the meantime, it doesn't serve any purpose anyway, I can duck down and go by and he won't see me, he's up high, he can't look down if I go close to the wall right below him, this wheelchair is handy for some things, I can keep my body low and throw this thing up so it blocks off his view, perfect, it's caught up there, well sort of, it's hanging on something oh lord, oh lord, the Asian woman, of all the times for her to come in here, "What are you doing, Preston?"

"I'm busy. Go away." She's staring straight at my crotch. "Get out!"

Instead she comes around behind my wheelchair and scoots me toward the bathroom and says, "I think we'd better get the sheet off the mirror," and closes the door and I'm left here by myself soaking wet and smelling and humiliated.

She leaves me alone for a while. I'm cleaning myself up when she calls in, "Are you all right, Preston?"

"Go away!"

"You're not the only person this happens to. It's nothing to be ashamed of. It happens all the time."

"Go away!"

"I'll find you something to change into." She actually sounds quite gentle and understanding, I need friends here, I can't make an enemy of everyone. "I'll give you something to put on to take care of accidents," she adds. Something to put on! I've seen what they do. I'll be walking around like a damn baby. They'll think I'm a pig that pisses anywhere.

"Preston?"

"Yes. Thank you." I mean it, I do thank her, I have to get control of myself, I'm either angry or I'm crying or some stupid thing, why is this happening to me, why, why dammit, I'm losing control of everything.

I suppose it is sensible. Old people aren't in control all the time, our bladders get weak and we have to accept that. I have to accept that. At least I know if something does happen, it's taken care of. I feel dry. She's found some loose baggy pants, made of soft cloth, with this cord at the waist. I've got underpants on with paper inside of that, to absorb any accidents. I hate it. I hate the feeling of it. She's peeling off the tape on the cabinet and putting it back on better and I must say she is doing a good job. "You're hired," I say. She smiles. She really is a sweet little girl.

"You have a lot of music in here," she says.

"What's left." I'm watching as she works on the cabinet, she's put me in the chair by the window but I can look across the bed and make sure that everything is all right, I cannot afford to lose any more of my things, I'm losing everything. Everything.

"Richard told me you were worried that people were coming in here and taking your CDs," she says. She's psychic. "He said you asked him to take them home bit by bit." She's having some trouble peeling the tape off that got wrapped around where it shouldn't be. "It's a shame," she says. She stops for a moment. "There's some lovely things in there. I can see Schubert and Brahms and some Mozart. You are quite a collector." She leans forward to look in the cabinet more closely. "Mahler. Quite a few Mahler. Six. I don't know much about him. My boyfriend could tell me. He loves classical music. He tells me I need to learn more, he's always on my case, we talk about that sometimes, on my case." She peels off and resets more tape. "Does Beverley listen to it much?"

I can't remember.

"We find that music helps. It seems to calm people down when nothing else works," she resets tape, "especially those who can't communicate any more. It says something to them. Maybe, later, if you don't mind . . . ."

The little house is deserted. Across the gap between one part of the building and another someone pulls a curtain across a window. "I'll have to come back and do some more later," I look back at her as she stands up and gives me her lovely smile. "That's the best I can do for now, Preston. I think your CDs are protected. I'll come back and do some more later."

"You're hired."

"We don't let people use speakers. What we find is they turn up the volume too loud, especially those that can't hear so well any more. But we don't mind earphones."

"They've taken them."

"I'll keep an eye. Richard says there are a number of your Beethoven he still has at home. I think he's hoping you'll change your mind."

"They take them all."

She comes around on the other side of the bed and squats down and takes my hand, like she would a child. I feel like objecting but I don't, her touch is pleasant. "Do you feel better?" she asks. I nod.

"Don't worry, Preston, there's nothing wrong, we know what we're doing, you can depend on us." I nod.

She straightens up and leaves. She's always leaving. Everybody is always leaving. She's left me in this chair so I can't move, so I can't get over there to see what she's done with my CDs, I need more tape, I've run out of tape and she's made sure I don't have any more tape, the wheelchair is over by the door again, that's deliberate, she doesn't want me to get out of here, none of them, none of them, want me to get out of here, well to hell with them, this bed is too high but it's good for propping myself, I can manage to get over there if I take it slow, across that gap, where the wheelchair is, folded up, I need to get exercise so I don't have to do this, so my legs are strong and they hold me up, I will get over there, I will, if I can make it to the wall, I don't want to panic, stop, gather my strength, go on, to the wall, to the wall.

Good.

And prop myself along, leaning on the wall, inching to the chair. She's left the door open. The first thing I'll do, when I get to my chair, once I open the damn chair, I need a better chair, this damn mirror, right in the way. I'll have to lean against it, get my fingers all over it, mucky it up, it's rocking.

How are you, Preston. How are you today, Preston. You look shitty Preston. So do you. Asshole. As the young ones would say.

Inch along. Don't knock the mirror over. Careful.

God. Half way across my room like I'm climbing Mount Everest. And now to get the damn wheelchair open. I need a new wheelchair. Stupid chair. Stupid, stupid chair . . . .

Done. Open. Sit down and rest. God. I'm exhausted.

What was it I came over here for? I have no idea. Whatever it was I'm too exhausted to do it. Just close my eyes and black out. Rest. Rest.

Damn you.

O damn you.

What kind of a world have you created? It's bad enough we get old. Do you have to make fools of us as well?

"Dinner," my little nurse says softly. She's standing at the end of the hallway beside the door to the washroom.

I don't feel like meeting anyone right now.

"Dinner?" she says, taking a couple of steps forward.

"I don't feel like dinner."

"It's good tonight," she says briskly and comes to the window where I'm sitting in the wheelchair, jammed in here.

"I'm sick."

She shakes her head like my mother used to do when we weren't feeling well, leans down and puts her hand on my forehead. "Your color's good. Is your stomach upset?" I nod. She clips a thermometer on my finger and squats in front of me, holds my hands, and looks up. "You'll feel better if you get yourself away from this room. You need some company. It's not healthy to stay in your room all the time." She has a soft voice. "I'll take you in the hall for a bit. If you feel like dinner, you can go down there. You don't have a temperature."

"I want it here."

She lets go of my hands and stands up. "I can't do that, Preston. You have to go to the dining room if you want to eat. We don't bring it to your room. Do you understand?" She tilts her head and looks down at me, like a mother looking at a child that is under the weather. "This is not a hotel."

"I'm sick."

"Did your son phone?"

"I don't know."

"I guess he didn't. I can't make you eat." She leans down, takes the thermometer from my finger and looks at it. "No temperature. You're completely normal."

"I'm sick."

"Think about it. You won't get anything to eat until tomorrow morning. Understand?" I nod. "I'll be back in a little while. If you're feeling better, I'll take you down for dinner. They might not like it, they like to have people down there on time, but I guess they'll have to put up with it this time. It isn't going to happen all the time. Your son didn't phone?"

I shake my head.

"You need to fit in here, Preston, no exceptions," she turns and goes out without looking back, she is very cold, they don't care here, we're nothing but numbers, we could starve to death and they'd go on with their work as if we never were born.

It was nice of her to ask, though. I'm not feeling well. I can't go to dinner when I'm not feeling well. I can hear them going by in the hall. She didn't say what they were having. If I go down I can have a cup of coffee, if I don't feel like anything more.

"Last chance," she says, standing in the doorway looking serious but not angry, she can talk me into anything. "Why don't we comb your hair and get you freshened up a bit," she says when I wheel to the door. "They can wait for a while."

"Well his majesty has decided to join us!" says my plump outspoken friend when I wheel myself into the dining room and pull up at my place. "Was it something we said?"

I have to smile.

"Well?" she demands.

I flutter my hand to signify I wasn't feeling well.

"Are you feeling better now?"

I nod.

"As you can see," signifying her plate, "we haven't left much. You'll have to make do with what's left." The silent woman is silent, the bent over man is drinking his coffee, some of the diners are getting ready to leave, I feel like I've missed out on something. We're having chicken and a boiled potato and some peas, and soup to start with, all set down at once by the woman who serves us and tells me she's glad to see I'm feeling better. "You're lucky," says my outspoken friend, "I was all set to have it myself. It looked so good."

I can't talk properly, I don't know the names of any of these people. That's the first thing I used to do when people came in my office. Call them by name.

"So what have you been doing?" my friend asks. I shrug. She shrugs back and goes back to her food. She hasn't touched her potato and picked at her chicken and asks for another cup of coffee, which the woman who serves us brings her. She takes a sip and goes back to her chicken.

I sample some of the soup, which is all right, but I don't have much appetite. "I should," it's getting harder to get words out, my friend cocks her head, waiting, "know your name."

"Gladys." She doesn't look up from her plate. "You'll have to find out about these two for yourself. Although you shouldn't expect too much from her," cocking her head at the woman beside me. The woman pounds her spoon on the table. I bend forward and look at her closely to encourage her to get out what she's trying to say. "Bob and I have been arguing," my outspoken friend says. Gladys. Her name is Gladys.

"Sylvia," says the bent over man. Bob. His name is Bob.

"Sylvia?" I ask the silent woman. She stops pounding and I imagine a suggestion of a smile, but there isn't much change. When the end of the world comes, the damned in Hell will be sealed inside their fiery cells forever.

She's there now.

"You never told us what you did," says the plump woman. Gladys. Gladys.

I try some more soup. "Things."

"How very mysterious." Gladys, Gladys, puts down her fork and knife and takes up her coffee cup. "Can you be more exact?" She watches me above the rim of her cup. What I did, it's been a long time, sometimes I remember, brief flashes, like mist rolling away, at other times I don't, I can't, and I can't predict when I'll remember and when I won't. It's not in the soup, which isn't very good.

"Well?" she demands.

I shrug.

She shrugs, "You're as bad as Sylvia," and drinks. When I get the chance, I'll have to write this down. Gladys. Bob. Sylvia. Gladys. Bob. Sylvia. I hope I can remember long enough to get to a pencil and paper. I can't do it here, it's rude. I don't mind these people, she was right, my Asian friend, it's healthy to get out and meet people. What is her name? I don't know her name. I'll have to ask for her name.

Sylvia, Bob—what?—Gladys! Gladys!

I ate more than I thought I would. I must say hello to the people in the hall as I wheel back to my room, I need to get out, these are good people, I've been sitting in my room too long feeling sorry for myself, the worst thing I can do is feel sorry for myself. Gladys. Gladys. I'll stop right here and write it down. I'm in the way. People are coming back from dinner, the ones that can't do it themselves are being wheeled, some are walking, limping, I'll pull over to the side and find a piece of paper and a pencil.

I don't have one. I must always carry paper and pencil. There's a lot to remember here. Names. Gladys. Tom. Sylvia. Gladys. Tom. No, not Tom. There's pencil and paper in my room, somewhere, I'd better get back there and write this down, what I remember. Gladys. Bob. Bob. What—Sylvia. I'll say hello later, I'm in a rush now, that's the woman who's always sitting in the hall where the corridor turns, every day, smiling, nodding off, waiting for lunch, for dinner, around the corner, heading for home, Gladys, Sylvia, Bob, Gladys Sylvia, Bob, hello, how are you, can't stop, Gladys, Sylvia, okay, sharp turn, two wheels, spin in, here we are, here we are, paper and pencil, where, where?

Here we are, on the table beside the lamp. Paper. Pencil. Sylvia. Bob. No Jim. No Bob. Who? Gladys! Gladys!

Exhausting. You wouldn't think something like that would be so exhausting.

Bob. Sylvia. Gladys. That's right. Gladys is the loud one. How could I forget Gladys.

Oh God!

That scared the hell out of me. The phone never rings. Who would be phoning now? I'm tired, I don't feel like talking, who would it be, I've had enough company for now. They can call back later.

It rings.

Damn.

It rings. It rings. It rings.

"Hello!" I don't sound very friendly, I'm angrier than I want to be, calm down.

"Preston." Beverley! "Preston?"

"Hi sweetheart."

"I'm glad I got you." It's hard to hear her, she's hoarse. She clears her throat.

"How are you feeling?"

"Not bad, under the circumstances." She sounds hoarser than usual, her voice is usually soft and lovely, there's something harsh.

"I feel terrible, Beverley."

"Don't honey. It was an accident, you didn't intend it to happen."

"I feel awful."

"Preston, it's all right." Her voice is firm, rather impatient, she doesn't want to discuss it any more. "How are you?" she asks.

"Better when I see you."

"Thanks." There's something more, the way she said thanks, I can't pin it down exactly. "Richard is okay," she says. I don't answer. "The house needs some repair, apparently, it's not as good as he expected. Apparently."

"You're better?"

"Yes." I know Beverley, that tone means she is not well, I know that tone, she makes me angry sometimes, she never looks after herself, she's always looking after other people first. "I wanted to talk to you," she says. "You haven't talked to Richard?" No. I don't think so. "I told him I wanted to tell you first. I know what he's like. He tends to get people upset, the way he presents things. He doesn't intend to, the poor dear."

She is talking in a special sort of tone that is hard to describe, as if whatever she wants to say is sad for me. I really don't like pity, even from her, I can handle this situation, I've gotten used to it, there is no need for pity. But that is Beverley, she is very caring.

Neither of us is saying anything.

"You're feeling all right?" I ask.

"Yes, Preston, it's just a severe sprain. It's nothing you did." Now she sounds impatient.

"Will you be coming to see me?"

She huffs, she does this when I'm being irritating, I don't know what I've done, but I can pick up on what she's feeling. "I'd like to. I've been tired lately," she says, after a pause to get over her irritation. "I told the doctor I've been passing a little blood."

"I was hard on you."

"He asked if he could give me something called a CT scan. It's actually been scheduled for a while. I didn't want to tell you."

I don't know these medical terms. "Did that help?"

"They discovered cancer."

I can't think. I don't understand. It can't be that. She was always healthy. I was the sick one.

"Preston? Hello?" I can't answer. "I wanted you to know. I wanted to tell you so myself. Hello."

"Will you die?"

"Not in the least. I'm lucky they found it when they did. I don't want you to worry about it. It's not good but the doctor is looking after it. I wanted you to know before Richard went charging over there."

"You're not going to die?"

"No, I am not going to die. Don't even think that."

"I wouldn't know what to do if you died."

"I am not going to die. Get that idea entirely out of your mind. I am not going to die." She's always trying to hide things, she looks after everybody else, she never looks after herself. It should be me. I'm already sick. It should be me.

"Richard is on his way over there," she says. "I couldn't stop him."

I push my wheelchair to the space between the window and my bed and roll to the chair. I lean forward and place my hands on the arms of the chair. I remember and sit back and put on the lock on the wheelchair so it doesn't roll away. I lean forward again and put my hands on the arms of the chair and take my feet off the foot rests of the wheelchair and rock forward and shift my one hand to the other arm so both hands are on the same arm and turn myself on my foot, pivot, and drop in my chair. The drop punches air from my body. Then I lean forward and push the brake off my wheelchair and shove it away. It rolls and turns against the bed and the wall and gets stuck there half sideways.

Something is going on outside, down below. There are blank windows across the space between this building and the next, and something is going on down below. Clapping and singing. My wheelchair is in front of me. I'm sitting in the space between my bed and the window and something is going on down below. I don't know what is going on down below. It means nothing. Nothing.

He comes striding in, "What CDs do you want me to take now?"

"How is your mother?" I ask.

He's carrying some magazines, drops them on the bed, comes to the window and stands on the other side of my wheelchair, which is sitting in the way. He stands facing me, across the wheelchair. "I can't stay long. I'm supposed to ask how you are. How are you?" He says it quite harshly. I'm finding it harder to answer questions and he doesn't give me long enough. "She has bladder cancer, so she isn't very well. What did you expect?" He waits for me to answer that. He's standing in front of my wheelchair in the space between the bed and the window. I'm sitting here on the other side of the wheelchair and I feel trapped, but I'm glad I am separated from his anger. "What!" he demands.

"Is she . . ." I want to say "in pain," but he doesn't wait to let me say it and huffs in disgust and turns and goes to the other side of the bed. We glare at each other.

"You really are disgusting," he says, very low. He picks up the telephone, listens, slams it down and comes back to the window. "Your phone is working just fine. Funny you couldn't even phone to find out how your wife is. Your wife, you know, your wife, the one you made sick!" He's raised his voice and is not facing me any more, he's staring out the window at the people down there sitting at chairs and tables on that sort of cement whatever it is, beside the little house. "Answer me!" He talks to the window, he won't look at me.

There are a number of people down there and something smoking from a black thing and people sitting in chairs with glasses and some balloons hanging from the little house.

"She was bleeding and you didn't give a damn!" declares my son. He lowers his voice, he's talking too loud. "She was too damn busy looking after you—YOU, damn you. She didn't have time to look after herself. You didn't give her time to look after herself. It was you, always you."

"I didn't . . . ."

"Oh hell," he turns and walks back to the telephone and picks up the receiver thing and holds it above his head. The spiral cord stretches out and the rest of the telephone lifts off the table. "There is nothing wrong with this!"

"How is she?"

"She has bladder cancer!" Does he think I wanted his mother to have cancer? Does he think I didn't know his mother is sick? "She was bleeding and you didn't give a damn! She could have bled to death and you wouldn't have given a damn!"

My Asian nurse comes in. I don't know her name. She comes up to my son and places a hand gently on his back, "Please calm down," she says, very softly. My son snarls. He snarls. My little Asian nurse steps back and says nothing and my son turns and slams the receiver back on what is left of the phone. It jangles on the table.

My son turns and steps toward my nurse. "I am talking to my father, all right! Is that all right? Is that all right with you?"

"You need to be quiet," says my nurse quietly. "We can hear you down the hall."

"I want to talk to my father," my son says, more loudly.

The big man comes in and stands behind the nurse and looks down on all of us.

"Get out of my way," my son says and moves toward them both. They step aside and he strides out of my room and they follow and I can hear him talking loudly in the hall and then he is sobbing and then the noise goes away in stages and there is silence in the hall. Usually there is all sorts of noise out there.

In a while my nurse comes back. "What is your name?" I ask.

"Don't pay any attention to what your son says, Preston. He doesn't mean it. He's upset about his mother, it doesn't have anything to do with you." She steps forward and bends down and wipes my face. "He doesn't understand. People can be cruel when they don't understand."

"How is she?"

This little girl knows what I mean, who I'm talking about, she knows me better than anyone else.

"They've found it early," she says. "That's good. She'll start taking treatment right away."

"I want to see her."

"I'll see what we can do. Don't be upset. It's good they found it early." She goes around to the other side of the bed, picks up the phone, listens, and puts it back together. "Your son needs to calm down. He's causing more trouble than he's curing."

"He kept shouting."

"We heard him."

"He kept shouting for no reason. I didn't do anything. There was no reason."

"He's upset, Preston. People get cruel when they're upset."

"He thinks I don't care about his mother. I knew his mother long before he did. I love his mother. I don't know what I'd do if I didn't have Beverley."

She comes back to my side of the bed, bends over and hugs me. "We'll make sure you see your wife. We can set up some kind of visitation." She pats my back, bending over. "Your son isn't the only one upset, is he? I don't think he should come back here until he's calmed down. I doubt if they'll let him."

I did not make her sick. I did not.

"I don't know if it would help," she says, and squats down in front of me holding my hands, "Maybe you want to get out of this room for a while. There's a birthday party going on downstairs. One of our residents is a hundred years old and we're having a little celebration. Everyone's invited. She doesn't have many relatives and her family has invited everyone in the home who wants to come and join the celebration. There's cake and wine."

"I might go."

She stands up. "I think that would be a good idea. I can take you down if you like, but you'll have to make your own way back. We don't want to make you completely dependent, do we? I'll see what I can do to arrange for some sort of visit with your wife, depending on how things are right now."

"I'd like to phone her."

"We'll see if we can use the phone at the nursing station. Your son has shaken up the one in here. I'll have to get Jim to look at it. We have to get you out of this room."

Gladys talks

Gladys talks about everyone. If I want to know who people are, I listen to Gladys, gossip central. Sylvia is not at the table today, and Tom, Bob, I can't remember because he doesn't talk much though I kind of think we have more in common than I have with Gladys. Gladys is talking about my wife, how is she, how did the operation go, she talks about the excursions the home organizes, I have to get out, she says, get my mind off my troubles, that little Asian girl Mei Li keeps telling her she should push Preston to get out, I don't leave my room from one meal to the next, I'm a prisoner in my room, feeling sorry for myself. That is not true but she rushes on and I don't get the chance to make my point, if I don't interrupt I never get to say anything, people rush on and by the time I know what I want to say, the chance has gone to say it. She talks about my son, your son seems so full of energy, he never rests, where had the cat gone, she's onto the cat now, her mind works that way, from one thing to the next nonstop, that black cat that used to be out there on that balcony, has anyone seen it? Maybe a coyote got it. They eat cats. The nurses talk about coyotes. She didn't think coyotes were here, in Ontario, Gladys didn't, she remembers all her friends out west, how they used to talk about coyotes, coyotes howling in the night.

But we never had any here. But they say they are, and they say they kill cats that are allowed to wander, we used to have cats all over the place when I was young, she says, cats would just wander in the house and set up shop and her mother could never resist them, we always had strays, maybe the coyotes got that cat. It's unbelievable, how people treat cats, just like people, cats are cats, people are people.

"You aren't saying a lot today," she says, turning to me, "of course you never say a lot, you've been here for over four months and you haven't said four words in all that time, I've never known anyone to clam up like you, unless it's Sylvia. Got something to say? Spit it out."

"I listen."

"Of course. You're always listening. It makes me nervous. I ask myself, what is that man thinking?"

"Where is Sylvia?" Bob asks. Or is it Tom?

"How am I supposed to know," says Gladys. "I don't know everything."

"I thought you did," says Bob. Tom.

"It's flattering you think so. Keep thinking that. What do you think?" She turns to me again. I hold up my hands. "Is that all you've got to say?" she says. She talks and she talks. Sometimes I hear what she says, but after a while I don't, she can sit right beside me nattering on, right in my ear, and I don't hear a thing. "Snow," she says. "That's what they say. Tomorrow. Snow."

I smile at the woman in the hall as I wheel by her post, where the corridor makes a corner. Sometimes she sleeps there. She always smiles and says hello. I wheel myself down the hall and a woman who looks sort of familiar says hello from the door where she stands outside her room and I nod, I don't know who she is. She calls me by name, Preston, hello Preston, you look rushed today, what's the hurry, no place to go here. The hall is wide and long and I can see all the way to the window at the far end and the bright light coming in way down there, my eyes aren't so clear, I can't make out details, and here we are, my room, turn in and check my glass cabinet and count the CDs in there. I lose count. I can't tell, maybe some more have been stolen, or not, I don't know, the tape is still in place, the tape isn't see through, it's grey and stronger and all the way across the cabinet. I try it and it can't open, which is good, what is my nurse's name, she said she'd come down and help me do this. I've got tape. Big strong tape on a grey roll. It's hard to get it off and I need scissors to cut it. The lamp is there, and my leather chair by the window and the TV and the pictures on top of the TV and a flower of some sort, she keeps bringing flowers and I water them and they die. Water has spilled around the bottle and it's marked the

TV. Clothes in the closet. A jacket and pants, and many shirts, and black shoes and brown shoes and white shoes with dirt on and boxes shoved in the back, and a brown and orange blanket thing with holes that my fingers get stuck in. The phone is black and gets covered with dust and I lift up the receiver thing to dust off the thing that it sits in and the numbers and I can hear the numbers beeping, black shows dust, I hate dust, a voice talking to me, please hang up, and a strange beeping, I set it down and dust the bottom and put it back on the table and set the thing back down on top and the beeping stops. Around the lamp. Dust makes me cough.

She comes in. "Hi, honey," I am so glad to see her, but I am kind of sad too, "I haven't seen you for months."

"I was here three days ago," she says. I have a chair for her and she puts a bag with handles that she brought along beside the chair and sits leaning against the back of the chair up against the wall underneath that thing that I'm always afraid will fall off and cut her head, it's her favorite place to sit. I can see the wall above her and part of a bed.

"How are you feeling?" she says.

"Not too well." I have this pain that pinches the back of my eyes.

"I'm feeling much better," she says. "I'm thankful I can get around. It's taken so long though, waiting, and then going through all that operation business and getting back on my feet. Richard doesn't want me to strain myself, he says, he'd much rather I lie in my bed all day apparently and let him take care of things. Which he says he'll do but the trouble is, he is so busy with school and his girlfriend and so on and so forth. If I don't do things myself they never get done. It tires me out."

I nod. I don't like to interrupt her.

"I don't think it's the same one though," Beverley says. "The girlfriend. He doesn't keep me up to date. Girlfriends come and go."

"Why do you have that?"

"This?" She lifts it up and looks at it. "One of those canes you made for yourself, many years ago. I can remember you doing it, carving away, carving away. I didn't think you'd mind. It helps me get around."

"It's cold in here."

"I never liked that window. I think they should move the bed. I see you've put more tape on your CDs. You never listen to your music. You used to love listening to Beethoven. I kind of miss it. Strange isn't it? I didn't really like it at the time and now I miss it. Maybe it's you I miss, in fact I'm sure it is. I think I'll have to leave the apartment, it's too hard to keep up. Now that I have other things to worry about. And besides that I get tired more easily, what with the operation and so forth."

She talks a lot more and it's harder to follow, I have to concentrate and think what to say and by the time I've thought what to say she's on to something else. It exhausts me and I doze off and when I wake up she has some of my shirts laid out on the bed. "I think I will take these home and clean them up. You have enough to get you through. I get around pretty well, you must admit. Snow!" she says and looks up at the window. "You used to love the first snowfall. I never understood it." She brings the bag over to the shirts and takes out some books and puts them on the bed and stuffs the shirts in the bag. "I'll bring these back all nicely cleaned and pressed. You said you wanted these."

"Don't go."

"I have to. If I don't go I won't be able to come back, will I?" She smiles and comes over to my chair and kisses me and she's gone.

Gone. And I'm alone. I'm mostly alone. There are three books lying on the bed, one quite big and the others not. She's left them on the edge and I try to reach across from my chair but I can't get at them from here and I'll have to shuffle away from this chair and get myself to the wheelchair and wheel over there and pick them up and see what she's left. I haven't been reading, I need to get back to my reading. I sleep a lot and waste entire days. And now it bugs me, exactly what those books are that she's left me, and I can't decide whether I should get up and work my way over there or sleep here for a while, and I can't sleep, and I stand and work my way to the wheelchair, leaning on the bed, and when I'm settled in the wheelchair I tootle around to see what books she's left for me.

Du Fu. Robert Frost poetry. And The Divine Comedy.

I recognize the big one, the cover. Dante. It feels familiar. It looks familiar. Poetry. I haven't read anything worth reading for so long.

Forget the big paragraphs, I'll go straight to the poetry. Canto I. Roman numeral one.

A man, in the middle of his life, leaving the straight way, alone in a dark wood. "Death could scarce be more bitter than that place." A light above a little hill in front of him. He climbs. He is stopped by a beast that drives him back down the hill, away from the light.

I have read this. I must have. My name is right here, in the front of the book. My handwriting. Not sloppy like it is now. I don't remember any of this. My name, in this one too. My handwriting. And this one too.

I feel like that man in the dark wood. "So bitter is it here that death is little more." The light right there, right in front of him, and he's driven back, down, back down the hill, by a beast. A ravenous beast.

"You had a visitor!" My nurse. Breezy and chipper, breezing in. "Whatcha got?" she asks and comes to the bed and picks up a book. I show her what I'm reading. She takes it, flips through it, reads a passage and hands it back. "How can you read that!" she exclaims. "I can't understand a word. You are one smart man."

"What is your name?" I ask.

"It's not important."

I hand her the book and she picks up the rest and takes them all to the table beside the chair that Beverley was sitting in. "Mei Li. My name is Mei Li."

"Did you tell me that before?"

"A couple of times." She comes back. "I'll take your temperature. Your wife looks better."

"Could you bring that book over here? The big one."

"The big one? I thought you didn't want it." She goes back to the table and brings it to me.

"I was reading it," I tell her, so she knows what I've been doing, so she won't deprive me of what I'm doing.

She clips the thermometer on my finger, all business, and I put the book on the bed. She feels my forehead. "You seem pretty good," she says, and smiles. "Pretty healthy."

When she's done and taken the thermometer away, I wheel myself to the chair by the window and arrange myself there. "Do you want the book?" she asks, picking it up.

"No."

She puts it back on the bed, out toward the middle. "Someone will be in with tea and cookies," she says, "in about an hour."

"What is your name?"

"It isn't important."

"I want to know."

"Mei Li," she says. "You should try to read your book," and goes out the door.

I need to get out. I need to get out that door. My whole world is inside this room. I need to get out somewhere, I need to get out and do something, it isn't healthy in here.

I stare out the window, angry, angry at what has happened to my life, angry at the prison I am in here, angry at everything, angry at being stuck inside when the world is out there . . .

Little white specks coming down. Drifting sideways, drifting up, sticking on the window, transforming to water. Little specks of water.

I take a deep breath and look over at the book, sitting where she left it. She's put it in the middle of the bed, just within reach. And I can reach it, and settle down, and open it up, and start. I'll get some paper and make notes. I can remember better if I have notes.

Bright light. White dimpled all along the windowsill outside, a cap of white on the little house and brown birds squabbling on the ground below it, scuffling the white into dark scratches. Gravel pits at the base of the pole holding up the little house. The lamp on the table beside my bed is on and the top of the bed is angled up, there's a book on the floor with the pages scrambled where it fell. And some papers scattered beside it.

No need for the light, lots of light outside. Motion in the hall. Mealtime? "Good morning!" My little nurse. "How come you slept with the bed up?" She picks up the book and papers. "It looks like you were reading." She helps me get up and make my way to the bathroom and goes off once I'm in, to help other people get up. In a while she'll be back, so I have to get done. Morning business, do my teeth, rinse my mouth. Like my note says, stuck up with tape on the mirror. Get moving Preston. I'm feeling good today. I have to concentrate on what I'm doing. Step by step. This used to be automatic, get up, business, brush, rinse. Now I have to remember, every step, make sure I don't miss any. It can be embarrassing. The woman down the hall can't do anything. They have to take her to the toilet, do everything. I'm glad I don't have that job.

Concentrate on your work, Preston.

I don't know how long I've taken, but I'm ready. Pajama top off, shirt on, pants buttoned up, belt notched tight, shoes on with socks. My shoes are untied but I can't reach down and do them up. Actually I don't feel like it. My feet feel better loose, not so bound up.

So I'm settled in my wheelchair and I have time. They haven't called breakfast yet. I'm hungry. Some go down and sit at their table, waiting. I don't want to get in that habit. They'll be there hours before the place opens and hours before the food is brought out. They have nothing but food and sleep. Their whole day.

So this book on the floor. And papers, with notes.

This is my handwriting. I used to be a neat writer, I'm sure of it. Not any more. It's hard to make some of this out. The Divine Comedy. These must be my notes for this book. Divine Comedy. Strange title.

"A man in the middle of his life. In a dark wood. 'So bitter it is that death is little more.' Standing on a little hill, the light above him, driven back by a ravenous beast. 'She caused me so much heaviness . . . I lost hope . . . .' 'While I was falling back to the low place, before mine eyes appeared one who through long silence seemed hoarse.'"

I guess I must have written that. It's my handwriting. Nobody else was here last night. I've never seen this stuff before.

"Lines to think about," it says. I've written.

"Those who are contented in the fire." What is that? "Mountain of purgatory" I've written in the margin. I wrote margin notes on my own book notes.

"Those who are contented in the fire." What does that mean? "Think about it," I've written.

Us? We are those in fire? I understand that. Everything we've ever been is burning up. "Contented in the fire"? We are not content! No, we are not content!

"Through me, is the way into the woeful city; through me, is the way into eternal woe; through me, is the way among the lost people . . . Leave every hope, ye who enter."

Everyone who enters. Here.

I thought that exactly when I came here. Why do I remember that? Why not all the other things I try to remember?

"Strange tongues, horrible cries, words of woe, accents of anger, voices high and hoarse." Like here. No, not like here. Mostly it's quiet despair. We don't have strange tongues here. We're more like Sylvia. No tongues at all.

All this comes from this book? I've written these notes, I know, I can see my handwriting. These notes were laying beside this book. Some of them right inside.

I don't remember any of this. I don't remember reading any of this.

"That . . . choir of the angels who were no rebels, nor were faithful to God, but were for themselves."

I have known people like that. Most people are like that. A note in the margin. I have to turn the paper to read it, written slanted. "Most people are like that." Incredible! I already thought that and wrote it down here. I must have done that last night. It's like meeting myself. Will I wind up babbling the same thing over and over and over and everybody looks at me and thinks to themselves, what a babbling idiot.

I am not a babbling idiot!

Calm down, Preston. Don't panic. The worst thing you can do is panic.

I need to explain myself more. These notes aren't very helpful. I must have thought I was understanding this. I didn't absorb what I thought I did.

Calm, Preston. Calm. No panic.

A sheet of paper, stuck in the book, at Canto Roman numeral three. I've written on it, "I stopped here." I actually read to here. I don't remember a thing. Oh my God, here it is, right here, in big letters at the start of Canto Three. "Through me, is the way into the woeful city; through me, is the way into eternal woe; through me, is the way among the lost people . . . Leave every hope, ye who enter."

I read this. I read all this. I don't remember a thing. It's like it never happened.

"Breakfast," says my Asian nurse, singing it out as she breezes by my door and hollers in. What is her name? I don't know her name! I know she told me her name! I don't know her name! It's like it never happened! It's like she never told me her name!

I am not hungry. I was feeling good, but now I feel rotten.

Don't panic, Preston. Don't you dare. You know what is happening. You know it. You can accept it, or you can fight it. You can't stop it.

Oh god. I know what is happening.

I have dementia. It will never get better. It progresses. My brain is dying. Every so often another switch turns off. It's a disease. I can't stop it.

Don't panic. Don't give up. You are not a person who gives up. I will not give up. I can look around me and touch the window. Which is cold. And touch my bed. Which is soft—or hard when I pound it. My chair arm which is, sort of cold but hard and when the Sun comes in and lights up everything in here so bright I have to shade my eyes and look for my sunglasses—when it does that, the chair arm warms up and feels sort of glowing.

Wordsworth, a kid, when Wordsworth was a kid he used to reach out and touch things, just to confirm that they were there. That it was real. That it wasn't a dream.

How did I remember that? Why do I remember that and forget so many other things?

Who cares. Really, who cares. It proves my brain still works.

Can still be stirred up.

I am living. I touch things. They are real. I don't give up.

They give us a thing, this sheet, this sheet I've been using as a bookmark, that I ripped up and taped back together, and wrote on, telling us what's up with the home. This is my home. Beverley is leaving the apartment. That home is gone. This is my home. These are my people.

So where are my people going? According to this sheet. That I ripped up and taped back together.

To see Niagara Falls. A big bus, with people in front waving. This is where we're going. Niagara Falls. This is the bus we are taking. "Let the staff know," it says, "Everyone invited."

I'm not really interested in Niagara Falls. But I am going anyway. As soon as I see my little nurse, whose name I still can't remember, I'm telling her I'm going. I've just decided. I can still decide. I can still do things.

I did some reading last night. I know because I can see my notes, I can read what they say.

Reading is good. It is. I forget what I read, but reading is good. Something may stick. It exercises my brain.

This thing that is dying on me.

"Breakfast, Preston. Last call," my nurse sings out on her way by.

"Coming."

There is someone in my room, I saw the person just as they went in, far down the hall. I'll lean into my wheeling so I get there as fast as I can, catch them in the act, I'm out of shape, I'm already getting winded, spin in the door.

"Richard!" He jumps like he's been caught at something and turns toward me. "How wonderful to see you!"

He smiles hugely as soon as I say that, comes over and hugs me hard and long. "I can't stay. I'm on my way to school. I'm sorry, Dad. I'm always rushing in and out."

"Wonderful to see you."

We move away from each other. "You look good," he says. He sits in the chair that Beverley takes and I'm facing him with my chair brake locked.

"How is your mother?"

"Getting better."

"Not in pain?"

"No. She's awfully tired." We run out of things to say and stare at each other. "You called me Richard."

"That is the name we gave you."

He laughs and laughs, though I don't see any reason for laughter. "I was afraid you'd forgotten."

"I do forget sometimes."

He says how much he loves me and I tell him how much I love him and there's another big pause. "How is school?" I ask

"The same." I don't know what that means. "You're looking good," he says. I'm an old man, I can't look that good.

"Your mother is okay?"

"Getting better. She is awfully weak."

"I wish I hadn't been so hard on her."

"That was a terrible thing to say. I'm sorry, Dad."

"I probably deserved it." He objects, no, I didn't deserve it, he had no right to say a thing like that. There's another big pause. I think we've had this conversation before.

"We're going to Niagara Falls," I tell him. "We talked about it at lunch."

"Good. Wonderful. You need to get out."

"Maybe you'd like to come along."

"When?"

"Some time. There's a thing on the table, inside the big book. The table by the lamp."

"What about your wife?" he asks.

"Do you think she can?"

"She's awfully weak."

And there's another pause.

"I wish I wasn't such a burden," I say, I mean that, Beverley is so sick and instead of concentrating on getting herself better, she has me. Richard insists I am not a burden and I insist I am, and we exhaust that topic of conversation also.

"It looks like we're getting winter," he says and we talk about the weather in jerks and starts and then he looks at his watch and says he has to get to school, he's late already, it's amazing how fast the time goes, there is never enough time. "I don't know about the trip, Dad," he stands up, "I'll have to talk to Mom. I don't know if she'll be able to go."

"I need a chaperone," I point out. "All these women are after my body."

He smiles. "We can't have that, can we," and leaves.

When we first brought him home, everyone told us he was the tiniest baby they had ever seen, so vulnerable, so perfect, he fit in the crook of my arm, unlike Renata, who was huge. Now I have to beg him to visit me or have anything to do with me, he keeps apologizing and staying away. I make him feel uncomfortable. I unlock my chair and turn and wheel to the table with the lamp and take the big book with the bookmark and look at the picture of the bus on the bookmark and the people smiling and waving and Niagara Falls printed below the bus in big surprised letters and a picture of the Falls behind the bus, tumbling over it. I put the book on my lap and take paper and pencil and put it on my lap also and wheel to the window and turn so my back is facing the window. The Sun spills on my back and on the page of the book as I open it. I start at Canto Roman Numeral Three "Through me, is the way into the woeful city," the Sun is warm on my back and too bright on the page so I turn my chair slightly so the Sun is at an angle and doesn't fall full on the page, a young cat with white and grey stripes walks in the door and walks along by the wall and underneath the chair that Richard has left and comes by the TV in the corner and underneath my wheelchair and over between the bed and the window and leaps up on the leather chair at the head of my bed that I usually sit in and up on the window sill and sits in the Sun, licking its paw and wiping its face. Cats are sneaky. I should swat at it, but it's too far away so I'll ignore it and read my book, ignore it and read my book, "Here sighs, laments, and deep wailings were resounding through the starless air," the cat is still grooming, "what folk are they who seem in woe so vanquished?" it's purring, "the wretched souls . . . of those who lived without infamy and without praise" they are sneaky and they walk quietly you never know where they are or where they go or why they sit where they sit and why they want to sit where they sit and come into a room when they want to and wander away when they want to and there is no reason why they come in or why they go away, "Master, what is so grievous to them, what makes them lament so bitterly? . . . These have no hope of death," and it lays out on the windowsill in the Sun as if it will never leave.

She chooses my outfit because she knows what colors go together. I don't know color from anything, she says. I don't argue with women. I've got myself ready but she combs my hair. My son is coming, she says. I don't want my son to think his father isn't dressed up. Do I? No I don't, she says. I haven't said anything.

She inspects my hands. She praises me for cleaning my nails and files them down. Her fingers are thin and delicate. I don't know why I'm going. I didn't sleep very well last night. I'm tired. I don't want to go out with a bunch of people I don't know. "I don't want to go," I say.

"You have to. Your son's waiting. He's really looking forward to it, he told me, he says he owes it to you. I told him I'd have you in the lobby half an hour before the bus gets here. The bus gets here in half an hour. We're late."

"I don't feel well." She ignores me and eases me from my chair to my wheelchair. My new wheelchair is much better, she says. The wheels are better lubricated, it runs more smoothly, I'll motor down the hall much faster. "We may have to put up speed signs," she says.

She pulls a sweater over my head and combs my hair again. She puts a blanket on my knees and a shawl on my shoulders. "I don't want this," I say and shove it off.

"You can give it to your son," she says and folds it up and puts it on my knees with the blanket. "It snowed last night, it's cold out, maybe your son will need it. You don't want your son to get cold?"

"No."

"He might not dress warmly enough," she gives me a hug and goes around to the back of the wheelchair. "I'll push you down. Just this once. I expect you to get yourself there next time."

"Where are we going?" I ask. I don't want to go anywhere, I didn't sleep well last night, I'm tired and I don't feel well.

"Niagara Falls."

"I've been there already."

The hall moves by, a woman says. "Hello Preston," a white and grey cat comes out of a room just before we reach the place where the hall bends and it walks fast beside us as we roll along, "It's cold at the Falls," my Asian nurse says behind me, "there's ice on the trees and the mist comes up off the Falls and it's almost like an ice storm sometimes. It's beautiful, especially if the sun comes out and lights up the ice like a chandelier. You'll like it. The Falls is lovely in the winter."

She hits the plate with the buttons and the elevator door opens and the grey and white cat gets on with us and rides down and follows us out to the lobby. "Look who's all dressed up," says Gladys, I remembered her name, Gladys. "Hello Isis," she says to the cat, "what are you up to?" It ignores her and pads to the big windows by the driveway and sits there grooming its face.

"I'm leaving him with you," says my Asian nurse.

"What did I do?" Gladys demands. "Why me?"

"Because you're lucky," says my Asian nurse and wiggles her fingers goodbye.

"So what am I supposed to do with you?" says Gladys. "I thought your son was coming."

"I don't want to go," I say.

"You won't get a refund," she says.

Everybody ignores me. It doesn't matter what I say. Nobody pays any attention. "So how will you get yourself up there on the bus?" Gladys says. "In that thing?"

"Fly," I tell her.

"Here he is!" Gladys says, looking at a big man bustling in the door in a big thick blue coat with a hood and high topped army sort of boots.

"Sorry I'm late, the damn car wouldn't start. The roads are all right. I assume the bus has snow tires. There's a lot of snow out there," this person talks and talks, even if I had anything to say I wouldn't get it in. He leans down and squeezes my shoulder. "How's my favorite Dad?" I hand him the blanket and the shawl.

"You slept all the way," he says.

I don't know where we are. We're sitting at the front of the bus. There is a great sheet of water falling in curled lines, brilliant in the sun, falling on the other side of a big trench in the ground, a big ravine with snow at its base and all along the trees above it. "Do you remember the first time we saw this?" he asks.

I don't remember anything, I just woke up.

"Do you?" he demands.

"Was your mother there?"

"Your wife was always there." I am not meeting his requirements. I don't say anything. It's better if I don't say anything, I don't get myself in trouble. "We came here after midnight," he says, "after all the lights were off. We could hear the Falls and we couldn't see them, just a white blur. I was ten. Do you remember?"

"A long time ago."

"We begged you for months. We want to go to Niagara Falls. We want to go to Niagara Falls. We drove you crazy. You don't remember?" I shake my head. "I think Renata pushed it because her little brother said he wanted to. She was older." He stops for a moment, The veil of water up in front of us is hypnotizing. "You were so busy all the time. We came here after midnight."

A man has come up the aisle and stands beside us flashing his camera at the windshield. The driver asks him to sit down and we turn and move along the street with the Falls to one side. There is snow beside the road and a few people walking along edge of the ravine, by a stone wall. Mist rises above the street up ahead of us.

"You told us all sorts of facts," he said. "You said we were looking at Lake Erie falling off a precipice. You called it a precipice. It sounded so much higher than a cliff. We had to take your word for it, because all we could see was a blur. You told us six million cubic feet of water drops over the Falls every second. I measured out a cubic foot with my hands and tried to imagine six million of them. And you told us about the people who went over in a barrel. I wanted to see the barrel." The driver turns on the wipers as we get close to the mist and tells us it's coming off the bigger Falls. There's a bigger Falls up here.

"We drove along this road," he says, "and we got out and stood by the wall where the water goes over. We could see it up close, even with the lights off. I remember the way the water was so smooth and shot out beyond the edge and curved down and the dull rumbling thunder of it when it hit the bottom. It was hypnotic. I remembered that last year, when that little Korean girl stood up on the wall and fell off and was gone in a second. Your wife made us stand back."

We can hear the Falls and see part of it on the far side of the curve as we drive by.

"You said the big one was called Horseshoe Falls and I was really disappointed when we couldn't see the horseshoe. What really impressed me, though," he says, "was the story you told about the first person to go over the Falls in a barrel and lived to tell about it. A sixty-three year old woman. A school teacher. That really turned Renata on. I was in Grade 4 and I thought of Miss Johnson going over in a barrel. Some of us wanted her to."

We have gone up the road beyond the Falls and reached a circle in the road, we swing around it and head back the way we came. "I looked it up," he says, he's launched and nothing is stopping him, "You were right. It's a neat story and my kids loved it. Her name was Annie Edson Taylor. It was back in 1901. She was almost in the poorhouse, she'd lost her job, so she came up with this scheme, to make money by going over the Falls in a barrel. She had this huge big barrel made out of oak and iron. But no one had done it so they didn't know if it would work so they put in a cat and dropped the barrel in the water and sent it over. The cat lived, so three days later Annie Edson got in. She took her lucky heart-shaped pillow and had the barrel stuffed with mattresses. They screwed down the lid and pumped in air with a bicycle pump." We go by an old building with "Hydro" something or other written in the brick. "They plugged the hole with a cork and dropped her in the river."

We can see mist rising above the edge of the Falls as we go back towards it.

"She went jouncing down the rapids, avoiding all those rocks over there," he points, "and went blink, off the brim, just like that."

As we drive by the Falls again there are hundreds of people wearing heavy coats over at the wall, mist rising behind them like a smoking steel plant. "She did it to make money but she didn't make much and her manager stole the barrel." He stops. I don't say anything. "So what do you think of that?" he demands.

"Look after your barrel," I suggest.

"That's exactly what you said! Exactly! Word for word! You don't remember?"

"Not all that."

"I do. Renata was there."

"Who?"

"The one who grew up and became a policeman. The one you wouldn't stop talking about, like I didn't exist." He turns away. "I never could please you. And now you don't even remember her."

We don't talk any more and the bus goes back to the town and lets us off at a casino. From the excitement at the back of the bus, it sounds like this is what all these people have come for.

It is dark and noisy, the machines are lighted and have pictures of women and cowboys and flowers and playing cards. Numbers flash and a red light blinks and a bell jangles. Old people crowd the aisles with plastic cards on lanyards around their necks, most of the people here are old and can't afford this and they are spending all their money. I can't hear what my son is shouting, the machines ding and make shushing sounds like water and gravel on metal and they flash and people sit around tables and shout and young people in visors lean over and shout and spin wheels and take hundred dollar bills and shove them in slots. More people keep coming up the moving stairs their heads emerge and their bodies rise and there's a bar where people sit and fiddle with machines and lose money while they drink. There's machines in aisle after aisle, all the same with different pictures and noises and spinning wheels and people stick plastic cards in and slips of paper come out. There is no money.

Plastic cards go in, slips of paper come out. Except for the hundred dollar bills that the young people in visors shove in slots.

Richard sits beside me and pushes buttons and wheels whirl and he groans and shouts and I sit here in my wheelchair and watch him losing plastic. He says I forget things and he's mad that I forget things but I notice he forgets all the plastic he's lost and goes ahead and loses more. I suppose it's good to get out and see what the world is up to. Crazy as it is. I'm better sitting here than sitting in my room being glum.

"It wasn't like this the last time, was it?" Richard shouts. He has to repeat it, I can barely hear. "No casino."

I do remember that his mother and I were too busy trying to keep our money. Not losing it.

It's too noisy. Too flashy. Too many lights and jangles and people bumping at my back and pushing through the crowd and standing behind me, seeing what I'm up to and all I'm up to is sitting here in my wheelchair to please my son. He seems to want to do this, mad as it is.

"This is fun," he shouts and leans over and says something else which I can't hear.

"What?" I shout.

"Love you," he shouts back.

Whatever makes him happy. As long as he's having fun I can sit here and share his enjoyment. I need to go. I have no idea where the washrooms are, he'll have to take me but I don't want to say anything, he's enjoying himself. If I didn't have to go so badly I'd probably fall asleep. He's exhausting.

Beverley looks

Beverley looks tired, her face is drawn. I think she has lost weight, her eyes seem to have receded, there's a suggestion of a shadow around them. She looks strained and I'm sorry to say, a little ghoulish. I tell her to take care of herself and I know she doesn't, I know her backwards and forwards. After all, we've been married all these years.

"That is true," she says.

"You are not putting me off, young lady. You are not taking care of yourself."

"Actually I am," she insists.

"You are under strict orders, do you understand? Take care of yourself."

I think she is going to say something more but changes her mind and just smiles.

"I mean it!"

"That is lovely of you, dear," she smiles some more, she has always had a sweet gentle smile. "How are you feeling?"

"Tired. I get tired a lot," I say.

"Do you wake up at night?"

"I think so. I sleep in my chair a lot. Probably."

"Do you eat well?"

"I think so. The food isn't very good. I eat it anyway, as much as I can."

"That's good." The conversation stops, it seems we've run out of things to say on this topic. But that's never a problem, our silences are as good as our talks, maybe better. She picks up the shopping bag she brought along and looks inside. "I brought you some more books."

"I haven't finished the ones that I've got. I wouldn't know where to put them." She sorts through the contents of her bag.

"I also brought some tape."

"Wonderful! I'm running out."

She takes out some transparent tape in a small plastic holder and puts it on the table.

"Do you have any more of that big grey stuff?" I ask. "The one on the big roll that sticks to anything?"

"I can bring some, if you really think you need it. I'm worried though. I'm afraid I won't be able to get in here, one of these days." She stops and smiles. "You'll have the door taped shut."

"That's not such a bad idea," I stop. And smile. "Not you of course. I'd always let you in."

"But would I get out?"

"I'd like to tape you in and . . . ." Wasn't there a song like that? "And . . . ." I hum it and sway my upper body and she hums and sways too.

"Am I interrupting?" says my little Asian girl, leaning on the wall next to the bathroom.

"Hi Mei Li," chirps Beverley.

"How are you feeling?" my Asian girl asks and they talk about things I know nothing about. I feel a little left out. Beverley gets some medical advice, which I am happy about, though I don't understand what the topic is and what the advice relates to. My nurse takes my pulse and my temperature and records something or other on a small black tablet she carries about. She and Beverley start off again, talking about my health and I let them go on, I'm finding it harder and harder to follow conversations and I find it's better to just let people have their head and go on with what they want to go on with and eventually they'll come back to something I can concentrate on. Things are more confusing now.

"Richard says he enjoyed your day out together. I'm so glad. You used to have such terrible fights. I'd curl up and cover my ears," Beverley says. The nurse is gone. I don't answer, I don't think an answer is expected. "He said you had some nice conversations. Things you hadn't talked about for a long time." I nod. She half smiles. "There were some problems at the end, he tells me." I guess. I don't know what she's talking about. "Personal hygiene."

"Yes." That seems a safe enough answer.

"I think you probably took on a little too much."

"It was a good day." I'm sure it was.

"I was wondering, Preston. Might it be better to plan something not quite so ambitious, the next time?"

"Yes."

"The home has a number of shorter trips they organize around town. With members of the staff along to help out. Should something arise."

"Good idea." Whatever the problem is, I am sure a shorter trip would solve the problem.

"He said the Falls were beautiful."

What falls?

This tape isn't strong enough but it will do until I get some stronger. The cabinet is as strong as a bank vault. I can't make out the CDs in there, especially the names of the composers, with all the tape. I think some are missing. I can see gaps in there and CDs fallen over. Mozart. Schubert. A gap in between. The tape is solid. Nothing has been broken. Whoever got in sure didn't get in this side. There is no point complaining. Nobody listens. They probably got in at the back. Why didn't I think of that!

It's all open at the back! Why didn't I turn the thing around? I can see right through. I can reach in and touch them, by god I can take them out. That's how they did it. By god I'll show them this. They'll believe me now. Why didn't I think of this before? So busy sealing up the front and forgot the back is wide open. I'll have to get some boards, big strong boards, and nail this shut. Or maybe send it all home. That's what I'll do. Send it home with Beverley.

No point doing anything now. I'll have to get some boards and block this up, at least until I've sent it all home. In the meantime I'll shove it against the wall with the back to the wall and jam some tables and things against the cabinet so I'll know if anyone has moved it. They'll have to turn it around to get at the back to take the CDs out. If I jam a table up against the front like this, they'll have to move the table and I'll know. People are pretty smart though. I'll just have to be smarter. Especially thieves. Thieves are smart. Sneaky like cats. Get out of here cat.

Doesn't pay any attention. Jumps up on the window sill and walks along the windowsill looking out. As if it owned the place.

I don't want to hurt it. Get out cat. Scat cat.

Pays no attention. Just like everybody else. Can't even have a room to call my own.

Well, if you can't beat 'em, join 'em.

I need to get myself sitting down here and do myself some reading. Use it or lose it. Good for the brain. The book on the bed so I can reach it when I go over on the other side to my chair.

Forgot my notes. Always forgetting. And paper. And pencil.

Where?

Here.

Here we are.

All these notes. I need to get them organized. Number them.

Okay. Book on the bed within reach. Notes and paper and pencil beside it. Wheel around the bed, lock down, swing myself over on the chair, before the cat gets there.

Sorry cat. Beat cha!

What was that? First come first serve. Well I got here first, my friend.

You like the sun? You like the sun, don't you. Warms the bones. Wonder what I'm doing here?

Would you like it if someone walked behind your head like that? Walked along the back of the chair right behind your head. I suppose you wonder what I'm doing. Reading behind my back. What was that?

We all have to put up with things, my friend. You are a friendly one, aren't you. If you don't mind, I'd like to do some reading.

I don't want to be rude, but you're getting in my way. Sitting on the back of the chair like that. Purring in my ear. Kind of pleasant. I shouldn't alienate you, should I.

You're the only friend I've got.

"Hi Preston, whatcha doin'?" The Asian girl.

"Hello."

"You have a friend." She comes around and reaches behind me and pets the cat, I can feel it standing up and savoring her attentions. Now it's really purring.

"Is it bothering you?" she asks, looking down at me. No, it isn't. We were reading this book. "What have you done with your table?" she asks.

"Thieves."

"I'm worried about your lamp. It's almost falling over. You shouldn't move your table unless you unplug your lamp." She goes around to the other side of the bed and puts her hand on the table in front of the cabinet. "Is it okay if I move this? I'm afraid the lamp will fall over. You didn't unplug the lamp when you moved the table."

"Yes." I might as well agree. I can move it back when she leaves. This Asian woman.

"You had a nice visit with your wife. I like Beverley. You made a good choice. You're obviously a smart man. Of course she tells me she made a good choice too," as she unplugs the lamp and moves the table and picks up some papers off the floor. I can move it back when she leaves. I need to put more tape on. The cat has deserted me and follows her out.

This vehicle shakes and rattles. It's some sort of bus with windows all along the sides and a slab thing that hums up and down. Gladys is rattling on as if nobody else is here, sitting in a seat behind the driver like a queen. Half this thing is full. Some of us are in the middle, strapped into our wheelchairs so damn tight we're gasping for breath, and tied to the floor. The driver yammers on with Gladys and the big guy is sitting at the back, saying nothing, watching us. Most people are in the seats. The windows shake and the door up front rattles. The door at the back only opens if something happens, like a fire or a head-on collision. Not much good for me, there's a seven foot drop, I'd pitch forward and land on my nose with the wheelchair on top.

I can't make out what Gladys is shouting so I won't bother listening. I suppose they're talking about the condition of the roads or something they heard on radio or the TV or heard from someone they're not supposed to talk about. Though Gladys doesn't need anything to talk about, she'll talk about it anyway and make it up if nothing else is available. I like the woman. She keeps things lively.

I've been told she kind of likes me but I'm married. Maybe that's not true, but I'll believe it until someone tells me different.

We're going to a mall. I don't have anything to buy but I've got money, you never know. It gets me out. I need to get out. Nobody visits me so I might as well get out and see the world. I've got tables rammed up against the cabinet, so if someone tries to steal my CDs while I'm gone they'll have to move the tables, and I've taped all the tables to the floor. So they'll have to break the tapes and I'll know it.

Nobody talks but Gladys. The rest of us stare and watch the world. We're not a very talkative group. Gladys has remarked on it. And the world goes by out there, or we go by it. Trucks and cars and buses and motorcycles and people walking across the street or jogging along the side of the road. And a bunch of tiny kids on a rope. And cars lined up row after row like they live in a beehive. And people swarming in and out of glass doors.

The ones who can walk or hobble with canes get off this thing first and the ones in the wheelchairs wait. I'm the only man in a wheelchair, so I have to go last. Women and children first.

The big guy helps the girls. It's my job to help myself. I can't be everywhere, he says and wheels the last one to the door and inside, leaving me to get off by myself and as soon as I do, the bus drives off and I'm here on the sidewalk and everybody has gone. The last one off before me, the woman the big guy wheeled away, was swinging her arms about and nattering nonsense and he was talking back, trying to calm her down. When I go in, he's up ahead still doing that and the others have gone on and he's looking to see where they're going and I turn sharp and lose myself down an aisle among coats and suits and when I peel some suits back and peek out I can see him wheeling the woman off, trying to catch up, thinking probably the bus driver is back there, looking after me. I drop the suits and close myself off and wheel as fast as I can in the opposite direction. I am tired of being ordered around. I am a grownup man. I have things to do.

In among the women's dresses and sweaters and unmentionables and scarves that catch at my coat as I wheel by and aisles that end so I have to back myself up and turn and find my way through, into cosmetics. The odor bothers me. Beverley hates the smell of candles, it bothers her allergies, and cosmetics, some of them too, and I can see. Yes, I can see. The pictures, the things they advertise. A man bending a woman over who, if not naked, looks naked from all we can see and they've cut off the interesting parts farther down, beyond the frame of the picture, so we have to imagine. And we're meant to imagine. And I do. Old Preston. I sure do. And a woman in an expensive white silk gown slashed down the front to her navel, I assume, the gap is still open when the picture ends. When I was young I'd be arrested for even looking at something like that. Not that I object. I'm a grownup. I can handle it as well as the next man.

Which isn't very well. I'm wasting time. I'm out in the open here. Through a gap between two funny uprights with holes at the top. Someone behind me sets off a bell and the woman who has done it stops in confusion and looks around and turns back and someone else goes through and sets off the same bell and keeps going and nobody does anything.

So here I am. Out in the real world. Shops all down the corridor. As far as I can see. Which isn't very far. Clothes. Clothes. Clothes. More raunchy pictures. A woman with her leg draped over a man's shoulder and the man, wearing a cowboy hat, grinning at her and what is she doing? Smiling with her mouth open wide and teeth showing, looking off somewhere else, as if he was some kind of I don't know, post, to hang her leg on and tickle her. Control yourself, Preston. A chocolate shop. I pull down a box and three fall off and a woman comes over and assures me that it is all right, can she help me dearie. I am not a dearie, but I buy the chocolates.

And roll along. There's a moving stairs thing, but it's too narrow for this wheelchair and I'm a team with this damn contraption, where it goes I go, where it doesn't I can't. So I sit looking down on a floor below and people at tables drinking. Coffee, from the smell.

Cakes, it looks like. I really wouldn't mind some, but I'm up here and they are down there.

Some kids come rushing from a store stuffing something in a bag and looking around and laughing and shovel the bag in my hand, "Hold this," a girl says who is young, maybe, I don't know, young, still a kid. They scamper off and I'm left, holding the bag. A shopping bag with handles. And it looks like a shirt stuffed inside. I'm still examining the thing when my wheelchair spins and starts moving rapidly back the way I've come and the big guy says, "You tricky old bastard."

What can I do? Jump off the chair and break my nose? Jam on the brakes? There's no point. Besides, there wasn't much to see out here, so why bother. My chocolates slip off my lap and he runs them over and doesn't stop and he's going so fast I'm more concerned about running someone down than getting back my chocolates.

My tables are exactly where I left them. No one has broken the tapes.

There's a shirt in this bag with a funny thick plastic thing clasped through one of the button holes and a knob, sort of, where the clasp comes out and attaches to the rest of the plastic rig. Someone has painted red on the plastic, but it's mainly a creamy white. I can't get it off. I don't want to rip the buttonhole. I don't know why they would put something like this on a shirt and make it so hard to get off, how is a person supposed to use the damn shirt with something like this on?

The cardboard tags are easy, cut them off and cut them up and throw them in my waste basket. But this plastic outfit is something else entirely.

There is a thick sort of plastic arm coming out of the body of the plastic thing and it goes through the buttonhole and it's so thick it's stretched out the buttonhole so, if I'm not very careful here, I'll rip the shirt getting it off. Why in the world they would put something like this on, I really don't know. I need a saw. Maybe I should ask for one. The big guy is mad and won't do me favors. So is my Asian lady. I've disappointed her, she says. What she has to do with it I really don't know. I've tried prying with my scissors but the plastic is tough and slick and I don't want the scissors to slide off while I'm trying to push at this thing and slash my leg or something. The plastic is really slick and hard. I could take it to the bathroom and try hammering this plastic thing whatever it is on the edge of the sink. I don't want to break anything. This is a tough whatever thing.

"What do you think?" I ask but the cat doesn't answer. It sits on the windowsill wiping its face with its hand, licking its hand, wiping its face. They are clean animals. Not like dogs. "So what do you think? What is this?" I pry with the scissors but nothing happens. So I'll take it to the bathroom. "Aren't you coming?" It doesn't move.

So I'll have to do this by myself. If it doesn't want to come. I'll close the bathroom door. "Coming?" I shout. No answer. I shut the door.

I hammer the thing on the sink. It's hard, pushing the shirt away so I can hammer on the plastic doohickey thing without the damn shirt, getting in the way. The cloth will soften the blows so I have to pull it back so it doesn't, without ripping it on this idiotic plastic thing, tag, whatever they call it. There is nothing to pry with and I don't want to damage my scissors. I cannot wear the shirt with this ridiculous plastic thing stuck on the front. I can't get the buttons done up, not with this thing there.

This is the toughest plastic I have ever encountered. I need a crowbar. The only thing I've got in here is a toothbrush and a shaving machine thing, and Listerine and other bottles and toilet paper. Can't do anything with that.

Try it again, pull as hard as I can.

Damn. There's some kind of blue liquid stuff inside this thing. It snapped and spilled this liquid all over the shirt. And my trousers. Damn. And my hands. And my wheelchair. I'll wash it off with soap.

All over my hands.

It's not coming off. This damn liquid blue stuff is not coming off. It's ruined the shirt and my pants and I can't get my hands clean and everything I touch, gets stained. What is this damn stuff? Why would they put a stupid tag like this on? It didn't have a price or anything. It served no purpose at all, except to ruin the shirt and my pants and get my hands all stained and everything I touch. Those kids never came back. They left me with this thing and it's completely useless. They'll never sell shirts with this going on.

I'm not feeling so well today. I dropped my spoon at breakfast and round little cereals and milk splotches scattered all over. I tried backing up and almost ran over the hand of the woman who serves us, who was bending down to pick up my spoon. I could hear the little Os crackling underneath the wheels as I backed up. She handed me my spoon but my hand was shaking so much I had to put it down and it clattered as I put it on the table. Gladys said nothing. I was extremely rude and told the server the goddamn cereal was stale and the milk was sour, take the damn thing away. And I was wishing she'd take my hand too and bring back another that didn't shake. I was very rude. I'm ashamed.

I couldn't put my toast in my mouth and kept missing and snapped at it as it went by and almost bit off my finger. There was no point trying to drink my coffee, I couldn't hold the cup still long enough, so I rattled it down and left it on the table, hoping the shaking would calm down enough so I'd be able to have something to eat. I was hungry. The more I couldn't eat the hungrier I got. Toast was best, but toast is dry. I didn't realize how much I depended on my coffee to moisten my breakfast. I was able to manage orange juice. And some toast. I need my coffee. My day doesn't start without coffee.

I feel so damn weak and useless. I am not in control. I hate it. I have to wear a bib. I splatter things. I can't hold things. I choke. There are people at other tables who have to be fed. It's bad enough that I wear wet pants. I'm not going to think about it. But I know where I'm going. I'll be sitting with my mouth open, being fed.

Maybe if I read a bit, I'll calm down. My hand is still shaking. No notes today. Notes from, my last notes I think. Notes. "They are among the blacker souls." I can hardly read this. Both hands shake. "A different . . . ." I can't make out. "A different sin weighs them," stop it, dammit, stop it, "down," dammit dammit, "to the bottom."

I'm exhausted. The cat is staring at me. I can't blame it. This old fool can't even read one damn sentence.

Give it a moment. I'll get it together, cat. I'll just take a deep breath here and relax. Close my eyes and relax.

"There is no greater woe than to lie in misery remembering the happy time."

God. I read a whole damn sentence. Incredible. A whole damn sentence.

"You don't know where that comes from, do you?" I say. The cat licks its hand and lowers its head and swipes its face. And doesn't answer. Sun. A bird, landing on the windowsill. The cat runs along the sill, the bird whirls away, the cat stops. "It's outside, you fool!"

It doesn't answer. Not that I blame it. I wouldn't either, not when I was called a fool. "Sorry old fella. We have to stick together." I say.

It lies down and waits, for the bird to come back. There is no greater woe. Even cats have troubles.

Take the book. Hold it with both hands and prop it on my lap, so I have something stable to control it with. Canto VII. The Avaricious and the Prodigal. The Wrathful and the Sullen. "This is where I stopped," the bookmark says. I can hold the book with both hands and rest it on my lap and it doesn't shake so much.

The cat lays its head flat, with its feet underneath ready to spring. "Don't be sullen, old fella. You'll go to hell. It says so right here." It ignores me. Like everybody else.

I have to hold this book down, to stop the shaking. To control the shaking. My hands still shake. I wish nobody could see the damn shaking. It's humiliating. "Be silent, accursed wolf! Consume thyself with thine own rage."

Another whole sentence. I read this whole book. I know I did. Some time or other I read this whole book. I'm sure of it. I was like that. I'd inhale books.

Gladys is alone when I come for lunch. "Do me a favor," she says, "if you can manage it. Park your chair and shift over here to Bob's place. Think you can manage that?"

There's a parking space at my spot, waiting for my wheelchair to pull up, and an empty chair at Bob's place. So I park my chair in my parking spot and manage to shift across to the straight backed chair beside Gladys without tipping the table and everything on it.

"You heard what happened?" she says. I shake my head. "He's in hospital, in a coma. They don't expect him to last out the day. How are you feeling? You look better."

I take my time getting settled, which gives me the opportunity to sort out my answer. "Good," I admit.

"You don't say a lot, do you?" I shrug. She always says that. Even if I was sitting here with a whole damn encyclopedia to talk about, I'd never get the chance, she wouldn't let me. "We all get these spells," she says, "It comes with the territory. I've taken the liberty of ordering your coffee," she takes the white ceramic pot in front of her plate and pours coffee in my cup. "I understand you can't get along without your brew, so I thought I'd accommodate

237

you. Sylvia's had another of her spells," she nods her head at the empty chair on the other side of her, "so it's you and me kiddo, all by our lonesome." She spoons up some soup. "Which is another advantage to our present arrangement, you see. If it looks like we're expecting someone, where I've had you park your vehicle, they won't try to impose another body. Especially since I've parked my satchel in Sylvia's spot." She lifts up a big net bag with a book and some knitting and what looks like some kind of electronic device inside, and sets it back down in Sylvia's chair.

My hand has a bit of a tremor but not bad and the coffee tastes wonderful. "Does this bother you?" she asks. "All this coming and going?"

I need some time to think that over and she waits, she's quite understanding, actually, which is why we get along. "I'm used . . . to it," I say.

"That's what bothers me. We shouldn't get used to it." I shrug. "What's that supposed to mean? What's a shrug? What does that mean?" My hand is fairly steady. "It just bothers me," she says, "that everybody in this entire institution acts as though every person who ever passed through has never been here. Here today gone tomorrow, as if they never did exist, never could exist, never will exist. Like they'll act when you and me aren't here, never did exist, never can exist, never will exist."

I don't know what I can say to that. There's a line of poetry, I think. Who cares. I've given up going through hell trying to remember these things. "Too busy," I offer, which is not very poetic.

"That's the problem, isn't it, everybody is too damn busy." Which is not quite what I meant. We're too damn busy dealing with our own problems. And that's not what I mean either. I don't know what I meant. More and more of my life is missing. More and more gaps. More and more things I want to say and can't.

"I'm happy to see you're better," she says, taking more soup. "These things come on, don't they. Just when we're working our butts off dealing with the last problem, here comes another one. I didn't sign up for this old age nonsense. I'm really not suited to it."

"It seems."

"You said that awful quick. It's not polite to agree with something like that, you know. You should know that." She's been served her soup already and I'm waiting for mine. "Never agree, when a woman says she's old." She spoons her soup. "I've been given to understand, you know, you've got the hots for yours truly," spooning her soup, looking at her soup, "not that I believe it, of course, I mean you know how these things get started, someone who hasn't got anything better to do tells someone else and they tell someone else and the next thing you know, it's gospel. Which makes it awkward, since your wife has asked me, as a special favor, to keep my eye on Preston, she calls you Preston, not my husband, not my sweetheart. Make sure you've got everything you need. It's a terrible responsibility."

Some women and a man are sitting at the table in front of me playing cards. Loud music is scrawling, screeching, making noises indescribable. There are tables all around me with people playing cards talking loudly. Gladys is over on the other side of the room but you can hear her above everybody else. Some people resent her, but she's quite popular. The big fish tank is bubbling, I can't hear it above the noise, but I can see the bubbles coming up. There's a draft from the glass doors. Someone is moving around inside the room next door. There is a hole in the wall and a sort of counter and I can make out various items on a shelf in that next door room and the person inside will come to the counter from time to time and pass through drinks or some other item. All the tables are full and I'm watching. I don't like playing cards. There is a big fireplace over on the side opposite the room with the hole in the wall and flames are coming up from the enclosure at the bottom, behind glass. A big sign on a long roll of paper is hung across the bricks some distance up the fireplace. Cords are attached to both ends of the roll and someone has written, I can piece it out, three words, "Bobby Burns Day," written on the roll and some kind of criss cross pattern in greens and reds and oranges and yellows. An old bent lady in a wheelchair is sleeping in front of the enclosure with the flames. I'm inclined to suggest to someone that they should turn her around so she'll get roasted evenly on both sides.

That is not a nice thought. I need to think nice thoughts. This is my home. I'm worried about the CD cabinet, but I've added more tape and I don't think there's any danger. My little Asian lady is quite popular, she goes between the tables and peeks at the cards people are holding and some of the players hold the cards up so she can see what they've got and she makes approving remarks and then they scold her for giving away their holdings. And then someone else holds up their cards so she can see what they've got. And some hold their cards so close to their bodies no one can see, not even them. And others can't be bothered and lay their cards out in rows so everyone can see. A few argue about what someone is writing down.

I don't know anyone here. Some seem familiar, but I don't know them. I know Gladys, but she is on the other side of the room, making herself noticed.

"Hello dear," a soft voice in my ear and I turn and Beverley kisses me and I look around for a chair. The Asian lady calls over to her and brings a chair and they hug. My wife was always very popular, I've always counted on her to smooth the path, I tended to be unfriendly with people, but my wife more than makes up for it.

She touches my head. "He had a fall in the bathroom," says the Asian lady.

"What have you been doing to yourself?" Beverley asks me.

"He said his legs gave out," the Asian lady announces. Everyone talks for me, they don't give me a chance to answer.

"Let me see," says Beverley and I bend my head down and I can feel her peeling back the bandage a little and I guess looking at the scab and then laying the bandage back in place again. "Just skinned a bit," she says.

"He keeps us occupied," says the lady and goes off, saying goodbye to everyone and a number call out goodbye.

"Name," I say, but my voice is weak, sometimes it gives out on me, other times it's strong. Beverley leans close to my mouth. The people are shouting, and laughing and it is noisy in here. "Name," I repeat.

"Name?" she asks.

"There."

"Oh. Mei Li, you mean. Mei Li. It's not a very familiar name is it? Are you enjoying yourself?" I shake my head. I point to the roll of paper above the fireplace.

"Bobby Burns," she says. "A Scottish poet."

I point towards the hall and the elevator thing.

"You want to go?" she says. "You never did like card games."

"Hi Beverley," Gladys shouts as my wife wheels me by. Beverley smiles and says hello, but I want her to myself and I wonder about the CD cabinet, I closed the door, but I can't be sure, sometimes I will close the door and I haven't and I can't lock the door to my room, they won't let me, anyone can come in any time they want.

"I really don't think there are many Scottish people here," says Beverley as she pushes the little silver button and the door rolls open and she rolls me inside the little room. "I suppose it's as good an excuse as any for a party. I remember how you used to recite Bobby Burns, with the accent and the cadence and everything, it has a lovely sound if it's done properly and you always did it properly. I used to try, but I never could. I depended on my spouse. It always astonished me, how many poems and stories you knew from memory, and how many accents you could mimic. You are still a very smart man. And you're mine."

I don't know what I already read in this book and what I didn't. I can't read my notes, they make no sense when I do. I open the book, read things that make no sense, open another page, they make no sense either. The words don't connect. Just words. Just words. The cat is sitting with its back to the window staring at me. "What the hell are you looking at?" It doesn't answer. I shouldn't swear. It probably objects to my swearing. For which I can't blame it. It's hard to read this thing, the type is too small.

On the cover are two men with long thick robes. Only their faces show. Both wear a circle of leaves. One figure stares down like a stone carving. The other wears long ear lugs. His face is thin, he is starved looking. At their feet is a grave lined with thick stone. Out of the grave rises a man naked except for thin shrouds around his groin. Half of him is out. He cannot escape. A glow like white hot steel rises from the grave. A stone slab all set to be clamped down on the mouth of the grave leans against the cliff face behind the man. The man's head rests back on the stone slab, he looks up at the other figures. All the man's ribs are outlined on his chest and groin. The muscles in his arms are tensed up. His diaphragm is sucked in. He is in terrible pain.

"I've got something to show you." Gladys, standing in her walker in the little hall with the open door of my room behind her. She's opened the door and come in. I closed it. Everybody comes in here like it's a railroad station. "What else have you got to do?" she asks.

She turns the walker and sits on the chair built into it, moving back and forth on the roller wheels, impatient, waiting for my reply. "Reading," I say.

"You can come back. The book will be here, right where you left it. If you don't come now, you won't see what I've got to show you. It won't be there later. Your book will. What are you waiting for? It's worth it. Trust me."

She waits for me to answer. I don't know what she wants. "Don't feel . . . ."

"I don't feel like sitting here talking to you either, but I am. I can't wait. Get the hell out of there and get in your damn chair pardon my language." She jerks her head toward the door. "Let's go. You need to get out of here. It isn't healthy."

It's better to go than to argue with her. I lean forward, set my hands on the arms of my wheelchair, swivel myself around, plop down, back out, turn at the end of the bed, and wheel toward her. "This is something you don't see every day," she says, stands, turns and pushes her walker out the door and I follow. We turn down the hall toward windows at the far end. A couple of people in blue outfits, slacks and tops, are standing at the windows with their backs toward us and move aside when we get close.

"They've been there five minutes," says the blue outfitted woman.

The other one is a man I haven't seen before. They step behind us when we pull up to the windows.

"Right there," the woman says, leaning and pointing. "They're grey with maybe a suggestion of red, right there, by that group of trees. You can see a white tree trunk down there, half way down the hill, there's some bushes to the right and some other trees around it. They've been eating the tops of the bushes. Can you see them?"

"Deer," says Gladys. "Right there. I'm looking right at them. Down the hill, by that birch tree, near those bushes, right there." She's pointing and flicks her finger at whatever it is she wants me to see.

All I can see are trees. Some houses up on a bank.

"Look for white, if they start to waggle their tails," says the woman, letting her long dark hair drop on my shoulder and talking in my ear.

"Which means some jerk is down there scaring them," says Gladys. "There's five of them, women, slim and young, ready for mating season. Beautiful animals. Really beautiful. Worth seeing. Well worth seeing. Better than some damn book."

"This is the first time we've seen them this year," says the woman.

"Didn't I tell you it was worth seeing," says Gladys. "Get away from here you damn cat," which is rubbing its body along the side of her leg. The woman behind me reaches down and picks it up.

"Can you see them?" Gladys demands. I'm leaning forward, trying to figure out what it is she wants me to see, there are trees, bushes, some weeds, water down at the end of the hill, houses up on a bank far to one side.

Gladys looks up behind her toward the woman who picked up the cat. "He doesn't react any more," cocking her head toward me, "You have to wait ten minutes before he answers a simple question, like talking to a post."

My wheelchair is backing up and turning around.

"Look at that," says Gladys behind me, "Would you look at that! I've never seen anything like that before," and my chair is rolling down the hall back toward my room and the woman who is pushing me is leaning her long hair over my shoulder and saying in my ear, very quietly, "Don't pay any attention to Gladys, she talks that way, it doesn't mean anything, she has a good heart and a loud mouth."

I'm glad I'm getting back to my room, the door is wide open and there's people in the hall walking by there all the time.

"Look at that!" says Gladys, loud, her voice carries all down the hall. "Just look at that!"

I am not a post.

The woman turns me in my room, asks me if she can get me anything, I ask if she has some tea and she goes off to get it.

The book is on the bed. I open it and look at the words. Words all over the page. Read, dammit. Concentrate. Try to read out loud. Follow the words with my finger. Each one. Throw all my mind into it. Concentrate. Concentrate. Concentrate on each word.

"I   wept   not   I   was   turned   to   stone."

I wheel to the table that is rammed up against the cabinet, open the drawer, put the book inside and shut the drawer.

I am

I am not hungry. People are going down the hall. A woman comes in and says, "Lunch, Preston," and goes off before I can answer. Nobody waits for me to answer. I don't move as fast as I used to, that's just the way it is. There is no law that says I have to travel at the speed of light. I need to get clean. I can't eat unless I'm clean.

I'm tired. I think I slept in this chair. The bed is clean and neat and the sheets are straight. No wrinkles. I hate wrinkles. I can't sleep in a bed with wrinkles. There are no wrinkles.

It's hard getting from this chair to that thing with wheels. Someone parked it too far away. My legs are useless sticks. It would be funny if it weren't so damn maddening. So here I am leaning between one thing and the other. Slowly toppling forward. With my head on the wheeled thing and my feet sliding underneath the chair I was just in.

"Let's get you up here," says a voice and the wheeled chair is pushed closer to the other chair, "push up with your feet. He's stuck," stronger arms lift me, "thanks Jim," a man's voice tells me there we are, I'm okay, I'm turned around, "There we are," says the big man, grinning down at me.

"Are you okay, Preston?" says a woman's voice, she leans over me, darker face, young face, beautiful face. She smoothes down my hair, "We're okay now," she says to the big man who leaves, sort of disappears from the horizon. "You must have had a weak spell," she says.

It's confusing, I don't know exactly what's happened, I'm sitting in the wheeled chair and the lady is putting soft things at my back and asking me if I can shift up and she puts soft things underneath me, "Stupid," I say, I don't mean she is stupid, I mean I am stupid, I hope she doesn't think I think she is stupid, she got me out of here, I don't want to alienate anyone who helps me like this, she is a tiny person, everything is miniature about this beautiful little woman, I hope she doesn't go away, everyone goes away, I hope she doesn't think I think she is stupid.

"We'll get you all put together," she says. "Have you washed?" I shake my head. It's better than trying to talk, I get in trouble when I talk. The wheeled chair turns and I'm moving toward the opening, turning into a smaller room, white things. "I see your wife brought some flowers. Daffodils. They look pretty, don't you think? They tell us spring is coming." She talks loudly as if I was deaf. Everyone talks loudly, like they're talking to a child. I am not a child. "You haven't been reading lately," she says, the cloth is warm and feels good, "we'll do your hands," she announces and the warm cloth is on my hands, "and your hair, we have to get you fixed up." Her hands are soft and tiny.

"Nice," I say. "Nice."

"Well thank you, Preston, that is really nice of you to say that," speaking with her voice rising, like she's talking to a child. Everybody talks simple, like I'm simple. "So now we've got you all fixed up here, we're all set to go," and I'm wheeled out and down a long corridor thing to a room with tables and a table where a loud woman says, "Well if it isn't Astor's Pet Horse!"

"No, Gladys," says the kind lady who has brought me down, "this is Preston. Maybe you would be good enough to introduce him to his new table companions."

"Absolutely Mei Li," the loud mouth says, "whatever you say, your wish is my command."

"I do," says the lady, pretty sharply, and leaves me with the loud mouth.

"So you decided to join us after all," says loud mouth. "This is Fred, the euchre champion." There is a man on the side, he nods. He is huge, with a vast beard and a big grin, bigger even than loud mouth, who is pretty big. "And Phil. Phil doesn't say much, he's keeping his powder dry," she says. "He and you should get along just fine." The man right in front of me, on the other side of the table, is very thin and wears a peaked hat that says something, U. S.

251

Something. I am not hungry. "Coffee," says loud mouth, and pours in a cup she puts in front of me. "I didn't mean anything about the pet horse comment, Preston, you know me, I am harmless, that's what everybody says. Preston and me are old friends," she says. "Old friends."

The two big people talk and talk. Someone puts some food on a plate in front of me. I'm not hungry. These loud mouths have ruined my appetite. I put the plate on my lap and back up and turn and wheel to the door and turn along the direction I think I remember I've gone, it seems kind of familiar, a woman in a green suit is in front of me. "You can't take food from the dining room," she says.

"Who is going to stop me!" I snap and accelerate and she has to step aside to avoid being run over. If you let people know who's in charge, they get out of the way.

"I am really disappointed, Preston." The woman is standing in front of me. I'm eating my food and she came in so quietly I didn't know she was here until she talked and I looked up and there she was. She is young. She has long black hair resting on her shoulders. She looks very sad. "We don't let people eat in their rooms. It attracts bugs. Ants. Awful bugs. Bed bugs. You don't want bugs in your bed, do you?"

I shake my head. She is right about that.

"I thought I had dressed you up so you looked nice, so you could meet your new table mates and make a good impression."

I nod.

"You say that and you're here. You weren't very nice to the kitchen staff. You almost ran over one of our nurse's aides. That's not like you, Preston. You're not like that. I know you."

I nod. She holds out her hands and I give her the plate.

"If you want this you can come to the dining room. Do you want it?"

I shake my head. She takes the thing from around my neck.

"You won't need this either. Will you promise me something?"

I nod.

"Promise you won't do this again. It makes me very sad."

I nod.

She pats my cheek and takes my food away. I'm still hungry.

Nobody talks. I'm glad. It's too hard listening and understanding what someone says and then figuring out what I should answer. My thoughts work slowly, and I have to work at it. But nobody talks. Everybody eats. Gladys hasn't said a word all mealtime. Gladys. She looks at me, I can sense her looking at me from time to time and I refuse to look back. I caught her one time peeking, she seemed embarrassed and wishing I would say something. Let her wish. She poured my coffee. I looked over and nodded, but that's all I did. She nodded back.

"I wish you two would talk to each other," says the big man with the beard on the other side of me, "It's spoiling my digestion." Gladys makes an indefinite noise and I don't look at either of them and when the thin man opposite me looks up and our eyes meet for a bit, we both look down again and mind our business.

I have to concentrate anyway. I'm just as glad not to have to talk, it's the best thing that could have happened. I have to think, how do I get these round things to my mouth. They roll around on the fork and I have to balance them carefully and they roll off, some of them, and most fall back on the plate. A few just disappear. And turn the fork as I open my mouth and place them on my tongue and remove the fork don't put the fork in too far and take the fork out so I'm not chewing fork and concentrate so when I swallow the chewed food goes down the right way and I don't choke. I forget to chew sometimes and the food chokes me when I try to swallow. If I don't think what I'm doing and concentrate on what I'm doing, water can choke me. I'll drink when I'm thinking of something else and I choke and it's embarrassing and very unpleasant.

"I didn't mean anything," says Gladys. "Open mouth. Insert foot."

"Happens all the time," says the big guy. "Lots of trouble. I've been there."

I have to cut the potato in small chunks and stab each chunk and raise it to my mouth and place it on my tongue and pull out the fork and then chew really well before I swallow.

"More coffee?" Gladys asks. I shake my head. "We're old friends," she says.

"Never lose old friends," the big guy says, he talks louder than Gladys. Sometimes I can't talk at all. "Old friends are the best friends."

"Amen," says Gladys.

"How long?" says the thin guy.

"Forever," says Gladys.

"What's your experience?" the big guys asks me. I'm chewing and I can't be interrupted or I'll choke and spew things everywhere. I raise my hand and chew and nobody says anything and it gives me a chance to think.

"Yes," I say, and stab another piece of potato.

"We're old friends,' says Gladys.

What happens when I can't do anything or say anything or think anything and I'm all alone inside my head? Sometimes people can't hear me and they ask me to repeat what I've just said and I can't remember.

"His wife is a wonderful person," says Gladys. "We're good friends."

"Never lose friends," says the big guy.

"Thanks," I say, nodding at the coffee. She gives me a huge smile.

A train? There's a train? The woman who comes in here is going by toward the noise. And it stops. I used to go down to the tracks and watch trains. How did I remember that? When I was a kid, after we moved. There were three railroads. I used to hear them at night. It was hot and I'd lie with the windows open and hear the trains. Lonely sound. The noise would go on and on. Long freight trains. They always sounded louder at night.

Gladys coming down the hall, duck back in and close the door. We're friends, but, too much friendship isn't good. I feel like a kid. I guess because I'm acting like a kid. I should open the door and go out and say hello.

Next time.

I used to watch when they had new engines and long freights and passenger trains. We never had sleek trains like they used to . . . . Who?

It used to give me a strange feeling, to hear trains at night.

Again? It's really close, next door practically, loud squealing, like freight cars going around a curve.

Stopped again.

I should get out of my room anyway. I'm beginning to hear things. Maybe, if Gladys is still there.

"Is she gone?"

The big man, the guy at my table, standing in his door bending forward looking out in the hall, in one direction, and the other.

"Is that woman gone? Mei Li?" I roll out in the hall and turn toward him, I'll go down to the end and see if there is anything and come back, just to get out and see what the world is up to. "She came in and gave me hell for my TV," he says. "I guess I had the sound up. Come on in, my friend, I want to show you something," and he hobbles out with his cane, hooks it on the arm of my chair, turns me and pulls me in his room. "My son set this rig up," he explains.

There is a long train going around a curve, on his TV. A big TV.

"I'm a train nut," he says, "and my son set me up so I can pull videos straight off the Internet and throw them on the screen. Don't ask me how he did it, all I know is, it works." He parks me in front of the big screen and picks up some earplugs. "Listen to this," and he claps the earplugs around my head.

There is huge squealing, big freight cars going around a curve and there they are on the screen and some louder thrumming noise and a big orange and yellow engine going backwards coming around the corner at the back of the freight cars and passing. This is exactly what I used to hear, god I can remember, I'd sit below a big curve at a sort of embankment and the trains would come around the corner and the wheels would squeal just like that. And now there is a long line of track going off in the distance and some mountains beyond and a frame above the track with lights, I remember this kind of thing, I have no idea what it's called and a train comes around a curve down beyond the frame and straightens and rushes toward me underneath the frame blowing a loud horn that changes pitch and gets lower as it races by with several engines behind it, some pointed forward, some going backward and a long long long line of black round cars with knobs on top. This is the sound I used to hear at night. I'd lie there trying to imagine how long the train was and sometimes I'd fall asleep before the noise ended.

"Wonderful," I say.

"A man after my own heart," he says and shakes my hand. "Even the cat likes it," he adds.

It's sitting on his windowsill.

"It showed up the first day I came here," he says. "It's been here ever since, pretty well every day. It has some sort of routine, like all cats. It shows up about two and hops on my chair and grooms itself and jumps up on my windowsill and lies in the sun for maybe half an hour and then gets up and yawns and stretches its legs and grooms itself some more and then it hops down and goes off wherever it goes. I like it, it's good company. We don't get much company here. What do you want to see next?"

I shrug.

"She's right. You don't say a lot. She was really upset when you grabbed your food and took off like that. I think she kind of likes you. This video was taken in a place called Hershey, Nebraska. It turns out that Hershey, Nebraska, has nothing to do with chocolate. What it was, was the home of one of the few Japanese Americans who flew during the Second World War for the USA. Pretty remarkable, when you consider this was just after Pearl Harbor. Reminds me of my days on the prairies. They run these coal trains full out, right through this little town, village really. The only thing you can hear, when the trains aren't going by, are pickup trucks whanging across the tracks and the sound of some kind of heavy machinery in the grain elevators you can see just down the way beside the track. The remarkable thing, though, is how many trains go through, some of them racing each other. And long things, and just when one has gone by you can see the headlights of another, way down the tracks in the distance."

After a while the noise bothers me, and the memories begin to fade and I thank him when I can get the words out or word out, I have to get going.

"Heavy date?" he asks.

I want to answer but he turns back to his TV and I don't know what I'd say anyway, I should have said I am happily married, I don't need dates. The cat stretches out on his windowsill and doesn't look like it's going to go anywhere.

I need money. There are papers in the drawer underneath the lamp and a book hidden among them, and I took them all out and searched them all and there was no money. The drawers in the bureau on the other side of the room, near the mirror, had clothes and stamps and envelopes and blank paper and I searched every one and got out all the clothes and junk and there is no money. All the pockets of the shirts and pants have kleenex and pencils and elastics and everything but money. I did find some coins, a few, not very many, not enough to do anything, with the prices the way they are today. The cat is rattling among the papers on the floor. It hasn't been here for months. I don't know where it goes. I think this is the same cat. It's enjoying itself and I'll let it alone. I need the company. The loud mouthed woman goes by my door and doesn't look in or say hello. They all ignore me.

"What the hell is going on here?" says a big guy with a beard and a cane. He's standing at the door. "You've stolen my cat," he says and stays where he is. I shake my head. "I'm joking., for godsake," he goes on, "You have no sense of humor."

I don't know why he's here.

"What are you up to?" he asks. I don't want him in here stealing my clothes and I pick them up and stuff them in the drawers. "Are you going on this trip?" he asks. I keep stuffing clothes in my bureau. "I won't interrupt you," he says and when I look again he's gone. I had money. Lots of it. It was sitting in one of these drawers and it's gone. "Some sort of bee in his bonnet," I hear him saying in the hall. I'll have to borrow some money. Not a lot. Just enough. Two dollars. One of those orange bills.

"Good heavens, Preston." She comes in and picks up the cat and takes it to the door and drops it in the hall, and comes back inside. "What are you doing?" I don't answer and stuff the rest of the clothes in the bottom drawer and try to shove it shut, but it won't go. "You'll never find anything," she says. "Can we pick up these papers? Somebody will trip and hurt themselves. Probably me. Your closet! What have you done to your closet?"

"Money," I say.

"There's money at the front desk," she says. "Your wife has set up an account for you, Preston. All you have to do is go down and ask. How much do you want?" She starts picking up paper and looks around with her hands full. "I have no idea where to put this," she says. She has black hair in a ball on top of her head, hair straggles out in strands. It makes her face look thin and sharp. Her skin is a fine smooth lovely tone. "I just don't know what I'll do with you," she says, still looking around, frustrated I think, but she talks quite nicely. I like this woman, I hope she comes back. Nobody comes back. They stand at the door and don't come in and nobody comes back. She puts the papers on the bed. "I'll deal with these later," she decides. "Why don't you sit down and I'll take your temperature? They're leaving in an hour, we have to get you ready."

"Who?"

"We're running a trip to see the blossoms, up along the escarpment. I understand we'll be stopping for ice cream afterwards. You need to get out, Preston, you've been in here too long, all winter. It's time to get out. Besides that, your wife is coming. What do you want to wear?" I shrug. "Why don't we have a look and see what we've got," she says, "if I can find anything in here," and she smiles, very gentle and understanding. I like this woman. She is short and delicate, a lovely little package, her top knot makes her face look thin and sharp. She pulls the wheeled chair over and I sit down and she clips something on my finger and sorts through the clothes I've stuffed in the drawers. "Beverley will be here and we'll have to get you looking nice. She asked if I'd choose something good, I don't think she's feeling as well as she has been. To be honest, Preston, if it wasn't for Beverley I don't think the people here would be quite so understanding, even though we're paid to be. I'll get you downstairs and then I'll try to straighten things up here a bit. Is that all right?" I nod.

The big bearded man is standing at the door. "Are we ready?"

"Go ahead. We'll meet you downstairs," she says.

"I don't know why you put up with this character," he says. "As far as I can see he's more trouble than he's worth. You're damn lucky to have Mei Li, old fella. Most people wouldn't put up with you, trust me." There's something wrong with his one eye. He's gone. They all go. I should have asked to borrow some money. I never think of these things til it's too damn late. He'll have some money, I'm sure he won't mind lending me some, just for emergencies, just in case I need it. I'll give it back right away. I'm good for it. I've always been good for it.

She's combed my hair, helped me wash and clean my teeth and get ready, it's always good to have assistance with this kind of thing, it makes me feel aristocratic, that I have my staff along to help me out with these things, people I can depend on. She rolls me to the door and operates the pad with the buttons, she does it so quickly

I can't follow. The loud mouthed woman gets on behind us in her vehicle and we have to jam in, she makes jokes and talks with the woman who is taking care of me, they seem to know each other and she takes over as if I'm not here and the only people in this room are her and the woman pushing me, she nods in my direction from time to time, the loud mouth and the woman behind me says shush, we have to be respectful, as if I am a cadaver they are laying out in a box for viewing, and the door opens and I am rolled out but the loud mouth is left to take care of herself and I can hear her behind me talking loudly to everyone in the hall as if she was a queen greeting her subjects and there is Beverley, sitting in a chair by the window and she makes to struggle up and the woman behind me tells her to stay where she is, she'll park Preston beside her and we can talk to our heart's content.

"It does make my heart content," says Beverley and I'm parked and the woman who brought me is hustling off to some other chore, wiggling her fingers goodbye, I like that gesture, it suits her perfectly, she is a miniature.

"So this is the little lady our Preston has been talking about," says the big man with the beard who has come over and is standing in front of us. He bends down and takes Beverley's hand and kisses it.

"I thank you sir," says Beverley.

"Quality has its due," he says, and talks to my wife as if I'm not here and finally goes off to a big group standing by the fish tank in a rough sort of circle centered on the loud mouth with the walker.

"Alone at last," says Beverley, and takes my hand. Her hand is tiny, and thin like paper, and her skin looks like paper, she has lost weight and her voice is not strong the way it used to be. I am worried about her. "How have you been?" she asks.

"I haven't seen you," I can talk to her more easily than anyone else.

"I have been over," she says. "Not as much as I'd like to. We're getting older, you and I." Not you, I think. Maybe me. Not you. There's laughter from the group beside the fish tank, they are all loud mouths. Sometimes I don't feel like this place is home, they are nice, sometimes, but sometimes I just feel alone. "The weather has been wonderful," Beverley says, "so mild, I'm glad we're getting you out. I haven't been able to do that as much as I'd like to, Preston, and Richard is so busy, and besides that you don't seem to be very enthusiastic about the trips the home offers. The blossoms are supposed to be very beautiful this year in particular, better than average they say."

"I need money."

"I have some," she says. "I can give you some if you'd like."

"Yes. Please." My Beverley takes care of me, I can always count on Beverley. She gets a purse she's been carrying, it seems, from the space between her chair and mine and gets out some bills. "Do you have your wallet?"

I search my pockets and bring out the contents. A handkerchief, some papers and a pencil, and some kind of small black circular thing. "Your magnifying glass!" she says, so softly and so beautifully, I love the sound of her voice the way it comes out so gentle and caring. "I haven't seen your magnifying glass for years. You used to carry it everywhere." She takes it from me and turns out a glass thing that is hidden inside the black circle. "You had this huge dictionary with tiny printing, with every word the English language ever created, I think. It had tiny print and you used to use this magnifying glass to read all the tiny entries, beside the major words. You'd tell me the origin of any word I ever wanted to know about, way back to Anglo-Saxon times and earlier and you'd tell me how every word originated and how it had changed down the years. Richard would groan, every time you got that book out, but I actually found it quite fascinating. I miss that, all your lessons." She gives me such a glow.

"All right," the big guy says, "enough of this. The bus is here, you two. Madame," he holds out his arm in a crook and Beverley struggles up and takes his arm and I'm left to wheel myself behind, though she looks back and smiles to make sure I am following along. He is not stealing my wife.

"I'm right behind you," says the loud mouthed woman, right behind me. "No hanky panky," she says. The people are talking, laughing, talking in high voices. "Wonderful," says loud mouth behind me as we go out the door, "wonderful, I love Spring, and Sumer is icumen in, lhude sing cuccu or something. What was that you said one time, Preston, it's Anglo Saxon, isn't it, or something like that?"

"Middle English," says Beverley, detaching herself from the big guy and coming back to stand beside me and claim me for herself.

"Would you look at that," says Beverley. Trees with white spots and green flat on the ground a pole going up behind them and a green something moving between the trees. "Are they spraying or something, do you think?" she says. "The blossoms are beautiful, I am so glad I came. I haven't been out myself, so very much." She pats my hand. "We both need to get out and see what's going on in the world." I nod. It's cold in here. Loud mouth has opened a window and is yattering on to whoever is unlucky enough to sit beside her and I can't hear Beverley, her voice is softer than it used to be and she sounds hoarse, I think, but she is still my Beverley, the only person I can count on. She's put a blanket on my knees and I take it up and wrap it around my shoulders and she asks if the window can be closed and I feel tired.

"You really missed some beautiful sights," Beverley says to me. "You mustn't have slept very well last night." The people in the lineup behind us are talking and laughing and I can hear the big bearded guy, the one with the cane, he's even louder than loud mouth, "You know what they say," he shouts, "man is the only animal that can be bald and sixty years old with a beer belly and still think he's sexy," they laugh back there. Mostly men, "With a cane," someone else says, "With a cane," the big man says and they laugh again, "You can't hear yourself think," says loud mouth who must have moved up because she's right behind us. "Hi Beverley," says a woman beside us, short and sweet with a soft voice.

"Mei Li," Beverley says and they embrace.

"You look really good," the woman says.

"One day at a time," says Beverley.

"We all do," says loud mouth but they ignore her.

"What kind of ice cream can we get you?" Beverley asks.

"I couldn't, Bev, I'm trying to lose weight."

"If you lost any more you'd disappear," says loud mouth.

"You can have that room," the woman tells my wife. People ahead of us move and I turn my wheel and Beverley holds back talking to the woman and loud mouth is right behind me.

"What was that all about?" loud mouth asks, "What were they talking about?" I don't know but I wouldn't tell her if I did. There is a big sign right above where the people in green wedge hats are moving back and forth and reaching down and digging at something and coming up with colored balls on slight brown crumbly things pointing down. "Sir?" says a young woman when the man and woman and children in front of me move away.

"Vanilla, Rocky Road, Banana, two scoops," says Beverley who has come up behind me and slipped by loud mouth.

"You are bad," says the little woman who has been talking to her.

"It's famous ice cream,' says Beverley. "People drive for miles."

"We all want treats," says loud mouth and everyone ignores her.

"You know what they say," says the big man who is still some places back behind us and there's a confused babble of noise and voices and everybody laughs.

"I told them it was our fiftieth wedding anniversary. I think I'm allowed a little white lie, don't you think?" says Beverley. This room is not familiar and I'm worried about my CDs. "It's only one night," she says. "We need some privacy. You always wanted privacy. You can go back to your room tomorrow. One night won't hurt, will it?" There are two windows and a corner, with windows on each part of the corner. There's trees out the window. Beverley is in the bathroom talking to me, her voice is louder. "I had them bring your sleeping togs," she says, and comes out wearing a long gown that I can partly see through, her body is like a ghost inside, moving. "I thought for once you wouldn't mind a regular bed, instead of the things they make you use here. And I was hoping you wouldn't mind company."

She gets in beside me.

"They call this the honeymoon suite," she says. I have missed her so much. Nobody comes to see me any more and I don't like anybody in this place any more and the only one I want is Beverley.

She takes my hand and grasps it and I can't move it. "I'm still recovering, Preston." her voice is very soft and sweet. "I'll need months to recover, I'm afraid. I wish it wasn't that way but I'm afraid it is. You'll hurt me. I know you wouldn't want to hurt me, would you?" I shake my head. "I've had a serious operation but things are better. I can't do what you want to do, not tonight. Not for some months, I'm afraid. But I wanted you with me, I really did, I miss you so much. I so wish we could, my darling, I truly do, but we can't. But I'm glad there are some things that you haven't forgotten." She smiles. "It makes me feel better. To know you want to."

I put my arms around her and she sort of hums, "Sumer is icomen in."

"Lhude sing cuccu," I reply.

She starts shaking in my arms and laughs and laughs and I join her.

The cat walks by and goes next door. Everybody walks by and goes next door. He is a loud man. There is a lot of movement in the hall. I recognize the woman who comes in, a small lovely little woman. She smiles. "Aren't you ready?" she asks. I don't know what she is talking about. People here make mysterious remarks. "Your son is coming. It's Father's Day. You need to get ready for Father's Day." She talks down to me and I resent it. I'm just as good as she is.

She stares at me, sitting in my chair. It's rude to stare. "It looks like you've worn your best pants to breakfast," she says. "Maybe there is something else in here." She goes over to my closet, rummaging through my clothes. I'd say something but she is the only one I like here. Everybody else gives orders. "I need to find something to match," she says. "Will this do?" She turns and holds up some pants. I don't like them. "Let's try something else," she says, "but I'll put these on the bed, just in case."

"Is his majesty ready yet?" says loud mouth at the door.

The woman rummaging in my closet steps toward the hallway so she can see who it is. "Hi Gladys," she says. "You look really good this afternoon."

"In other words it's none of my damn business," says loud mouth and backs out and walks herself off.

"We do need to get going here," says my little woman softly, which makes such a contrast to loud mouth, she takes out two more sets of pants. "It's kind of a question of what's the best of a . . . ." she doesn't finish her statement. "It's probably not a good idea to do your own alterations," she says, lifting up a set of pants that someone has ruined by sewing it up around the crotch and the waist and getting the material all twisted. "I don't think we can use this, do you?" I shake my head. "I have a suggestion, if you don't mind." I nod. "I'd suggest that the next time you need some alterations you ask someone here to do it. We have good people. If they can't do it, we'll send them out to have them done professionally. Will you do that next time?" She's looking at me with her soft brown eyes. I nod.

She sets the pants on the bed and looks over the selection she has brought out. "It's the beige or the brown," she says. "What do you think?" She lifts up two. "Make your choice. It's your choice." She gives me a lovely smile and I point to the one that has a rougher sort of material. "The brown it is," she says and puts it back down on the bed and takes the others back to the closet and hangs them up.

"So now we'll have to match it up," she announces and goes to the tall thing near the—shiny thing—mirror and pulls out a— drawer. "Oh my heavens," she says, quietly, "what have you done to your shirts?"

There's people in the hall, a woman who says "Hello, Preston" when we pass a room, a big TV inside and hundreds of flowers in a jug, a long jug that gives off flashes. The woman who dressed me is pushing, we turn the bend, come out by a desk. "Mei Li," says a tall lady holding a black thing. "You know who," she adds, lifting the thing.

"I'm busy," the lovely woman behind me says.

"He asked for you."

"I don't have the time right now. Say I'm busy."

"I told him you were here."

"As if I have the time," she says sounding disgusted. She rolls me around the end of the counter, tells me she'll be right back, don't go away, and leaves but I can hear her at the counter, "I was just taking him down."

The big man with the beard comes along with his cane. His legs are bare, his arms are bare, his white shirt thing is wet. "It is hot out there!" he says. "I went out there for my regular walk and had to turn around half way. It must be, I don't know, a hundred something out there. I am ready for something liquid." A black cat pads by up close to the wall. "What are you up to, Preston," he asks, "have they abandoned you?" His face is wet and red and he's panting.

"We do the best we can," the woman who was taking me down is raising her voice and drops it back, I can't hear any more.

"Problems," says the big man, looking towards the counter and back at me, "always problems." He taps my arm lightly with his cane. "You heard about Phil? Our table partner. Some sort of tests. Always tests. He'll be back in a couple of days. Always tests. I thought we'd graduated." He smiles. "You don't say much, do you?"

"Yes, we will do that," says the woman.

"A bunch of people are meeting in my room," he says. "We're going down below later. I thought you'd be there." I shrug. "That's okay, I'll survive. Is Beverley coming?"

"I will," says the woman," but I can't promise anything."

Loud mouth wheels by with her walker. "Your father coming, Gladys?" the big man says. She doesn't answer and keeps going. "She thinks Father's Day is for her," he says. "She thinks everything is for her."

The loud mouth woman stops and turns when she reaches the elevator, punches the pad and glares back at us.

"Got to get going," says the big man, staring back at her. "My son and my very beautiful daughter-in-law will not be honoring us with their presence today, despite the fact that I am the only damn father they have got." Loud mouth wheels out of sight. "The only damn parent they've got, in fact, but you know how young people are today, busy, busy, busy, no time for the old folks. Sorry you couldn't drop by, would've made it worth your while." He leaves me and passes by the woman who was pushing me down the hall. She says hello, but doesn't stop. He shrugs and keeps going.

"Your son will be coming a little late," she says and gets behind me and pushes me down the hall pretty quick. "You're lucky you have people who care about you, Preston. Most people don't. I get more calls about Preston O'Shaughnessy in any one day than I do for everyone else for the rest of the year. So it seems, anyway. Your son keeps me on my toes. A replacement for actually coming here and seeing his father for a change." Her voice is tense. She punches the buttons on the pad, hard, like she wants to punch them through the wall. She turns to me while we wait. "Not that I need any encouragement. You really are a lovely man, despite all your faults. It's just that some people are not willing to give it a rest." The door opens and she rolls me inside.

Tables with people, the big guy with noisy friends at one, the loud mouth woman, kind of sour and unfriendly, at another, and me at another with some people who don't talk and don't react. A woman comes around with tiny sandwiches and I take one to be polite. A man comes around with a bottle and glasses, puts a glass in front of me, and pours. "I think they've had enough over there," he says. The noisy table laughs again. Someone important, a woman, is up front above the heads of all the people, talking about Father's Day. She asks everyone to applaud for all the fathers. People do that and a big man appears behind me, bends over me and whispers, "Don't applaud, you're a father." He squeezes my shoulder. "Sorry I'm late."

He goes off somewhere and I try to move my chair to make a space because I believe he wants to sit down beside me. I'm right. He comes back carrying a chair, puts it down, moves me over more than I've been able to do, and once he's made a space, slides his chair beside me and sits. And sets a pot of flowers on the table. "It's the first day of summer, you need something to brighten up your room. Sorry I'm late. Didn't you get some cookies? The cookies are wonderful." Before I can answer he's up and off somewhere and comes back with a plate and some thin cookies. "There's just a suggestion of lemon," he says. "I'm assured they're non-fattening." He picks one up and crunches it in his mouth and hands a cookie to me. "Where did you get the wine? Did they bring around wine? Did I miss the wine?" He gets up again and goes off somewhere.

I lift the cookie, hold it in my open mouth, make sure my tongue is out of the way and bite off a chunk. And chew and concentrate.

"The traffic was terrible," he says, he's got a glass with red something in it. "You are so lucky you're in here all protected. The world out there is crazy, take my word for it. Just crazy. And how's my old dad?" He stops. He expects something. I stop chewing and stare at him. He tilts his head.

The piano starts up and they all begin to sing, Row Row Row Your Boat, and the big guy with the cane is louder than anyone else. He's a good singer, I have to admit that. I'm concentrating on chewing.

"You wouldn't think he was such a good singer," the man beside me says. "With that beard."

I'm trying to understand what he expects me to answer.

"Did you?" he says.

"How many fathers are here?" a woman on the platform shouts. Men put up their hands and the man beside me takes mine and holds it up. I'll choke if I don't finish this cookie, it's very dry, it sticks in my throat. I want to take a drink but I can't do two things at once I'll choke. I'll take a drink later.

The piano starts again and they sing some other songs and I manage to swallow without choking. The man offers me another cookie and I shake my head and carefully take a sip from my glass. They sing Oh My Darling Clementine and I remember some lines and sing along, low and hoarse from the cookie, but I do sing, the liquid has lubricated me somewhat. The big loud guy is louder than anyone else. Finally everyone stops because we've run out of verses. But not him, he continues singing, verse after verse.

"That's amazing," says the man beside me. "I've never heard those words before. Is he making them up? What do you think? You're the expert. I never heard anyone who knew so many songs as you do. I used to listen to you all the time, I was fascinated, once I understood just how huge your repertoire was. Do you remember? Dad?"

"How I missed my Clementine," the loud guy sings, his voice rising rather ridiculously, "Till I kissed her baby sister, And forgot my Clementine."

Everyone applauds and he shouts out, "That's all folks." They applaud again.

"Hi, Richard." It's the little lady who dressed me and combed my hair really nicely. She bends and hugs the man beside me.

"He doesn't know me," the man says. "He doesn't know his own son. I knew this would happen. I knew this was coming." He is crying and the lady who dressed me rubs his back.

Breakfast is the best meal of the day. "Hello Preston," the loud mouthed woman says, when I park at the table. I nod. There is no point being rude.

"You never know," she says. "You just never know." She pours my coffee. "Yesterday he was singing and partying and entertaining everybody all day long, and he's gone just like that." She nods at the space opposite her. The chair is empty. "Just like that. We just never know."

I sip carefully. "Poor Richard," she says. She pours herself some coffee. "I know how he feels. It's hard when it happens to someone you truly love. And he does love you, Preston, there is no doubt about that, you're a lucky man. Maybe he doesn't show it, he's rough around the edges. Like you, I suspect. But he does love you." I concentrate on raising the cup to my lips and inhaling just slightly, not enough to let it down my throat to my lungs, but enough to get the coffee in my mouth. I need to learn to tip it in my mouth. It works, what I'm doing. I put the cup down. "As I was saying," she says, "Phil has some sort of appointment. We're on our lonesome once again, just like it was before."

I nod.

She drinks and puts her cup down. "My name is Gladys, Preston. I know you've got a problem. I appreciate that." She is talking quite gently, not loud. "We've been friends for a good long while and I don't want to lose you. We need all the friends we can get. My name is Gladys. I'd like you to do me a favor if you would, and try to pronounce my name. Will you do that? I'd really appreciate it." I want some more coffee. "Gla-dis. Would you say that? Please."

She's quite sincere.

"Gla," she says.

"Gla," I say, slurring a little bit. She smiles.

"Dis," she says.

"Dis."

"Gla-dis. Gla-dis."

"Gla-dis," I say. She's happy, she's smiling, she's satisfied. I pick up my cup.

"We need to keep our friends," she says. "I don't know what happened, it's probably my fault, what happened, what caused our friendship to go sour. I do have a big mouth. I don't mean it though. I care about my friends. And you are my friend, Preston. A good friend."

I nod.

"How is Beverley?" she asks.

I nod.

"Wonderful. Have your coffee."

This place

I am telling you, this place is a death trap. Don't just sit there. This place is a death trap. I asked where the fire exit was. I asked a man in the hall, it took a long time for him to understand. I went in the direction he pointed. It was a dead end. You may sit there and make faces but I tell you, this place is a death trap. If you think I don't know what I'm talking about, you try it. If there ever is a fire here, there will be mass panic. People will die. I know. I went the other way. The halls are confusing. You don't know where they go. They turn this way and this way and this way and this way and you keep going and there's another dead end.

He just sits there, staring at me.

What's the matter with you?

They don't care here. I ask for a blanket. It's cold here. Nobody comes.

They keep moving my chair. I put the chair by the window and I come back and they've moved my chair. Someone has taped all my records. I can't get in the cabinet.

You can see for yourself. Just look. Look! There's grey tape around and around and around this cabinet. I can't get in. I ask them to help me and they say they'll be back, but they have to do something else for somebody else. For another inmate. They never come back. We're prisoners here. Maybe you don't know it but we're prisoners here. They've got you in a wheelchair. Just like me. They've got you tied in. Just like me. So you won't fall, they say.

"Preston?"

It's a short woman.

"Why don't we get your trousers on so you can come down to lunch?"

"Is everything all right?" A tall man in green. At the door.

"Yes, Jim," she says. "Thanks."

He goes.

"Who?" I ask.

"Jim. That's Jim. He works here."

"Who?" I point.

"Jim."

I point, I jab my finger at him.

"That's you in the mirror."

"Who?"

"Let's get these trousers on. You shouldn't take them off. It wouldn't be polite for lunch."

That person is in my room. He won't listen. I tried to tell him about the fire. He wouldn't listen. This place is a death trap. I told him. He thought I was lying. I don't lie. This place is a death trap.

"I can't get them on if you keep fighting me, Preston."

A death trap.

"What's wrong, Preston. You seem upset. What's wrong? That's you. That's your reflection. There's no need to be upset. We have a nice lunch ready. You need to eat. Don't you want to eat?" I nod. "There'll be someone there to help you. First we'll go to the bathroom and get you ready. We'll wash your face. I'll comb your hair. It's all right. Everything is all right."

A death trap.

She brushes my hair back and touches my hand. "We're here, Preston. We do care. You are lucky to have people who care about you. Your son cares about you. Your wife cares about you. We care about you. This is your home."

She coaxes me and I feel better, and we go to the washroom and she washes my face with a warm cloth and it does feel better. I tend to get a little agitated. She smiles and I have to smile back. She brushes my hair.

"He's all right," says the woman pushing me. I can push myself. I don't need to be pushed. I'm letting her do it because she's been decent to me. Most people aren't decent to me. I'm at a table and a big woman is beside me.

"I was worried," the big woman says to the woman behind me. She pours coffee in a mug and sets it in front of me. My hand is shaking and I can't hold it. She puts her hand across the top of my mug. She doesn't want me to lift it. "I'll take care of him, Mei Li. If I can. If that's all right."

"Okay," says the woman behind me. I can see a hand reaching out to the big woman and giving her something folded up. I turn my head and watch the woman behind me going out the door. She is small. There are other tables and other people.

"Don't try to have your coffee right now," says the big woman. I look back at her. She's still got her hand on my mug. "Rest for a bit. The shaking will stop. It always does." She's talking softly and her voice is broad, she could make lots of noise if she tried. She's a big woman. I put my hand down. "I've asked them to bring you something soft. So you won't choke. Do you want that? Is that all right? Nod if it is." I nod. There's noises around me. I can hear rattling and clattering and people talking.

She unfolds something and holds it up. "We won't call this a bib," she says. "It's too masculine for that. I've seen big men wear things like this, eating spaghetti. It keeps their expensive suits clean. Is it all right if we put this on? It will keep your suit clean." She talks too much. I don't know what she wants. She's holding up a large sort of cloth with a big hole at top and long ribbons going out from each side of the hole. "Can I put this on?" she asks. I don't know what she wants.

A woman in white with an apron comes up. "That's all right," says the big woman. "It's better if I put it on myself. Preston and I are old friends. Aren't we, Preston." The white woman goes away. The big woman is still holding up the cloth. She gets up and moves her wheeled thing behind me and reaches the cloth over my face and fumbles around back there. "You are a handsome man." She takes the mug and puts it back away from me. "We'll get this later," she says, and moves back to the place where she was.

"I asked them to give me some carrots and peas. You like carrots and peas, Preston. I remember. Is it all right if I give you some? It's all chopped up. Pureed." She shows me a small bowl with some orange stuff. She takes a silver thing and puts some in her mouth. "Good," she says. "Want some? It's good. You like carrots and peas." She is talking like I'm a child. But she is being decent. I open my mouth and she puts some in. It is good.

"Your wife told me one time that she was amazed at all the knowledge that is packed into that head of yours." She puts more orange in my mouth. "She said you were always coming out with something new. Quite interesting too, she said. She said she misses that." She puts more in. "We had a long talk. I think we had some misunderstandings, but we've cleared those things up. She asked if I would be sure you were all right. Within reason, without interfering with your life." She puts more in. "Don't eat too fast. I'll give you some strips of bread. You can handle those, I think. She said it is really tragic that a man as smart as you," she puts more in. "I won't say. I agree. It is. My name is Gladys. You don't have to say it. Just think it."

She puts the thing down she's been using to give me the orange, and puts a round thing with strips in front of me. "Just think it. Gladys. Can you think it?"

I nod.

But I don't like being fed. It is kind of her to do that, but I don't like being fed. I go along because I don't want to offend her. It is decent of her, to do this.

"They'll probably give you some Paxil," she says and hands me a strip. "Take it slow. Small bites. That's healthy bread, Preston. Whole wheat. Your son has a problem with Paxil. That's what your wife says. Are you thinking Gladys?"

I nod. I don't want to be rude.

"Eat slowly. This is good healthy bread. It's important to eat healthy things. And act sensibly. Always act sensibly. Don't go out when it's hot as hell. I've known people to do that and come back red faced and sweating and have heart attacks. We need to hang on to good people like you. Good friends are rare. They're getting rarer all the time."

I feel much better. There are noisy people in the hall, some kids, a girl, a taller kid, a boy, a man and a woman, a baby in a wheeled thing, and an old woman they are pushing down the hall. I've got a hat and a sweater that buttons up the front, and some pants, very light, she laid them out for me, and I'm following the parade of people down to the thing. The woman punches the silver pad and the door opens and I get on with the rest. "Move over for the man, dear," says the woman and the tall boy does that. I'm facing the wall and the woman whispers something and the boy turns me around. The door opens and we all get off, the people are noisy, they talk to the woman in the wheeled chair and go out the glass doors. The man lifts the old woman into the square car and folds up the chair and they all get in and he slides the door closed and they drive off. It's bright. I have my hat. People come in the door and I move away, to the side, out in the light. It's windy, just slightly. There are other people here and a black table and they are talking, and an older woman moves me back where it isn't so hot and pulls my hat down so it isn't so bright. She asks if I want something to drink and gives me a bottle and lifts the top and shows me how to turn it on and off. I'm in a corner and it's hot. A wind comes once in a while but it's hot.

"I don't think he understands," says someone.

People come in and go out the glass doors. There are a lot of children.

"Are you going to the barbeque?" a woman asks. "There's a barbeque on the back patio. I'll take you down if you want."

"I don't think he wants to, dear."

"Everyone is out there. I can take you if you want. We're going there. We're waiting for some friends."

"I don't think he wants to."

More people come in and I'm rolling into the building, "They do this every year," a voice says behind me. "It's a chance for families to see their loved ones and have something to eat and enjoy themselves. Do you have family coming?" There are more children and people in chairs and with canes and with rolling things on wheels they can stand up in and black boxy things smoking and a little house on a pole and brown squeaky tables and hundreds of chairs and tables with people standing at them, "Could I get you a hot dog?" says the voice behind me, "I don't think he wants to," says another voice.

I am parked beside the little house on the pole. There are seeds scattered all around and the wheels of my chair crunch. It's very bright but a long darkness goes all along one side and people stand inside it and not many people are out in the bright area. A woman gives me a long bun with a brown thing inside. "Do you want ketchup and mustard?" she asks. I shake my head. "Bon appetit," she says.

Over where the people come out is a line of tall windows and Beverley comes out and walks over, with her wonderful smile. "Hello dear! I was wondering where you got to. Did you forget we had a date?"

I put the bun thing on my lap and take her hand.

"I often wondered what this place was like," she says, looking around. "I've seen it so often, from upstairs. It's strange, when you think of it, that I've never been down here in all the time I've come to this place. You look handsome today."

"Look who it is." The big loud mouth woman.

"Hello Gladys," Beverley says.

"He looks pretty good today, don't you think? How is Richard?"

"Just back from India. Where it seems he was looking at a number of Hindu temples with some pretty shocking illustrations, judging from his pictures. It's all very religious, I'm told."

"Have you tried the broccoli salad? It's quite delicious."

"Actually, Gladys," Beverley says, "Preston and I have a date, we're supposed to meet my son for dinner and fireworks. He's late, as usual. If you'll excuse us." The big woman nods and Beverley takes the bun thing and puts it on a table beside the door on our way through. "I really don't trust that woman," she says. "How have you been, Preston?" She wheels me along rapidly, dodging through the people coming the other way.

"Yes," I say.

"I really do miss you," she says. "Would you mind helping me, push on the wheels, if you would, I'm not quite recovered, though I'm much better. I'm thinking of leaving the apartment. It's too hard." We propel me along. "I had to talk Richard into this, Preston, he's not a very understanding person when it comes to old age. Be nice to him. Do you understand any of this? He wants to remember you the way you were, he says. Maybe it's better that you don't recognize him. I don't either, sometimes."

I feel dizzy. We get to the glass doors where the people come in from outside. We bump into people coming in, there's not enough room for us, and we wait outside. It's hot.

"Where is that man," says Beverley.

I lean forward and fall slowly. Beverley tries to stop me. The wheels spin away. I go down in a blur, my head strikes.

Confusion. People yelling. Beverley screaming at somebody. A black area and hard pavement. A line of grey. Blood. The noise of someone. Moving something. A blanket, it feels like. Beverley, are you all right Preston, are you all right. "This is the doctor, Preston.

Dr. Wilson." A babble of voices, one voice near. "I'm the doctor. We've met. I come here. Can you hear me? Nod if you can hear me."

I nod.

"Tell me if you can feel. I'm going to apply a little pressure on your arms and your legs. Can you feel that?"

I nod.

"That?"

I nod.

Someone puts something on my head. "You've cracked your head pretty badly. I'm going to have them move you. If you feel any pain, shake your head."

They move me.

I feel pain.

I shake my head, he asks me how bad it is, is it really bad.

I shake my head. He says it's probably the shock. He doesn't think there is any more damage.

I am being lifted. Beverley is talking, telling me it's all right, I've cut my head very badly, but the doctor is here, he doesn't think anything is broken, I've just cut my head, it's a very bad cut, but they think I'm all right, it's all her fault she says.

I shake my head.

She insists it's her fault. Another voice in my ear, a man's, oh my god, what have you done now, and Beverley telling the person to shut up, if you'd been here when you should have been this wouldn't have happened.

"We'll take you to the hospital overnight," says another voice, low, like he is telling me secrets. "I'm giving you a shot for infection and something to relax you. You've had a shock, but it looks like you'll survive. We'll send you to the hospital overnight, just to be on the safe side."

I can feel a sharp pinching and after a while, I don't feel pain and the sound of everything, goes away.

Voices. Light. Blurred voices.

"If you hadn't . . ."

Can't hear. Arguing voices.

"If if if if if . . . . !"

Not as loud. Not as near.

". . . wouldn't be here . . . ."

"If I hadn't been . . . ."

". . . . not fair at all . . . ."

". . . . all my life. . . . my fault. All my . . ."

Light. Shapes.

". . . not going to take the blame. I won't."

Angry. Loud.

"Your father . . ."

"He can't hear a damn thing. Thank God."

"We should go outside."

"He can't hear a damn thing."

"We'll be able to argue outside. Really enjoy ourselves."

"Sometimes you have a sick sense of humor."

"We'll disturb your father."

"Maybe we should."

"I will not help pay for your mortgage."

"Why?"

"Your father needs the money. We both need the money."

"Why?"

"Because, my dear, it is your mortgage. You took it on yourself. It wasn't my idea, it was your idea."

"They are going to foreclose, Mom."

"Perhaps you shouldn't have taken this trip to India. Perhaps you should have used the money you spent on your trip to India to pay your mortgage."

"I knew you'd say that. It's the story of my whole filthy rotten stinking life."

"Don't say that. It's not worthy of you."

"Bull!"

"Actually it was my understanding that the person who was living with . . . ."

"Don't talk to me about that bitch!"

"That the person who was living with you"

"I said!"

"Was supposed to pay half."

"Well she isn't."

"I am not paying for your mortgage. That's all."

"You'll get your stinking money back. Don't worry about that!"

"Like all the other times."

"Where are you going?" Fading noise.

"Outside."

"I hate your guts."

"You always exaggerate."

Voices going away. Not as loud. Arguing.

Blurred voices.

"Mom!"

Light.

Fading sound.

No sound.

Silence.

Light.

Fading.

Going away.

"Mr. O'Shaughnessy." A new voice. "Are you awake? Can you hear me? If you can hear me squeeze my hand."

I do.

"Do you feel any pain? Squeeze my hand if you feel any pain."

I don't.

"Your family is here. You're in the hospital. You're all right."

No. I am not all right.

The light above me is blurred. I need my glasses. It fades out at all the edges from bright to pale to nothing. Beside it are paler areas with indefinite traces of dark lines.

I have no feelings. I just register what I see. What I feel.

I see less and less. I feel less and less. I don't care about anything. I have lost control. I can only lie here and let what happens happen. I have tried to be positive. I have tried to see the plus side of everything. A sense of humor helps. I can't be amused any more. I can only lie here. I can only lie here and feel nothing.

I know who I am. I am Preston O'Shaughnessy. I have done things. When I try to think of what I have done, it's all a blur. I know it was important. I hope it was important. I think it was important. I don't exist any more. I am just a name. What happens when I can't even remember that? What happens when I can't even remember my own name?

"Preston? Preston? Can you hear me? Are you awake? You've been sleeping. That's good."

It's hard, I get it out. "Yes."

"Can you sit up? Do you think you can sit up? I have some pills I would like you to take. Do you think you can do that? I'll raise your bed."

I nod. The blurred light elevates until it ascends out of sight. Blurred shapes rise up. Hands hook something around my ears. The wall in front of me is clearer. A woman smiles at me. "Is that better? Can you see better?" Yes, that is better.

"How do you feel?" I don't know. It seems a strange question. I don't feel. "Your family was here. They left you some lovely flowers. I've put them on the table by the wall. Can you see them?"

Yes. I can see them. Colored splotches.

"Aren't they beautiful?" If they were beautiful you wouldn't have to tell me.

"You look better. I'm giving you some pills. Can you put them in your mouth. That's good. Have some water." I obey. I have no choice. Whatever I want doesn't matter. Whatever happens is someone else's choice. I might as well be a stone. It's hard to have a sense of humor when you feel like a stone.

"We'll have you up and out of here in no time. You'll be home before you know it."

Where is that?

Doors being hammered shut. I cannot weep.

I am sitting up. A doctor is here. Beverley is here. "He's had stitches," the doctor says. "We could do a catscan. If we find there is a blood clot on his brain we'd have to operate. But he'd never be the same afterwards. We could do that. I just want you to understand what the consequences are. You told me he doesn't want heroic measures." He is tall, young, wearing green with a funny cap on his head.

"I don't know what to do," says Beverley.

"Do you want to think about it?" the doctor asks.

I am here. "Are you . . ."

"What was that?" says Beverley, bending down to hear.

"Doctor," I say.

"Do you want to talk to the doctor?"

I nod.

He bends down.

"Do you?"

"Yes," he says. "Was there something you wanted to say?"

I take a deep breath, I push it out. "Do you want, take out my brain, look at it?" I am exhausted. It is so damn hard to say something. It's like climbing a bloody mountain.

The doctor smiles. "That's a good sign," he says.

"What is?" demands Beverley.

"He still has a sense of humor."

I'd like to see what you'd be like if you were here, smart boy in green. I can hear you. Don't talk like I don't exist.

"Do you want me to operate?" he asks.

I shake my head.

"Do you think he has a blood clot?" Beverley asks.

"I don't think so," says the doctor. "We can't be sure unless we do a catscan. There is no point if we won't operate." He comes close to me and speaks clearly and loudly. "Do you want me to operate?"

I shake my head as hard as I can.

"I don't want you to operate," says Beverley. "I don't care what my son thinks, I don't want you to operate. We have to respect what my husband wants." She takes my hand and I squeeze it hard. We are still a team.

I want this to stop. It won't stop. It just keeps changing. No matter what I do.

I want it to stop. But I do feel better. I don't feel down and I don't feel like saying to hell with it. I am me. I am Preston O'Shaughnessy. I am a person, I exist in this world. And I am going back to some place I know. I am not done yet. I am still here.

I'm lying on a flat sort of thing, there are walls all around me and rattling and Beverley is sitting here beside me and someone is saying, "Is everything all right back there?" and Beverley says that everything is fine and we are holding hands and I feel good.

If we want to talk she leans down and shouts in my ear. This thing is so loud that's the only thing that works. But we just feel good, holding hands. I can deal with it, if I can touch somebody. If I know I'm still here, that there are people here, that I'm not completely alone. It is not good to be alone.

I can feel a tightness on my head. There are stitches. I can feel the vibration of this thing on my back, this thing I am lying on vibrates, like I'm lying on the skin of a drum. I feel better. I can think clearer. It comes and goes.

There is a loud noise at my feet, "We're here. All out that is getting out," says someone loudly and I am lifted, me and this whole thing I am on and I can see the ceiling of this rattling thing moving by me and a taller canopy thing and I am lowered and there is a clicking and I am rolling, the canopy thing turns and I can see a lower sort of ceiling and noises of people talking and a much taller ceiling again, "Hi Preston," says someone and Beverley says, "Mei Li," in her warmest most loving voice that she reserves for those who are most precious to her. They talk, and the other person seems to be telling Beverley something about something and I can hear doors rolling and we are in a small room that jerks and Beverley talks to this other person and they talk and talk and more doors rolling and then down a hall with lights passing by and people saying, "Hello Preston," and finally I am in a place I kind of recognize, that seems familiar and I am lifted on a bed and people go off and Beverley is still here.

"Welcome home," she says.

"I have a whole bunch of pills," says a small woman with a lovely smile. "It is so good to see you, Preston. We were worried. You scared the hell out of us." She feeds me a pill, and another, and another, and another, I concentrate to make sure I get them down the right way in the right direction. "Your friend is back," she says. I don't know what she means. There is a cat on the windowsill, washing its face.

The woman goes away, but I am sitting up and she comes back into view, goes to the window, pets the cat, which stands up and stretches its back in an arch and moves along the windowsill and disappears.

"Could you tell me how many pills are in this box?" says the little woman. "Hold up your fingers." I do.

"Could you count how many fingers are on my hand?" She holds it up. "One," she points at a finger. "What is next?"

She waits. I guess. I tell her. She nods. It was a strange question. She asks me some other questions. I try to give her answers. After a while, she stops asking.

I don't know what she wants. She doesn't look straight at me. I haven't given her the right answers.

I want this to stop. I want to stay where I am. It keeps changing. I keep losing things. I feel good and then I don't. I can't go to the bathroom. I need help going to the bathroom. I can't take a bath. I need help to take a bath. I need help to go across the room, from my chair to my bed. When they ask me questions, all I can do is grunt.

A person carrying some bright colored things. She smiles. She has a wonderful smile. She asks me how I am. I don't know. She sits down. The cat rubs against her leg and she picks it up and says something to it and strokes its head. It makes a rumbling sound.

"Preston," she says.

I look at the cat. She puts it down and comes up to my chair. She strokes my face. "Preston?" I don't know what she wants. "What is my name, Preston? Who am I?"

I try to say something.

"Do you know who I am?" She strokes my face.

I think I recognize her. She is familiar.

"Oh Preston," she says. "Oh my darling."

"Bev . . ."

"Yes. Yes."

"Beverley."

"You didn't know me for a minute, did you?" she says. "I brought you some flowers."

She goes back to her chair and puts the bright things on a flat thing that is raised up.

"You can see them from here," she says.

Beverley says. Beverley.

It gets brighter and then darker. She looks at the window. "The sun has been in and out all day," she says. Beverley says. "It's getting colder."

She picks up the cat and strokes its head.

"I've been thinking, Preston. As I told you before, I can't stay in our apartment. Your son wants me to move to his place. Assuming he'll still have it. And help him pay the mortgage, which would be the only reason I would be invited to go there. I'm trying to think what you'd do, if you were in my place. I always try to think like you do, Preston, it's the only way I know to keep in contact, outside of coming here. And what you'd like. You always had very definite likes and dislikes. We really can't talk any more, can we. It's like those people we used to hear so much about. I remember how you used to tell me, they were nothing but charlatans. 'They're nothing but charlatans, Bev,' you'd say. You would even sound like that, so certain, so absolute. It made me feel protected. Nobody can communicate telepathically, you'd say. It's so ironic, isn't it, and kind of sad. That's the only way we can communicate now. Out of body experiences. One of these days you won't remember my name at all. I'll have to do something before that, won't I."

She puts the cat down. "I have a meeting. I just dropped by to bring you some flowers, so you'll have a reminder, how much I really love you. I'll be back later. Right now I have a meeting. Miss me."

Dark. I don't know this place. Creaking. The window is creaking. Wind lunging against the window. Pounding. Water pounding on the window. Sudden bright light, dark again. Very dark. Black hole. Inside a black hole. I don't know where this is. No lights outside. No lights in here. Light arcing in the door, going by, footsteps. Brilliant light flares up the building, outside the window, it disappears and I blink and can see faint spots wherever I look. They fade. I don't know where this is. Someone shouts. Voices. Light blazes up the building outside, goes dark, blazes again, spots when I look around, then fading. I don't know where I am. Another shout. More lights arcing in the door, going by. A voice, "There's no lights anywhere."

I am inside, inside a black hole.

Light blazes again.

I don't know where I am.

There are more voices in the hall and lights arcing and footsteps going by and then everything goes quiet.

Another blaze of light. Fading spots.

Then it's darker than ever. Wind pounds on the window.

I know how this ends. I know how it ends. It gets darker and darker.

Light blazes again.

It will go out, one time, and never come back.

I know that.

We are all the same.

We all end up, in the dark, alone.

The little woman is banging around, ". . . hear the storm last night, all that lightning," she says, helping me put on my pants, my shirt, a white shirt, ". . . . think it actually was a tornado . . . . motor home was flung across the street," my jacket, she has polished my shoes, she stands in front of me.

"We have to look special today," she says, she bends down, hugs me and brushes my hair with her hand. "I'll miss you."

We wheel out the door, along the hall, around the bend, the tall man in green standing there, "High five," he says.

"Hold up your hand," says the woman.

I do. The tall man slaps it.

We go by the place with people in green outfits, "There's Preston," they are all smiling.

The loud woman is standing in her walker, coming out from the room with the tables. "I don't know," she says. "Some people get special privileges."

"Big day," says the woman wheeling me by.

"Whatever," says the loud woman, she sounds sad.

We go to the door and wait there, the woman behind me pushes the buttons on the pad, the door rolls open, we go in, she's beating some kind of drum beat on the handles of my chair. "This is exciting," she says. "This has never happened before."

The room jerks, the light moves from one place to another, the room jerks again, the door rolls open. We roll down by the big room, the fish tank, the glass doors, we keep rolling.

"We're going to another section," she says. "No locks, no codes. Some people have cars."

We turn a bend and go by another place, the people smile, say, "Hi Preston."

I don't know any of them.

We are going fast along a hall by more rooms, the woman behind me says, "You're moving here, we call this the honeymoon suite."

She turns sharp in a room with two beds and another room, through a door with a big TV in there, boxes and crumpled wads of paper on the floor.

Beverley has a huge smile. The biggest smile I have ever seen. "Hi honey," she says, "How do you like our new place." She comes to my chair and smiles down at me. "I wanted to play 'Hail the Conquering Hero Comes.' I couldn't find your Handel." She looks up at the woman behind me, she smiles, I know that smile, it's full of mischief.

"I'll be going," says the woman.

Beverley goes over to her, I turn my chair around and watch them, they hug. The little woman comes over to me and kisses me on the cheek. "This is your home now, Preston, this is where you stay now." She whispers. "I have to be careful. Beverley is very possessive."

She puts things on my ears. Beverley.

"Beethoven." Her face is close. "It's Beethoven."

I nod. I understand.

"Restful. Very restful."

I nod.

Music.

"You're tired. You've had a long day."

I nod.

"It's Beethoven."

Wonderful.

Sonata.

"Sonata 32."

Wonderful music.